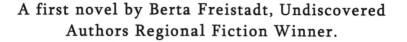

A first novel by Berta Freistadt, Undiscovered Authors Regional Fiction Winner.

Berta Freistadt is an award winning writer and poet, and a teacher. She has been published on both sides of the Atlantic and has lived most of her life in London.

ISBN13 978 -1-905108-47-3

Printed in the UK by BookForce

BookForce UK's policy is to use papers that are natural, renewable and
recyclable products and made from wood grown in sustainable forests where
ever possible

BookForce UK Ltd.
50 Albemarle Street
London W1S 4BD
www.bookforce.co.uk
www.discoveredauthors.co.uk

Acknowledgements and Thanks

Debts of inspiration are owed to the following authors who, among many others, lodged indelible images into my mind: Margaret Atwood, John Christopher, Jorge Luis Borges, Octavia Butler, Suzette H. Elgin, John Hersey, George MacDonald, Vonda McIntyre, Walter M, Miller, George Orwell, Marge Piercy, Olaf Stapledon, John Wyndham.

For encouragement, help and advice, thanks to; Lou Lou Brown, Sally Pomme Clayton, Kris Kleindienst, Danzy Senna and Steph Taylor; to Monique Charlesworth for support over the subjunctive, and to Cathy Phillips for her outstanding cover photo. Also thanks to Elizabeth Fairbairn for being the first to like the book, to Natalie Matthews who helped me fix it, and to Tim Hughes & Elaine Hutton, without whom...

Contents

~ ~ ~ ~ ~

Chapter 1

Little Ghost and the Word Count

~ ~ ~ ~ ~

It was the hour of storytelling at the cafe called Eye The Girls; in Paradise, at the Garden of Eden. The lanterns were lit and the bar closed and we were all sitting around waiting. It was my turn. This story came back to me then reminding me how Little Ghost had told it to comfort me, when I was alone. Whispered it in my ear as I sat by the sea writing to my lover. As I stroked the Fur One.

'One night when lightening cracked the black sky like a sudden golden tree and the wind blew and blew, the World grew tired and ceased her chaos. Not content with sudden tranquillity She looked around for mischief and seeing a happy group of women in a pool, towelling each other down and wringing out their hair and drying the horses, She sent them a word. We don't know to this day what it was; perhaps it was 'darling' or 'careful' or even 'turnips'. Probably not, for this first word was surely something of importance. Whatever it was, it was taken up with enthusiasm, thrown around, bandied about and quite exhausted.'

Little Ghost would tell this part better; she would say, '...and the word was whispered from one pearl ear to another, each syllable licked into shape by a snake tongue. If a lip slipped from the way a red tongue would push the other purple or coral mouth into shape until it had learned its lesson. Sometimes though, the lesson was passed back and forth so many times like Chinese Whispers that the Word became lost or mixed or changed. Word became words and words led to conversation. Then arguments and jokes and consensus and lies and sometimes, even silences became popular until no one remembered how it all started... '

Little Ghost knew about such things: things that you or I would not think of thinking about. And I'm still learning my trade. At this point I could see that all was not well at Eye The Girls. There was whispering and scratching and some were even snatching a quick drink of their beer, not really the done thing to a good storyteller. If only Little Ghost were here I thought — she had a way with her. But I plodded on.

'One day a man arrived dressed like death with his silver dog and a book of receipts in his bag.

"It's time to pay," he announced, "how many words do you have?"

The puzzled looks and soft conversation that resulted from this took a long time and at the end of it all, he was no better off. Some things cannot be explained by words alone.

"Words cost money," he tried again opening his big book to them. But it was no good, they could give no answer for they had only words and no numbers. So he explained to them that to use words properly they would have to learn to count and they looked at each other and some began to cry. He held up his fingers and showed them one to ten. Then he tried to explain that one to ten were more than new words.

"How interesting," said Chimi, who had always felt something missing from her life, but had never been sure what it was. Now it was obvious; something to do with this new number thing. Turning her back on the strange man she started to touch all the fingers within reach. Everyone seemed to have the same one to ten on the ends of their hands except for Tunda who'd had an accident in the butchery when she was an apprentice, and her special friend Mrinal who'd done the same out hunting when she was really old enough to know better. Of course, one thing led to another, and the day turned to afternoon, and the afternoon soon turned to after dark. Bellies began to remind them of the kitchen, and people began to drift away.

By now the Tally-Man was getting irritable, he had plenty to do and this job was just administration. So he shouted a little, enough to get their attention again. The silver dog, catching his mood, growled, but with nothing to get his teeth into he fell back to attacking his fleas and licking his scabs to make them better. In a sweat about his buying and selling the Tally-Man finally came to this.

"Well you can have a short while to learn, but they must be paid for. Nothing is for free."

The listening women were impressed with his persistence if not his ideas and in either case still looked very puzzled. He realised that it was quite hopeless and didn't attempt the issue of Time.

"You lot are hopeless cases," he said, and turned away abruptly to think how to organise them. The dog, jerked suddenly off its haunches onto its back by the tightening lead, leapt into the air and snapped in anger at the first thing near it which was its master's ankle. So angered was the man at this last indignity that he gave his faithful hound a vicious kick in its silver ribs.

The women had never seen anything like it before, and as they stared at him they began to search their minds for a new word to describe what they had seen.

"Who are you looking at?" he said, and he dug into his pack and pulled out a shiny little red book which he threw at them, for he wasn't used to disapproval.

"I don't help everyone like this," he told them.

Eyebrows, half moons of gold, dark seagull wings, rust snakelings, shot up at this; even more so when they began to pass the book around. Few words and many unknown marks, though Chimi tutted and turned the book up the other way, and wouldn't let it go when it was Daria's turn.

"You've got a week," he shouted, pretending he thought they knew what that was. And they both lolloped away.

So, since she seemed to understand better than any of them what he was talking about, they set Chimi to count up how many numbers there were. It seemed to them that might be a solution, for with a knowledge of how many numbers there were, they could know how many words they might have. This idea took hold and some of them grew quite excited. Hysterical almost. They left Chimi in a quiet corner with some sheets of paper and a pencil or two. At first she used the shiny red Book of Numbers the paymaster had left, but soon getting the hang of things she tossed it away and began to improvise. At supper time at the end of the first day Chimi refused to come to table, put her finger to her silently moving lips and motioned her friends away as they approached. At the end of the second day the same thing happened and at the end of the third too. Mrinal watched from the darkness and grieved, for where Chimi had started sitting tall and bright, now she had sunk against a tree and her lips, still moving, were dry and livid.'

At this point, when she told me the tale Little Ghost had wiped a tear from her eye. But at Eye The Girls they all sighed and shook their heads in disgust. Even Fleur and Jassy, who only came to kiss all night long, took their eyes from each other and listened for a while. There was no more surreptitious drinking and I began to relax a little.

'By the fourth day Mrinal wasn't having any of it, she told them all, and they agreed. It looked as if the numbers might never stop and Chimi being Chimi, who never broke a promise, had to be made to. For after all who cared? Who cared for the ones and the twos, for the tens and the thirties. Who cared that twenty was a parcel of either four fives or five fours or two tens. Or that nineteen was ten and nine and nine and ten and three fives plus one five minus one? It seemed like a game for children, very interesting, but really once you had the trick of it, what did it matter? Far more important was that a woman was counting herself to death. They would tell a lie; they would say that there were so many words and pay for that. That seemed enough.

So Mrinal, with some others, went to Chimi and said, "Stop. Enough is enough. We will pay for however many you have counted to this moment."

Chimi looked at her true friend and companion and said, "One million, seventy-two thousand, five hundred and forty-three." And fell over completely.'

At Eye The Girls a fight nearly broke out. Briony, who knew maths and science and made a point of letting everybody know, said you couldn't count to a million in four days. Jen swore that of course you could; though what she knew about it I'd like to know. Briony said it would take you at least twenty days if you did it straight off, no eating or drinking or sleeping and you'd probably need some help with the figures, and it would definitely be double that if you did.

'Did what?' said someone.

'Did the eating and things.'

Then she sighed as if we were all stupid and Jen said what we all thought, and called her a show-off. They both stood up at that and faced each other like two porkers in a field. I stopped the fight before it really began by promising not to finish the story, so they all sat down and glared at each other and me until I started again.

Little Ghost though, had asked me what million meant, and why it was and what one should do with so many numbers. I remember I couldn't answer at that time wanting only to forget and felt it wasn't reasonable for a storyteller to ask questions.

'At the end of the week the man and his dog returned. He wore a sly grin on his face but the dog was limping still. The sight of him brought feelings to Mrinal's heart that she had not felt before. As he approached she rose as was customary and polite and when he said, "Well?"

She said, "Why?"

Where it came from she couldn't say. It surprised her and the others too, for they gasped at the sound of it. "Why" was a word for children; no adult used it. There were always better ways of approaching puzzlement than impropriety. But the man appeared oblivious and said, "Because."

At this the women gave a second gasp and made valiant efforts to stifle their laughter. How was he to know that "Because" was the funniest word in the language. Naughty children had to be sent outside in ceremonies of thanksgiving for muttering it to each other to relieve their boredom. A lover might whisper it after a night of passion to re-kindle with laughter what had died in exhaustion. Workers would sing "Because" songs to cheer themselves up in monotonous work. But for a stranger to utter the word was unbelievable and they fell against each other helpless with laughter.

Frowning, the man tried to bring them to order.

"Now look," he said, "just because. . . " and they were off again. What he couldn't know was that laughter with them was a sport, highly developed and respected. Their stomach muscles and larynxes were trained to continue for hours without stopping. So it was that after several minutes the man backed away; he had never encountered anything like it and there were other places. Walking away he whistled for the silver dog, but the dog didn't hear. It was sitting as dogs do sometimes with its head on one side transfixed in ecstasy as a softly laughing woman scratched its back and blew into its ear.'

At Eye The Girls they put the lights back on and I could see the kissing my story had interrupted. Beer was served again and someone said thank you. As I got up to go home I remembered the sea light again and the weight of Little Ghost and how the Fur One had smelt in the hot sun as she gently clawed me.

'What happened to Mrinal and Chimi, did they make love all night long after that?' said Jassy.

I had to confess I didn't know for Little Ghost had in fact fallen asleep on me at that point.

A voice said, 'They should have killed him.'

And someone nodded. At least Jen and Briony agreed about something at last.

Chapter 2

Exit from the City of L

~ ~ ~ ~ ~

And then one day, two came. From far away. After, we were much changed. It was summer when the light never goes but only dims a little as if to bow in the new day. Some of us had forgotten to sleep that night and were sitting in the garden out the back of Eye The Girls. True, some were dozing, but most were just sitting watching the changing sky and talking about this and that and who was doing what with whom and when. The garden, though we called it one, was more truly a cobbled yard with weeds and trees, though that was pretty enough, the weeds being only a little wilder than those flowers we cultivate around the houses, and the trees full of flowers that filled the air with sweetness. The garden looked on to the one road that ran from behind the hills into this place we call Paradise. All our seats were placed to face the vista, as if having got our drinks, our one purpose was to sit as though it were a play and watch the proceedings. There were the cobbles and the weeds, there the ring of trees around the garden and there, held in a picture frame of branches and leaves was the road that led to us or away, depending on who you were and where you were going. Dusty, its margin fringed with green, it grew smaller the nearer to the far hills it went; a straight road, only veering a little to the left and then to the right as it climbed taking your eyes imperceptibly upward into those hills.

Of course none of us had gone that far. We were more forest people; all our hikes were beneath the safe canopy of the forest. Few, if any had risked wandering away out in the open to beyond, where who knows what lay waiting. There were stories. Old tales, from the beginning, of footprints circling Paradise. But the stories never told whether they were human or animal. And then on that day, that morning early when we should have been sleeping and never seen them coming, there were suddenly two on the road. It was as if they were there in an instant; we never saw them in the hills, though I have excellent sight; we never saw them where the road comes out of the mouth of the hills nor where the road, at first thin as a snake's tail, fattens into the body. No, as I say, suddenly they were there in the picture, walking towards us growing at every moment. At first we watched as if we didn't see: we were so lazy and lethargic that morning having drunk too much and talked too long. Until Ryo laughed and asked if we were awake or dreaming and made manifest these two who we had, all of us, at one moment, thought were nothing but a trick of the light, flecks across the eyeball.

At Ryo's outburst we all sat up a little, amazed. There indeed through the early morning mist, were two people. And what's more one looked like a male; though he seemed little more than a boy so perhaps he'd not give much trouble.

The woman he was with looked strong enough even though she was dressed in the old way. They came so slowly, all but empty handed, dragging their feet, sometimes stumbling, hauling each other along as if every step was pain. The boy was very frail and leant often on the woman and while you could see that she was finished still she helped him with an arm and a hand. This was a true drama in our pretty picture frame, that we had never seen before, and so it took a while, of wondering and calculating, before we came to our senses to realise that these were real people and not the phantoms conjured up by playmakers. Then again suddenly, Ryo cried out that we should hide, not let them come, run away and other nonsense. But most of us remembering hospitality and our manners shut her up and sent her home. How could we welcome strangers with her howling fear in our midst? By this time we were all on our feet and bright and awake and gathered in a group. Still none of us went out to fetch them; how strange that was, to behave that way. I seem to remember it felt more than the unwillingness to let strangers into your house; more than the effort required for good behaviour and hospitality. There was something else, I'm sure of it. Ryo again. She had a knack of unnerving me. I know she often dreams right, but she's too frightened of the gift. She can't control it.

When they saw us we must have been a comic sight, a bunch of women in their work clothes, further disarrayed by a night's drinking, gawking through the trees. I suppose we were as strange a picture to them as they were to us. Anyhow, the sight of us stopped them. Their eyes flared terribly and brightly for a moment and they clutched each other. Laughter and tears seemed to come at the same time from both as if seeing us was a reward, a goal, something succeeded. After that they pulled each other along faster to get to us and at last remembering our duties and our humanity we left off staring and came out to them through the trees to help them.

Out of the shelter of the garden it was a little chilly.

Behind on the horizon of the hills the early morning mist swirled, covering and concealing, and it was no wonder that we'd not seen them come down from there. Closer, I could see they'd reached us just in time. Both were at the end of their strength. The boy especially was a shadow. We seemed to catch each other's eye, as if he'd come 'specially for me, and despite all I knew I held out my arms to him and he fell towards me. Lifting him I hardly knew he was there. He lay in my embrace like a moth, breath shallow, rasping, his lips cracked and his skin burnt and flaking. The woman, as I said, was stronger, though she was weeping now uncontrollably and Pook and Delia had taken her, their arms around her, half carrying her back to the garden. She was a strong-boned woman with worker's hands and long dark hair streaked with grey curling down her back. I wondered if the boy was her son, or her servant. These things still happened in other places. I know; we're not so cut off. In the garden we sat them and fed them little pieces of last night's leftovers. Gave them water. We didn't let them eat their fill or drink too much. Too much nourishment on a starved system is worse than nothing. Then they slept. They just slumped where they sat and sleep came to them in an instant like a cloud on the moon in a storm.

*****

When I woke up it was to the caress of fingers on my face and for a moment I thought I was back home with Mary. Sometimes she used to wake me by stroking my face or kissing me. I thought it had been some dreadful nightmare, I willed it to be, pushing aside all I knew, the weakness and stiffness of my body, the pictures in my head, and I turned to her to tell her the terrible dream, to get from her, demand, the comfort I knew was mine. But it was a strange woman with her hands on me, an unknown face, a stranger. I was among strangers far from home.

But we'd made it, or so it seemed and at least I was alive for the moment. No way of knowing though for how long. When it wasn't Mary, not her beloved hands, I shrank from those fingers and would have pushed them away if I'd had the strength. She didn't seem at all put out, in fact her face was full of kindness; compassion was it? She murmured something soft and was wiping her hands on a cloth when I saw a glass bottle filled with a greenish oily liquid. Poison? Had I been punished in my sleep even here? But the woman rose and picked up the bottle screwing the top back on it.

'Your face will soon be better', she said, and smiled.

Then I realised that the tight, stretched burning sensation that I'd had on my face for weeks had gone. I tried the muscles; wrinkled my brow, blinked and even stretched my lips: all was easy. Such relief. She could see what I was doing and nodded. That a stranger had been kind to me in my sleep when I couldn't agree to repay filled my eyes with tears and my heart with hope that we had really found the right place. That this was really Paradise.

And then I remembered 'we'. Where was Charlie? But before I could ask, as my tears were spilling over, the unknown friend tut-tutted and gently patted the tears away.

'No wetness till it sinks in,' she said, reproving, but nicely. 'Sleep again, now.' she said and waved her fingers before my eyes in such a way that her face swam before me a moment or two and then receded into a dimness that was irresistible and I must have slept. Again I woke, but brighter and fresher, with less pain and a savage hunger. Then I remembered I had eaten, bits; some bread, some strange cold cooked things. When was that? Months ago? Or yesterday? Last night? There had been no night for a long time. That had saved us I think. Charlie and me. We'd given up trying to sleep and just gone on walking. Tramping foot before foot. Remembering the instructions and never daring to think it was a joke. Another terrible trap. If there'd been any night we might have slept and lost time and they'd have found us gone, and chased us and caught us and then what? Ah, Mary; that I'd had no faith in you. Perhaps you made it too. Perhaps even now you're here, your body healed by that woman. I wouldn't care how much she caressed you, how grateful you were to her, if only I knew you were alive.

Then I remembered the medicine. How long had Charlie been without it? How long had I been lying here? If this was Paradise we wouldn't have to hide it anymore; there was no risk. So I sat up, only slowly as the motion made me dizzy. They'd left me in my underclothes so I guessed it hadn't been long. As I was stretching to get my pack someone came into the room. She was carrying a tray and I could smell food. Suddenly hunger hit me and I could hardly stop my mouth from watering. As she put the tray down I could see soup and bread and milk and I was ready to die for it, but I thought of the medicine and knew Charlie'd be worrying.

'What can I get you?' the woman said.

They had such a strange way of speaking; the words were the same but they kind of lilted and shushed.

'My pack,' I said, 'Charlie needs something.'

'Charlie?' she said, 'is that a name?'

'Yes, of course.'

'Ah well, never fret, Charlie has all that is needed.'

'No, you don't understand,' I said carefully, 'Charlie needs medicine; it's in my pack.'

'We're healing her fine.'

But she gave me the pack and I dug into it and found the bottle.

'Will you let Charlie have this,' I said, 'please?' and she nodded. 'Promise?'

And she smiled and made a kind of sign over her heart with her hand. I hoped this meant she was telling the truth and so I fell on the food. The woman laughed and as she left the room she said, 'Don't gobble, you'll make yourself sick.'

And I remembered my mother, who used to say that to me when I was little.

*****

Jassy was laughing when she came from the sick room.

'What's the joke?' I said.

'We've a little wolf cub in there; I've never seen anyone devour bread like that. You'd think it was cake the way he grabbed it.'

Then she handed me a bottle of pills.

'I made a promise to give these to the woman. She's called Charlie, by the way.'

We never call women by men's names — it's bad luck, and we never give this sort of medicine. We treat with plants and the spirit. Most usually work. But a promise had been made and it wasn't our property. We could sort out the rights and wrongs of it all later.

'This is what I meant: strangers bring trouble.'

It was Ryo, and who better to know that. But life goes forward and times change. Each season the harvest grows a little different; each brewing of beer never quite the same.

What could we do? They came in need. Maybe sent to teach us something. So I shrugged and tried to look sympathetic but I took the bottle and knocked on the door where this Charlie was still asleep. There was no answer so I quietly opened the door and looked in. She was asleep indeed. Fast. Dead to dreaming. I went to put the bottle on the cabinet by the bed and, though I shouldn't, I stopped to look at her. It was a kind of stealing to stare at a woman you didn't know while she was unconscious like that. But my, what a lovely creature she was. We'd taken off her dress and coat and hung them up for her. Never get me in something like that. How could you move or run or work? Still women in those places had different lives to ours. I wonder why they came. Driven out or fled? We'd know one day soon.

I was admiring her cheekbones and the curve of her mouth and even, shame on me, fell to eyeing the soft breast that rose and fell with every breath, when she turned over towards me her hair tumbling across her face and with a gasp began to weep. Still deep in slumber she cried as if awake and her tears shone through her hair and began to wet her pillow. That was so shocking to me, to see a woman so deeply grieved that even sleep was no respite. My heart quite overcame my senses and I went to sit by the bed to try to comfort her. Though how you comfort a woman in her sleep I hadn't stopped to think. But no sooner had I stroked back her hair than her eyes flew open and gasping again she shrank back as though I was a monster. A fine nurse I was turning out to be. Lusting after my patient, assaulting her and scaring her half to death.

'So sorry,' I was even stuttering, 'your friend says you should have this medicine.'

A strange sigh came from her, like one of relief and she

smiled at me and said something which I took to be a thank you. She half rose on her elbow and brushed the hair from her face and the tears from her eyes with no comment. Then taking the bottle and undoing it, before I could pour her some water, she'd gulped some down dry. Then she lay back and damn it, I know it's hard to believe, but she gave me one of those looks. Moved her body a little so her breasts were even more revealed and smiled at me from under her lids and made a movement with her lips that got me, in the middle of the day, in the middle of my work, hot as a Saturday night and feeling like climbing into bed with her there and then. I reminded myself that this was a sick woman who had endured much when she said to me, 'What are you then? A man or a woman?'

That cooled me down I can tell you.

'A woman.' I said, as if it wasn't obvious.

And she drew in a breath and exhaled like she was disappointed, as of course she would be coming from afar. And then she said, 'Got anything to eat, I'm starving?'

So we fed her and she was as ravenous as the boy. Then she lay back in the bed and went again to sleeping and those two sentences were the last we heard from her for a long while. She slept like before, with gasps and tears only now with food inside her she was stronger and more active in the battle she was playing. Her tears were sparser and dryer, if that were possible, and she fought with unseen enemies making a battleground of the sheets and pillows. Every so often there'd be a respite and she would lie as if exhausted, before again with a shout of despair seeming to dive into the invisible fray.

*****

16

Charlie didn't get up for three weeks. I sat there every day first of all waiting for the sleeper to awaken so we could get our story straight. We couldn't tell them the truth. They were like children in many ways. I don't know how many generations they'd been here. I wanted to ask but I knew my questions would lead to theirs. As it was they treated me as sick as Charlie, only up. They let me sit all day in the sun and fed me and smiled and chatted in a harmless way. The one called Hashie came a lot and talked about her new job. I like her. But Jassy kept sending her back to work and one or two of the others were already looking at me as if they knew what a liar I was. How long could I carry this off?

After a while I knew Mary wasn't here. I hadn't really thought she was. If only. The rumours that those early transports had made it had kept us going. But if I'd gone then, with Mary and the others, I couldn't have got Charlie out. So I kept one promise, though Ma will never know. Oh Mary. If there was any hope, any word. No point in thinking like that, my life with her is over.

I wondered if they'd let us stay... when they know. To stop myself thinking I tried to repair Charlie's dress. They seemed surprised, but what they were surprised about I'm not sure. That anyone should attempt such a doomed task or that a boy should be able to sew. I think it was the last. Anyway the dress was mostly past it. I smiled to think of Charlie in trousers. Everyone wore them here that I could see. Ploughing and planting and harvesting were all trouser work. Nettles would sting Charlie's legs in a dress. It all seemed very funny.

I couldn't get a word out of Charlie who ate, slept, popped pills and dreamt nightmares and just checked with those big brown eyes that I was there. I soon gave up trying so I began just putting my head in at mealtimes. I'd wave, Charlie'd grunt, mouth full and smile and I'd take myself off before I yelled in frustration at the silly creature. What a way to behave! How long before our hosts got fed up with us. We were like parasites. But on the other hand, I said to myself, how long is it that either of us has been given kindness with nothing asked and nothing taken? Anyone would hide under a sheet after what we've been through. What we've seen. It's just a time of resting, I know that. Charlie sleeps and dreams and I sit and dream. It's the same really. We'll have to come clean, one day. Not to tell the truth would be spitting in their faces and we've both had enough of that. Wiped the spittle; got on with it. So we must tell them. When we're strong, and the blisters have healed.

There must be a place for us somewhere. You'd never get me to go back; not for anything, not even for Charlie, Ma, not even for Charlie. Oh Ma, you never saw the worst; what happened after you'd gone. The machines, the emptiness, the loneliness. They left us till last; our kind. And then one at a time: Angel, Susi, Jamal, Rori. One day there, the next gone silently as if they'd never existed. And what for? Who did we hurt? Who can help their nature? They even took those who'd tried to live differently. Charlie's friend Leo. He tried so hard to live as they wanted. When it was all but over; when they'd won, there was this dreadful stillness; while we waited. Some said they were too stupid to work out who we were. Which was which. It wasn't that. They weren't so frightened of us as they were in the past. Played with us never dreaming that any of us could escape. Such arrogance. To torture and destroy and then to be so careless.

*****

18

It was Ryo who saw it first. Saw through her. Then it seemed obvious. How silly we were. Us of all people. But still we didn't blame ourselves, it wasn't important. We had to admire her for the performance. The deepened voice, the shaved head, never using the communal washrooms. We took her at face value. She looked like a boy, therefore she was one. She certainly walked like one. At least one of theirs. Here of course, when we'd got it straightened out, she looked like one of us. Especially when her hair began to grow a little.

Ryo was in a bad state about her, at first. Only Dortha could calm her down and stop her throwing her out bodily. She saw it in a vision, a dream. A man who was a woman tied to a great metal box which measured her and spoke for her. It was a terrible, haunting dream she said. And we took notice this time. Paying attention. We let Dortha take her away but not before she'd uttered dire threats of what would come. That the machine would come for us and measure us too, and count us. We remembered counting, and the other stories, and it was hard to laugh, but we did, Jassy loudest. I for one prayed that it was Ryo's fear of her dream and not part of the future.

It was Jassy who checked her out. The sort of job she'd love; not known for her tact. She got talking to the boy about dreams and predictions and asked him, her, what she thought was meant by Ryo's dream. The poor girl hummed and hahed so much and blushed and stammered that I could have kicked that Jassy. I told her to get back to work and I sat down next to her. Compared to Charlie she was not much of a woman. Straight as a board with not a curve on her. When she'd fallen into my arms those weeks ago when she came in from beyond the hills and down the road she weighed no more than a feather. She was a little heavier now, more flesh on her face, but she had none of the assurance or the humour of women here in Paradise. None of the subtlety, the irony. She was a child in many ways; so serious, so one-dimensional. My heart bled for her. I asked her her name, which I'd never done before, not being polite with us. But I'd neglected to think that their manners were most likely different to ours and maybe I'd not cause offence.

'My name?' she said, and paused as if it were something she'd forgotten. 'They call me Johnny,' and most strangely she giggled and then burst into tears. 'Sorry,' she said, 'I'm as bad as Charlie.'

'Your real name though?'

'Oh, that one.' And we looked into each other's eyes, hers soft brown, and we both knew that I knew. 'Selena,' she said simply and looked down as if waiting for punishment.

'Welcome to you, Selena.' I said, 'I'm Noor,' and leant forward and kissed her on the cheek. She gasped as though there was no air and covered the place where my mouth had been with a hand. And it all came tumbling out, too terrible a story that we all half knew; that had already brought our mother ancestors here those many decades ago. As she spoke and cried, others moved near to hear and soon were holding hands for comfort, and to stop themselves rudely blocking their ears.

The Man-Woman Wars. We thought we were immune here and now we had these two broken women as witness to all we had escaped. I don't know now if I can remember all she said. She was unburdening herself, not telling a story. She spoke of towns how normal they could seem. Just like our mother's grandmothers used to tell. Ordinary streets with families; man and woman at work, children at school.

Cars, holidays, cats and dogs. Then at night through an open window a curtain would move and a howl of despair would echo down the ordinary street, a cry of terror. The cry of a captive wolf. How urgent it became to be ordinary, to fit that ordinary picture. She said that kittens were drowned if they were too beautiful and children scarred at birth for the same reason. How cutting and scarring became fashionable and how beauty was despised and plainness and ugliness were sought. There were hospitals, she said, with shut wards where machines would normalise the brilliant, subdue the vocal and calm the energetic.

'But,' we asked, 'who was in control? ' She didn't answer except to shake her head. We thought that was the end because she stopped for a while and sat staring into space. Then a bird began to sing and she jumped a little and began again. Another story, another history of despair. While all this was happening and was the normal way of being — she used that word many times — some other thing more desperate was happening. The left hand working separately from the right but both belonging to the same sick body.

She spoke quietly now of women who disappeared. Some in groups, some one by one. Tragic accidents, disease and plagues. Viruses that struck them down. Leaders, politicians, writers, public women, rebel women. All gone very soon. Then others, any woman who spoke out or up to any man. Some died in their beds, some in child birth, some went out for a walk and just never came back. Slowly, slowly the number diminished until in a street of two hundred houses, where four or five hundred women and girls had lived, perhaps only forty remained. Now we were quiet, not breathing, as if they might spring out and get us. But still it was not over. 'They were so clever, but not clever enough,' she said. 'They never foresaw what would happen. No one could imagine it. Before, it had been...' and she was silent, searching for a word.

'Terrifying?' someone offered.

'Yes. Terrifying; the disappearances, our impotence. But it was private, almost invisible. Now something so dreadful happened; so wild, so beyond understanding. They thought it would be simple, to get rid of the women they didn't want. And it was. But then... ' She was half way between shining and terrible, telling her story.

She went on with her tale and her words burnt into our heads. The disappearing spread to men. Men died; many, many men mysteriously killed, and suicides. Mostly suicides. Street corners piled high with the dead bodies of men. No sign of violence on them — as if they'd just laid down and died. And hanging from trees down the ordinary streets, men hanging two or three to a branch. 'It was a state secret,' she said, 'but everyone knew what it was; a disease of despair. Special squads were employed to clear up the bodies. We never knew what they did with them. And very soon there was hardly anyone left. Those empty boulevards with one car maybe driving any which way. The empty supermarkets; great halls with half filled shelves and one checkout girl with blank eyes. And rumour. There were still rumours. How did we know that the rest of the country was like our part. Those of us left, congregating in the odd bar clutching our drinks, listening, straining for whispers, but pretending we didn't hear the noise of the metal boots.'

'They called it the Vanishing Plague and no one was supposed to mention what was happening. Some slipped through the net; Charlie and I and some others managed to avoid the traps. We left everything. Friends, homes, pets, belongings.'

At last she stopped. There was silence. People moved away as if embarrassed by what they'd heard. Wanting to pretend that the end of the story was like the beginning. Just her and me. We didn't speak for some time, but sat in the cooling air and stared at the earth. Finally she looked at me and said, 'It's time Charlie got up.'

'You know,' I said to her, 'at first I thought you and Charlie were mother and child, and then I wondered if you were lovers. Then I thought, stupidly, that you were perhaps brother and sister.'

And she looked at me and said simply, 'But we are.'

*****

Later I couldn't believe what I'd done. After all our promises. I sat by his bed after I'd told her and tried to warn him. But he moaned and rolled over and pretended he was dreaming. I felt the anger rise again. I'm sorry, Charlie, I know I should have waited till we could talk about what to do. But you weren't here. A little sympathy and a woman's kindness and I'm done for.

But he still had his eyes closed and moved restlessly beneath the sheet. His lovely hair was matted up with so much turning. He was always so proud of it. After we got away we rowed because I'd packed matches and a knife and he took hair cream and a comb. He was always beautiful, even before he was a woman. Those curving brush-like eye lashes and his long elegant legs. After the operation, with the pills, he'd grown his breasts and become what he'd always wanted. What a pair we were. Me so pale, no eyelashes, no breasts to speak of. Ma used to laugh at us and make jokes about the milkman. But I liked to flaunt it. How we looked. North and south, fur and paper.

And I have been desired by women. Mary. Couldn't understand it, but I remember it. The electricity. Our bodies sometimes hardly belonging to us. Carrying on without us, even if we'd had a row. I remember everything. Your rough hands. You were always rubbing them with cream, not that it made any difference. Your hands on me, I remember that. And mine on you — your body smooth as a candle. And how we fitted. Physical synchronicity. Some kind of miracle. Remember the holiday on Isla? Remember Rosy the beetle. When the brakes went on that hill and you held her on the handbrake with that line of traffic behind us. Remember when I took you home to meet Ma? And how Charlie used to tease us? I remember it all. All past now, gone.

Looking at Charlie reminded me of all that was past. All that happened to us. All that happened to Charlie. How brave he'd been at school and after. The terrible things they'd done to him. The terrible things he'd been made to do when they took him away. And I thought about the time when I knew I was different too and was frightened and how Charlie had told me to be strong and true. And how he'd dressed up as a big tough brother and come to the playground and fought the kid who was harassing me. And how I did the same for him later. Then as I was thinking these soft things about him, my anger draining away, he began to weep again. When he'd wept before it sounded full of self pity, almost whining. Now at last his crying was healthier, as though a wound was fresh, not festering. Suddenly his eyes opened and with a great sob he awoke. Sitting up slowly he pulled the sheets round him and looked at me and said, 'You hussy!' He looked so sweet; so tousled and bleary eyed. He was my own brother again. And I climbed into the bed and put my arms around him. Cuddling each other it was almost as if it had never happened, and we were back home, children, waiting for Ma to come in and tell us to get back to our own beds and go to sleep. As if we'd never come to this strange place.

And it was strange, sanctuary or not. Like stepping into the past. And, apart from some little boys, all women. Promising for me, but what of Charlie? They were nice enough, kept their distance, most of them, not that I blame them for that. Noor's son, Bruno, he was about seven, came first to stare and then to talk. While I was still boy, I couldn't answer and nearly laughed, when he said, 'How do you be a man?' As if I knew. But then when I was a woman he came less often. Some nights I could hear them in this place that was half a cafe and half a bar laughing and singing, carrying on like we did once long ago. I went there a few times, once I got my appetite back. They made this grain thing like a cake, but with a kind of cheese and vegetables. I ate it all the time. After a while I stopped going; the laughing and the shouting and the quarrels were too familiar; I kept thinking of all that was gone. And sometimes I couldn't make out what was going on there. Noor's kindness to me was clear enough; but the others. As well as talking to each other they used signs and seemed to be able to speak to each other without words. Magic? Perhaps we won't be here long enough to find out.

*****

We met at Eye The Girls on the last night of the working week to discuss it. Outside again in the garden where it had all started, taking advantage of the warm night air which would be cooling soon and winter coming on. Story time was cancelled. There were a few complaints about this, but a decision had to be made and everyone had to be told so they could come to a conclusion. At least one woman was present from each household; a real crowd, even in the open. Drinks were free, or they'd never have come. We mustn't forget to pay that account or the beer will be water before we know it. The facts were easily told although I had to go over it once or twice. Some of the younger ones couldn't grasp the concept at first. It seemed a shame to spoil their innocence. But when innocence seems likely to become ignorance it's time to explain things clearly. I tried not to look at April-Mae and Bruno, who should have been in bed by now; I could see them whispering with the other sprouts. Hashana was trying to keep them in order, but since she was obviously telling them dubious finger jokes there was a bit too much giggling. I thought that wouldn't last long, once the meeting began properly; even so young they knew how to behave in meetings. As I spoke I knew other older women, like Susasima and Johana, weren't looking at each other. I knew they were remembering. Old stories. Most of us had been born here, but memory has little to do with experience and I wept inside myself to pass on those pains to young Briony and Jen and their friends. I'd never had such an attentive audience as I tried to explain it all. Stumbling. The things men did to women they all knew, but what some of them did to each other was another matter. But if they thought about it long enough it would answer many questions. It would even explain without explaining why we were here, why our mother ancestors had come.

'But,' it was Hashana, looking up from the sprouts, one ear on the meeting, with Bruno on her knee, 'why did they think a new body would change things? Why didn't they just go on being a different sort of man?' No one could answer that. And on and on, the questions. I reminded them of their history lessons, what they already knew. Save us, I had no answers. Though Briony, as usual thought to tell us what to think.

'They were damn fools. If they'd done more than mutilate themselves, if they'd looked beyond the end of their penises they could have changed the world before it was over.'

An easy answer; but some of us knew that two was not always enough when it came to who you were. In some places there was a wider choice. Look at us even. Women all; but hunters, nurses, singers, builders, hearth makers, adventurers. I'm rambling now. That's what happened that night. It got late; there were questions and answers and silence and argument. Not much drinking got done either. Plenty of yawning. Then suddenly, silhouetted against the lit doorway of the bar there was a tall figure in a dress. I wondered how he could stand after so much lying down. I said, 'Come in, Charlie,' so everyone would be sure to know that this was who we'd been talking about. Not that there was much room for mistakes. There was a movement in the crowd in the garden and people were moving away making a great space where there'd been scarce room to breathe. She, he, moved slowly on bare feet to the centre of the space and stood there looking at us. He had on the dress that his sister had tried to mend. It was a flowered thing in some light, heavy material that we don't have. The skirt part moved around his form swinging with his tread and at the neck which was low where his breasts just showed there was some narrow crinkly lacing. The dress was waisted and decorated down the front with some shining buttons that matched its colour. It must have looked very effective when it was new. It had pockets that you couldn't see for he reached in at his hip and drew out a comb.

Slowly and with great concentration he started to comb his long tangled hair. It reminded me of something I'd forgotten; someone rather; my grandmother. She'd sometimes wear a skirt and used to comb her hair like that. She never cut it though my mother used to be at her all the time.

'But doesn't it get in the way? Isn't it a nuisance?' Grandmother would just frown and tut; then she'd smile at mother and tie it back. But when there was no one around, only me, she'd get a comb and undo it and comb it just like that. Holding the bulk of it with one hand and with little tugging movements start at the end clearing the tangles, carefully working upwards until it was all flowing free like a swathe of grass.

His head was inclined over a little as finally he ran the comb through it, dark and curly with a little grey in it. I thought he might be a few years younger than me. Then he stopped and flipped it over down his back where with a life of its own it bobbed and bounced. Then he cleaned the comb of hairs with his fingers and rolled them into a ball between his two hands. It was such a performance — we were spellbound, breathless. What would he do with the ball of hair? He looked at us with a look and popped it in his pocket. Everyone breathed out. A collective sigh of approval. He might be a man but he was tidy, responsible for his own mess — one of the first things a child learns here.

'Charlie!'

It was his sister. When had she come there? She was standing in the lit doorway, a troubled look on her thin face with a hand held towards him. She was asking him something. The man-woman saw her and smiled and shook his head. Reaching into another pocket he took out something else. A little bit of paper. He wrapped it around the comb and put it to his mouth, began to blow and a strange buzzing sound, like a swarm of bees, filled the air. He was making music.

'Don't, Charlie,' came a frightened voice from the door. But Charlie ignored it; instead in the lowering light of the evening, under the cool eye of the stars, he began to sway, to dance. The man-woman began to circle the space, his feet pounding a rhythm, his mouth making strange melodies, his eyes far away, almost crossed with inner contemplation.

'Oh no,' once more from the sister who sat suddenly on her haunches in the doorway and put her head in her hands.

What followed was something I never saw before, nor will probably ever again. That Charlie was something special. No playmaker ever told a story like that. I don't know which was best done, the story he told or the way he did it. Such skill in a performer. He could have earned a fortune in the old days; perhaps even now. He had nothing but his body and the comb. And the light was fading so we couldn't see his face too well. But by the end most were stunned and some were weeping. He showed us all his life as if it were a word tale at story time.

We saw a little boy, unlike the others, liking the wrong things, wanting to be a girl. We saw him grow, bewildered, try to change, how he was beaten and tormented for his difference. He showed us the world we'd only heard about: what his sister had told us in words we now saw for ourselves. And the questions that had been asked, he answered, showing us the despair, the disparagement and most terrible of all showed us his answers. His own fears, self-disgust, and the mutilation. To a high buzzing melody that was both accompaniment and sound effect he showed us the terror and the transformation. We saw him change from man to woman. We saw his body shape alter before our very eyes. One moment it was male, spare, spiky and awkward, and the next it was full and rounded with breasts and hips and a waist. We saw the pain and the cutting, not something that I really thought April-Mae should see, but we were too numb to stop it. Even his sister watched. Finally, without stopping the music he reached behind him and with a little shake he let the dress and what he wore underneath drop. He continued to dance for a while letting us watch him naked and he was truly like a woman.

Who else watched and wondered a little how different it would be with him?

How it would be to hold him and caress him. To touch that curling mound and explore him deeper. But I remembered he was a man for all his looks; that without the medicine his pretty waist would thicken, his breasts vanish and his soft bottom harden up to nothing.

At the end we were silent; no one knew quite what to do. Jen started to clap but was shushed and stopped. Then Charlie did one more thing while he had our attention, from nowhere — he was truly a magician — he produced the pill bottle. Only Jassy and I had seen it but we all knew its significance from the dance. He unscrewed the top and turned it upside down. Nothing came out. They were finished. Then he threw it onto the cobbles. As the glass broke and splintered at his feet he put his hands on his breasts, those beautiful breasts, and shutting his eyes he slowly ran his hands over them, cupping them lovingly and then over his fine waist, his hips and his soft buttocks. For a moment only he did this as though it were a farewell gift he was giving us, or himself. Then changing, he smiled like a sprite, held out his arms as though to hug us and made a kind of obeisance, and suddenly he was gone. Running off through the lighted doorway back to the sick room with his sister on his tail. No one spoke. Dortha was sweeping up the glass as I picked up the dress and the other things. People were going home in two and threes. Arms around each other. No one would sleep alone tonight, that was for sure. But whether for shock or fear or desire, who'd know?

The little ones were all carried off to their beds. Bruno was out immediately but it took a little while to soothe April-Mae till she was asleep.

'Was that a brother? Like Bruno?' I nodded while she blinked with the effort of staying awake.

'But why,' she said, her brow wrinkled with effort, 'was he so big? Brother's are always small.'

I left her with Hashana on dream-duty as sleep felled her, before I had to think how to give her the right answer. I knew what it was in my mind, though not in my heart; the usual struggle for all of us with boys. But I felt a little bit proud that my daughter should be more puzzled by philosophy than biology. But there was no one around to tell. Then I looked for the strange two and found the sister crouched by her brother picking glass from his feet.

'Good job the bottle was brown,' she was saying angrily.

I said, 'Don't cut your hands, will you.' And she looked up at me and I knew where I was wanted tonight. I marvelled that the history we had just seen, that surely she too must have shared in some part, had produced two such loving, courageous people. Charlie refused the dress and asked for trousers and a shirt. I said we'd see about it in the morning. We bound his feet and he collapsed beneath the covers sleeping immediately.

She wasn't looking at me so I took her hand. 'Selena,' I said, 'come with me.' And she did. Followed me like a lamb. And it seemed that they did things there much like we did them here. Though there was a tension in her I've never felt before. But it was by no means unpleasant and after all the confusion she was precious for being a true woman. She wept a little, not much, and I think it was more because she had called 'Mary', rather than had wanted that woman. Finally we slept as the sun came up and I felt happy that her face looked more relaxed than it ever had since she'd arrived here. For myself too, of course. She was a beautiful woman. When I woke a few hours later she was gone. So were some of my clothes. Trousers, shoes, jacket; and my duck-egg blue shirt. They never said goodbye. I wondered how a woman who looked like a man, and a man who had the body of a woman would fare. What would he do now the pills had gone? I hoped she, at least, would return. She owed me for the clothes.

Chapter 3

Ryo's Crack

~ ~ ~ ~ ~

My name is Ryo. It was written on a wall, she said; a white wall near a place where there was fire and hot coals in a box. That's all I know. Except there were birds who fed on bread. They were sick; full of parasites. It was a story, I remember her telling me, I think. And smiling men who were kind, she said, but I wasn't to tell that. No one would understand. I don't. Are they memories? Or dreams or am I getting mixed up with the visions? Dorthy says it doesn't really matter, but I'm not so sure.

It's the only thing that never comes to me. I play the parts over and over. Tell the tale differently every time. The box bigger, smaller; square, oblong, clay, metal. The birds, sometimes a rash of them, the tiny ones that sound like stones falling into a quarry; sometimes the giant ones with the waterfall tails. Or were they those terrible ones that float on the wind with fingers poking out of their shoulders? Was it a big wall? Or a small one like you have outside your house, made of wood and painted? I don't know. Did she see it all just once, or many times? I look and look in the mirror but there's only other people's lives there, never mine. Never hers.

Last night a spaceship disintegrated into a million pieces

of light. I saw it in the mirror. For a moment it hung in black space silent, motionless but for a long curl of vapour twisting away from it. There was a silence. Then a cruel staccato ticking that the realms of space seemed to eat up. Then at its most still it exploded in the sky and below it, on Earth, a crowd of people screamed and fell on to their knees and wept. There were bags and baggage and children. Some of the children stood and watched the burning debris as it tumbled out of the sky. They were laughing. A woman was shaking one child and hit it till it cried too. I wish I hadn't seen that. Before it faded I knew it was more than a burnt out spacecraft. It was more than a picture. I knew, as well, it was a chance lost forever. It made me feel helpless. But they're not all like that.

There was the bridge. It was made of fine wire and stretched across the sea for a hundred miles. It swung like a spider's web and people ran on it and travelled over it quite safely. Voices and music rose from it into the sky and birds sat in its towers as though it was a forest. Blue and gold; blue and gold. I long to go there. To see where it lands. Only this side is clear, the other is so far away it's covered with mist. Or perhaps it's sea spray. I don't know where it is or why it comes to me. If I could go there I know I would be happy.

Of course it's not really a mirror. I don't know what it is. A tear in the cloth of the world? It shimmers from a little crack in the rock, or sometimes it's just under the floorboards. Just those two places. Nowhere else. It comes looking for me when it has something to be seen. One day it'll grow big and I'll fall through. I'll either float then forever, like dreams of flying, or I'll pop through with a big bang and be somewhere else so fast that my skin will singe and I'll smell of burning.

I have to be careful what I tell. How I tell it. I never

know the true meaning. Sometimes it's nothing but pictures till I'm dizzy. Sometimes there's something else. Still pictures but there's a meaning hovering around, like the spaceship. It's so hard to tell what. If it shows one of us at least I know who it's about. But I don't always know if it's then or now, or a warning of what's to come. I try and try to unravel it. But it's not like learning out of a book. You can't ever practise till it's right. It doesn't stay still.

I blame her for it all. I know that's wrong. Unreasonable. But I don't care about unreasonable. It was her fault, what she did. I was just a little child. Probably ordinary then. I'm sure I was. We are all born ordinary, aren't we?

I suppose there was no other way. She said the men would smile. What men? I don't remember. Just that little space I was crammed into. How quiet I had to be. Children hate the dark, don't they? It gives them the terrors. You wouldn't do it to an animal let alone a little child. Even to save a life. What a thing to do. I think that time was my time come, and she changed my fate by hiding me. Cheated Death for me. So now I have to repay. What I am is a punishment. I should be glad to be alive, of course. But life isn't everything. To be left behind. Without her. She abandoned me.

That's how I found it. Looking for her. To be with her again. To be cradled in her arms, safe. I was so tiny they didn't see me go. I crawled away on my hands and knees. Couldn't have been watching me, could they, to let a motherless child run away? They found me later in the rocks. The second time I cheated Death in one week. I spoke to them. I couldn't before. Not a word. I remember they were dragging me from the crack and I hated to leave it. I hated them. Rescuing me and feeding me wasn't enough; so I spoke to them. Well, howled.

It was just a pretty toy at first when I found it. But it was mine, I didn't want to lose it. Not lose anything else so soon. But they were adults and I was only a child. So after I yelled at them I didn't speak again, not for a long time. She was gone and they took away my beautiful thing. I kept dreaming of it. I always remember those dreams. How the thing glittered, like a patch of white sky at the edge of a forest. How it was so bright; so tiny, yet so huge. It'd be there shining like a tin star on a cradle with its people and moons and roads and bridges, all moving like ants all over each other. And I'd watch it and it'd get bigger and I'd see them all clearly; all at once, but separate.

They'd watched me carefully in those years. They looked after me with pity in their hearts, and gave me Dorthy as a playmate; but they said the forest was dangerous and we should only go there together. That I could only go alone when I was properly grown up. And even though I was so young I remembered where it was. I never forgot while I was growing up. It hung on to me. It called me, I think. And as soon as they took their eyes off me I was gone. I was seven by then. It took me some days, but I knew it was waiting for me. I was hungry to find it. And when I did I fell on it for I remembered this pretty toy. But that was spoilt. It was no toy now. It was changed just as I had. I could see straight away. Like when a baby sees a knife and wants it for the glittering blade, and later when it's grown it knows about sharp edges. The glitter is still there, but there's something else. That second time I knew if I didn't take it on, it would close right up. Vanish for me and wait until another came along. So I said yes to it. I said alright; I'll be yours and you'll be mine. And that's how it's been. I don't know everything about it though. I don't know why it's sometimes in the rocks and sometimes under the floor; if it's in both places at the same time or if it comes to find me at home when I'm not at the rocks. It's harder on the floor. Dangerous. I have to lie down flat on my face and put my eye to a hole. Dorthy said once that if anyone caught me I should pretend something, and that pretending wasn't the same as lying. So one day, I was about twelve, I was watching it in the floor and Auntie came in. I only just got up in time. I was so afraid she'd see it, because I knew they'd disapprove, and it was shining up like the sun on glass. Burning rays up the edges of the boards. I put my foot on the hole all the time she was in the room. I kept it there while she was walking about and swivelled round to talk to her.

'What a lovely smell, Auntie.'

That was no lie. She'd made hot rolls for breakfast and they did smell good. It was so funny my foot was stuck and my belly was grumbling.

'That's a lovely smile, this morning,' she said. 'Are you practising your dancing?'

I was bursting with laughter and afraid she'd see what I was doing. But she didn't say anything. I think she knew something was up though. I think she thought I was being cheeky.

I remember when they opened that cupboard the mother had gone. She didn't say goodbye before she left. But do you remember to say goodbye when Death is halfway down your throat? But if they rescued me, why not her? Why were the birds sick? My head is full of wild things. Singing spiders and ticking mice. Those were her words. One day the crack will open onto her face and she'll tell me all. The word Mother won't stick in my throat anymore, because she'll soothe me and explain. I'll understand everything then. I'll know all the answers. They'll listen to me properly and won't say I'm mad. If only I knew what I'm supposed to do.

Chapter 4

Red and Green

~ ~ ~ ~ ~

Nella was a fairy. And lived in a wide branched tree at the edge of the Garden, though why she lived there, nobody knew. The tree was a willow with deep scarred bark, silver-legged branches and pale leaves that twisted and flickered like fingers at a horse-fair. Nella herself was indistinguishable from the tree; her rest and her roost. She too was long and silvered and flickering, and would by the end carry many scars. I dreamed of her for many years, and I think, she of me.

Sometimes when walking in the forest on tea breaks or holidays, those from the Cafe would linger hopefully beneath the basket of branches straining for a glimpse of her. Some said she was a tall old hag; for some of them had been watching for her for thirty years and their mothers told the same story. Others said there was more than one Nella, a family of them like a clan of cats in a barn. Over a hundred years or so there's bound to be one black tom with golden eyes who would seem immortal, but it wouldn't be the same one all the time, would it? So it was with Nellas, they'd say. Some who were cynical and laughed at the obsession said she was a mirror of desires, a dream lover, a heart devil. And they asked me, but I wouldn't say; so the arguments batted back and forth over the years. What was certain was that Nella was compulsive and elusive, flashing only her favourites, so they said, glimpses of grey leg, lilac lips and a long silver plait. But peer and call as they might, Nella gave no one much satisfaction. Except perhaps in dreams.

But I had it in confidence that she did come down at moon-black and take the ice buns and day-old sandwiches left by somebody from the Cafe.

*****

This was something we'd done at Eye The Girls for I don't know how long. A tradition almost. No one can say when it started or who first thought of it. She's probably long gone now. I do it nowadays; or I did. It was the only thing I had to give. But it wasn't out of kindness that I used to do it, it was out of a longing, a deep craving to see her. To see if it was true that she looked like her tree, that her lips were lilac and her fingers long as willow leaves. I was half in love with her. Obsessed. But we all were, we all speculated about her in the long evenings at the Café, went home and dreamt about her and I was the worst and they used to tell me to shut up. But she held my soul. I'd lie under the tree and dream of seeing her; of saving her from danger; of being her. Those daydreams were full of adventures of love and sacrifice. I'd trip through the boughs chased by nameless dangers warning her just in time. I'd fight off mythical bears and wolves, I'd grapple with slimeys. I always won and there was always a wonderful scene at the end where Nella was grateful and loving.

Anyway I was so determined to see her that I used to do this thing. Then, I thought it was no end of a cunning plan.

When I'd put the buns under the tree I'd stand and yawn for a bit, to show how tired I was, for although we had fun, us girls at the Cafe, it was hard work, the shifts were long and by nightfall we were truly dog-tired. My feet were usually longing for rest and my body for bed. So I'd yawn and stretch and go sauntering off. Sometimes I'd hum or whistle or kick leaves, anything that made a noise. Then I'd tail it off, the noise, so delicately, so cleverly you'd think I was really stomping off home, and if you were the Nella you'd hear my footsteps receding, getting quieter, fading into the distance. Of course all the while I was only a few feet away from the tree and I'd creep back with all the stealth of a tracker, never moving a leaf or cracking a twig until I was crouching beneath the blue elder bush that grew nearby. But if I was skilled at silence, she the queen of Nellas, had a greater talent for patience. Never once did I see her descend for the buns. But they were always gone when I awoke for I slept every time. Every time I vowed to keep awake and I'd force my eyes wide and pinch my wrists when I grew drowsy. I can't blame it on a Nella spell, my eyelids would just close and I'd sleep sound and deep for several hours. Sweet blackness. Sometimes not till dawn was crinkling up the horizon beyond the trees, would I come to. Strangely I was never stiff nor cold and I always woke curled in a pile of leaves as though someone had covered me. Like in the old story. And there was nothing, no sign of her. No Nella, no buns.

I never told a soul about this silly trick; not even my sister, only Dream Mistress; she was different, though she laughed at me.

Once I thought I caught the sound of something high in the grey-green branches but it was only the tree humming to itself in the early morning air. Oh Nella, what a mystery you

were then. Like believing in The Faithful Watcher, there was
no proof. You just hoped, and said you knew.

*****

It was of course the Nella. The sound of her contentment.
She'd lie with her legs wrapped round a branch sucking the
sugar from the buns. Ice sucked, the Nella could have fun too
with the rest of the thing, flinging it in pieces to the gulls and
the hawks from the very tip of the tip of the tree. Flinging
and applauding their marvellous catches, those acrobats on
the wing. And in spring she'd use the bun bits to treaty with
the birds for their feathers, spiking the new buds through soft
bread; in autumn it was the same with the squirrels and the
thorns.

But such games were the exception. And the dreams of
the women were just that, dreams. The reality was much
harder. That a Nella had a job to do was unimaginable. It
was a life of Riley, they all thought, to be a Nella. Sad and
lonely maybe, with only a silly Nella's nature to keep her
from loving arms and a warm bed back at Eye The Girls. If
they had known, what would they have done? Gone rescuing
with nets and ladders? With torches and rice and burning
branches to flush out the evil? But they never knew, never
guessed that it was the Nella and I, not they, who were the
Watcher at the margins. It was they and not the Nella who
needed rescue. They lived all unknowing that beyond the
Nella tree, the willow, beyond where tall railings marked the
edge and they long covered, all but hidden by vines and
creepers and great piles of leaf-mould, where they still stood,
so high and straight and waiting, deep, deep where even the
tough and bold might never go was a small, small house.

It lay down in a ditch at the side of an ancient road. Long unused, it was overgrown and overhung, like a tunnel, endless, menacing. Where the house faced the road some broken fencing marked the boundary, and if you leaned on it as some may have done long ago, stopped as they passed and leaned out of curiosity, hearts in their mouths, dreading what they might see, this little house might be spied in the dusky gloom. Built into the side of the ditch it was more a hut than a house, its place in the undergrowth allowing hideous disguise so that its outline came and went to those who looked making them first dizzy then fearful of spells till they turned and ran leaving the house to the shadows of the Garden where it belonged. Yet shadows apart, still someone lived there. And that someone, the thought of them fills the heart with dread. And those brave souls doubting rumour and laughing at fear had leaned and looked and what had become of them? Most went by with heads averted, whistling, skirts kirted, thoughts on lucky charms, rushed on by, away and out of here, my dears. Let's not dawdle just now, my dears. Let's out into the open away from this cold gloom and the house in the ditch and whoever lives there. And when they found themselves there again in a dream, they came to me.

'What does it mean, Dream Mistress? What does it mean?'

And I would give them back their fee, for either I could not, or would not say. Except to tell them to run from here, to hide, to go far, far away.

Far away, though not so far. And if they'd known at Eye The Girls, not far enough. We kept watch as time went by and dreaded whose patience would dwindle first. And what a job it was. The holding. Holding off, holding on, holding up.

Holding at bay. Many ways it could be done dreaming, and be done it must. Far near enough and no further, was the motto. Eye The Girls was the fort at the edge of the desert. Though they knew it not. That old evils existed they didn't doubt, but never guessed it so near. And many a Nella had regretted their choice, wished they'd stayed with the old devil they knew. As for me ...

They'd thought of the life of Riley that Nellas had, and only when they'd climbed the sanctuary trunk did they learn the truth. But too late then. Escaped from who knows what, who knows where. Some pain and cruelty, some sadness, a little badness. Their own safety bought but no ease. A job to do. A training from one old Nella due long for retirement, only just holding the holding. But one always came in time. As though called. Some young thing scrambling up the tree, full of fancy ideas and energy. To be held and comforted, heard and soothed. And healed. Help me, hear me, heal me would become heed me, hide me, hold me. Eventually healing done and holding learnt, an old Nella might take a few years fun rest before she let herself go. Let herself fade completely into dryness and leaf dust and get blown away up and over, out of fingers reach and touch. Away from grizzling apprentice Nellas who had to do it all now, with only soft eyes below and the old icing sugar to make up. For with an old Nella gone, there was only one left to know, to see past leaf and branch, past trunk and twig, past the deep shadow that hid all.

There in the ditch, in the hut a witch stood big and strong. In the small bright room excitement radiated. In the pot on the fire a finishing spell was cooking. In the scarlet water that frothed and bubbled were the usual animal ears and droppings and fetid herbs: but even more powerful was immersed the bile, envy and anger, the venom and curses, the drawn out biding of a hundred years.

They had no idea that anyone hated them so much. For a long while after they were in shock, a kind of group malaise came upon them. Not at the thought of the near miss or at their stupidity, but in the face of such hatred. Paradise was unready. We were quite unaware.

Only the Nella knew. Could smell and see. Each day she'd slip to the highest high, where the boughs bent and the whippy twigs clattered like bone hands waving from a grave. Perched like a grey linnet warm in her cape of swapped feathers and fur she'd sway and croon and see long sight. Legs plaited, fingers woven to the tree, no wind could move her, no frost freeze her out. The groundlings were her business, her dot. She'd earned them and there was but one bead left. Ten hundred years ago there'd been a full row of them. Green glass beads, shiny with promise and a silver skin like alley marbles.

Ten hundred years ago in an ancient city, the story said, in a place now lost, a woman who was loved and feared wore the beads at the start of a journey. By the end of that journey the necklace had broken, the woman was dead and one bead had gone forever.

Who, Nella asked me, knew all the stories of the disappearing stones and their dead owners. How had they died? And how had the beads come from that time to this? Through flood and fire and famine. Through war and changing worlds into the Nella's hands. I couldn't answer, I'm just Dream Mistress. Dream me the answer, someone, and I'll tell you. I dreamt only of Nella and that first woman from that vanished time with her antiquated ways, strange clothes and customs, how she and Nella were as cousins. She had started something and with Nella it would finish. Each warning ignored for many a reason, a journey needing done, a battle unavoidable; ignorance, daring, obstinacy, belief in immortality. But even Nellas die. So she fingered the last pendant bead now hot beneath her breasts. She remembered with sadness her old Nella who had scratched out the eyes of a slimy as it slid up the tree. But somehow old legs got unbound, fingernails stuck and old Nella had tumbled, her long plait catching on twigs as she fell, unravelling like a sigh and holding her fast in the lower branches. Nella rubbed the wet from her eyes. It was bound to happen one day to all of us, it is our job.

But even today as she smelt the red, her destiny being cooked up, she could see old Nella swinging by her silver hair for a second or two before she faded. And in her reaching hand for Nella to take, a last green bead and its broken thong. The impact of the single bead where for years had been two remained to this day. The shock. The vanishing of her Nella. The sudden silence, the emptiness of the tree. How lonely she had felt in that moment. The moment in which her apprenticeship had ended.

Around her neck she knew the last pendant was her safekeeping. And since there was only one, she knew too that she must do more than hold. More than hold it away. She remembered the holding lessons. First a feather in still air, then a twig, then a bird or two if they were willing to play. Then old Nella herself; that was a day and a half. Old Nella smiling, she nervous, trying not to think of dropping. Then becoming adept, anything in breezes, gales and finally in the hurricane, where many old trees gave up their roots in exhaustion, a great sycamore itself. Held in mid air against the winds of that night, all night long. Old Nella had been pleased. Said it had been a good night for proving young talent. Hurricanes, she said, were always a sign of a new witch in town.

'Be yours', she said. 'Your one. Better watch out good now. Both of us.'

And five months later she was gone. So, all alone now, she waited. Held, watched and planned. Sucked ice buns and old sandwiches, played with the gulls and looked after sleepy groundlings. She wondered how it would be. An eye-scratching, or a pulling-the-legs-off? Maybe it would be the heart coming out of the body or a twisting into the centre of the earth. But win she would. Had to. Or how about her groundlings?

Of course, all the time they knew. They actually knew. Though masked by the deep forest the creature there could not hide completely, forever. As plans grew ripe and poison festered and budded, it slipped out. On the wind, in a bird's eye, even the holding was part of it. Part of the chance warning gives if you listen. And though they weren't exactly listening, being too busy with living, they were better in their dreams. For who had trained them? So then at night the truth would out. And he would be revealed. The long matted cloak blown back by dreaming's power and then, unmasked, the powerful red body, the gleaming teeth and the hungry envious eyes. Words they would never remember; his promises to regain what was lost. Retaken, his domain. Threats and laughter echoed in the night clouds as he flicked the scarlet poisons over himself and his watching sleepers. He knew them. He knew all their names, their secrets, their hopes and weaknesses. He knew their bed-talk, their mother's lineage, their secret languages, their loves, their little lies. He would come for them with gifts and jewels to take each as a bride. He had pleasure for them that they had never known and treasure; diamonds shot with ruby threads that would adorn their bodies and bind them, bind them to him forever as it used to be. I could do nothing; he had me too.

We all have the dreams. And wake with horrors and clutch a bed lover or a toy and hold and hold. Some with tears, some screams; all sweating and oblivious to comfort. The witch revealed; the red; the binding. Almost always the same. Different chapter, same story.

*****

Was that part of it? Who knows now? You'd think we'd have known better, wouldn't you? But it just so happened that the Dream Mistress had fallen ill and dream telling had been postponed that season. Due to sickness, it said on the board. But still we were intelligent women. I could never understand how it happened that not one of us spoke. Not even Delia and Pook, who were like twins and shared everything. Not even they spoke the details. A bad dream, it was a bad dream, hold me sweetheart, hold me friend and I'll be better. Hashana and I fought over nothing, like we never had before not even when we lived with our mother; so I never told her of my dreams, like I used to, the red ones; nor did she me. And why did the Dream Mistress just then fall sick, anyway? A fine piece of coincidence that was. Once in a while someone would fall sick, some young green girl, get ill with a nameless fear and take too long to find her courage. An old-life fever they said, and rubbed herbs on her and held her while she screamed. Then one of the little boys was found playing with a book. And that was something else to fight over; with his mother, with each other. And maybe in the middle of something, a kiss, laying a fire, sweeping water, you might stop and half smell something different on the breeze. Something that was bad, maybe very bad and wonder why it smelt so red. But it was only a glance of a smell and fire would be getting hot, water running all over the place or the kiss so sweet that your mind would not want to think of the vileness of that vapour. How many times was there a warning? So we put the dreams on hold. We kept them in, we hugged them to ourselves and staunched our trembling with bright smiles and hard work. Oh, a lot of troubles needed mending that winter, and a lot of unfinished jobs got finished. Sleeves shortened, old shoes soled, paintwork touched up, tools ground. Hundreds of letters written.

*****

Autumn always sends the strongest dreams: always busiest then. So I was sorry to be laid low, usually I'm so strong. Pook came now and again with gossip she called news, and so I learned what I didn't dream. How fearful a time it was. Did I ever doubt they'd manage without me? That I will never tell.

Her dreams began in the autumn of that year. Always the most difficult time for Nellas. There was still holding to be done but leaves were dropping so there was a little fading as well. Not too much, however frightened and tired she was. A little fading and transforming to be managed, so that looking up into the thinning leaves groundlings would wonder which bird had made such a strange nest.

'It always nests in this tree', said Clovis, whose mother and grandmother and great grandmother had all been artists.

'My mother has a watercolour of the whole grove under

snow with a nest in the willow just like this one.'

And when they looked at the painting they agreed it was the same extraordinary nest looking as if it were wrapped around the branch or tied on with scarves.

Willows drop leaves at the first cold. Others like the chestnut and the dog maple turn golden, almost red at the top. The Garden was full of those golden scarlet beacons. It was a time for autumn picnics. The children loved these trips and ran screaming and laughing into piles of leaves. They played catch and chase and sticky toffee and queen's ride. They found nuts and curly hazel twigs; they looked for the longest leaf and the smallest one, the reddest, the yellowest, the greenest, running further and further into the deep, daring themselves and each other to banish fear and polish their courage. The bears of the old myths were gone, like the wolves. No one could catch a fox or get to see a badger with all the noise they made then. The Garden was empty of danger, empty beyond the railings where no one could live so far away, so deep among the woven vines from comfort and help. The Garden was the Garden, giver of wood and shade and breath.

On one trip, it must have been the last for there were no more conkers and the leaves were almost all of them down, a youngster ran back shivering for a hot drink and a bun. Was it Matty? She'd lost her gloves which were blue and now wore a red pair. Someone in a red cloak had swapped them she said. And no amount of patient explaining that stories and lies ought not to be mixed up could make her change her tune. The lady was very tall and big and though she smelt bad, she had a shiny smile and jewels around her neck.

'Not a scarf?' said a friend hoping to cure the child.

'Oh no,' said the little one, 'she wasn't cold.'

Somehow it got forgotten, the gloves were just gloves. Except I felt Nella above in the willow, shiver so hard that the remaining leaves fell all at once on top of us.

And so it was that when the red figure began to be seen she was scarcely noticed. She pushed a pram that seemed to be full of something and once or twice people thought to ask her in for a rest, to feed the baby in the warm. But the woman was always wandering just beyond calling distance, her red cloak wrapped around her tall form and the pram never bumping on the rough forest floor. Through the trees, in and out, just in sight, like a wild animal smelling its prey. Pressing forward but always coming against the holding. Nella doing her job, proving her training. And all the while the red witch tore at their dreams, a wild scavenging thing in the night. But watching went on; and watching so hard and fierce with both eyes on red, Nella forgot the obvious.

'Behind you. Behind you,' they yelled in the old game, 'Behind you. Behind you,'

I called in my dreams. But Nella forgot to look behind her. Never took her eyes off day or night the circling figure, never ceased the strong hold. But always puzzling the contradiction between holding off and drawing near. For only with drawing near could the end be fixed. And how that was to be accomplished was hazy.

When winter came that year it came with special vengeance and beauty. The snow fell one night so fast and thick that roads vanished, high hedges halved and the landscape changed beyond recognition. What had been familiar was, that new day, a different place. That morning had them climbing out of windows with brushes and shovels to clear doorways. Larders were inspected and dogs and children admonished. It might look fun but drifts this deep were dangerous. Those with field animals went out in teams calling and digging. In sheds and byres horses and cows were patted and milked and told to be patient. The snow was white over the whole country; like a bedspread smoothed by a neat hand. White on ground and tree. White in the air. All colour gone. A pale sun leaned listlessly in the sky eyeing all beneath her. Softly blinking, her regard lit up the white, lending blue shadow and turning plain twig to glistening jewel. As the day progressed and a little warmth came from the sun some of the top snow melted. A steady drip, drip, drip could be heard and the wet carved long runnels in the hard gleaming casing of white. With some of the snow cleared and some of it melting the children were set free to play. Snow creatures were built, snow castles, and snowballs thrown all glistening and gleaming. A spider's web was found with a hundred frozen drops like a necklace or a crown they'd seen in a book of the old times.

While they were counting the drops, Matty came running to her friends with the biggest snowball ever, held tightly and with some effort between her red gloved hands.

'She threw it at me and I caught it.' So pleased with herself that they didn't point out that she could hardly hold it let alone catch anything so heavy. So dense and packed was the cold weight of it, they left it there in the clearing and notched up one more lie that would turn Matty, one day, into an Outsider or a Storyteller and loved for her lies, so no harm done. Perhaps a Dreamer? But that's to come. The heavy ball lay there sullen and unresponsive in the sun's weak light. As the day wore on and noon became teatime the windows of Eye The Girls across the way glowed as fires were lighted and cocoa and applejack punch chalked up on the order board.

As the customers came in stamping the snow from long

boots and short, each passed the snowball in their own way. Some, so intent on the items on the chalked board, didn't see it. Others gave the ball the little kick it seemed to invite. As it got smaller and more battered it became a football kicked between two of them, spattering wetly and travelling no distance at all. Not that it needed to. It was where it should be. The night was not a long one. Clearing snow and finding animals had made them long for sheets and oblivion. A quick drink and a game of rummy and they were ready for home. Tables were soon cleared and wiped. Washing up and adding up done, tips counted, cut and stowed, lights off and doors locked.

Outside all was dream dark, another moon black night. Dortha saw the snowball, dull and dirty, from all the games. In the light of her torch she looked at the fragments, another mess to be swept in the morning, and as the light swung like a thin beacon and the shadows moved like cloaked actors in a drama, the beam caught something in the heart of it all, something that was alive and vivid. A shining thing like the frozen jewels of the day just gone. Dortha stepped without breathing over the hard packed snow as if motion might melt desire. On the ground it lay glittering, not a transitory jewel of nature, but a more permanent thing, solid, real; a tiny, perfect and beautiful object. Dortha stooped, clumsy in her winter gear, gloved fingers so careful and precise, picked at it, lifted it for inspection. In the torchlight she could see it was an earring, a diamond or a crystal, brilliantly faceted and streaked with a darker vein. Where did this come from? She wondered for a moment. And then immediately knew it as a gift for Nella; and pocketed it. Oh, Dortha.

*****

And then came the best dream of all. It was the season of gift giving that ends the fall of leaves just before the fall of the snows. We'd had the first fall already. Early and unnaturally deep. I was feeling sorrowful because it meant the end of the midnight trips to the willow. So the dream was a gift and I knew it was more than the longings of my imagination. It was a sign I felt, a sign that she knew me special and loved me. What a dope.

I was deeper in the Garden than ever before. Chasing Matty and she'd outrun me though she was a little girl again. When I caught her she was standing in a trance with her red hand held out to me.

'For you,' she whispered.

In her hand was a tiny parcel. An autumn leaf gathered by its points into a little sack and tied with a thread of root. I knew what was in it and didn't even open it. I put it into my pocket and took the child's hand and we began to walk.

'It's a secret,' she said. 'We don't tell anyone,' and disappeared behind a tree.

Then my arms were laden with gifts. The trees were strangely full of leaves but they didn't rustle or make their papery noise. Instead I could hear bubbling, like a stream over stones, or water in a pot, boiling. I didn't know what the gifts were and I was excited because Nella would open them and give some to me. And on the top was a huge cake covered with sugar icing, with a lump of sugar crystal in the middle. Then it changed and I was in the tree and she was soft as velvet and was cooing and humming with pleasure and we were making wordless promises and I was her's forever. Then like a flash of light through the dream and the forest I knew I had a special gift that would please her and bind her to me. The earring. On the cake, the crystal lump I suddenly realised, was an earring. I had long arms like Nella now, so I reached down and plucked the jewel from the cake. When Nella saw it, she glowed with happiness and held her ear lobe out to me. As I clipped the thing on she held me tighter and we rocked together in ecstasy and love.

I woke with the deep conviction that it had been real and not a dream. Dream Mistress would know, I thought, till I remembered. And as I was battling with memory and the feeling that something very important had happened, and if it hadn't I could make it, the window flapped open and a cold blast of air slipped in to the room. It blew across me and chilled me for a moment. All the bedclothes were on the floor and my night gown gone. But the dream had left me so languorous I couldn't get up the energy to shut the window. And the floor looked wet too as if snow had melted between the window and my bed. I'd have to check the lock in the morning later when I wasn't so tired and hot and chilly. I pulled some sheets from the floor and went chasing the dream again but I fell into a deep empty sleep. And in the morning there was no open window, no wet floor though some dried willow leaves had blown in from somewhere. There were a few under the bed and one beneath the pillow. Later, I remembered the real earring that I'd found but it was gone. I must have lost it in the dark or perhaps I dreamed that too.

*****

And bound in my sick, restless sleep I saw it all; and could do nothing. Through the railings she came, flowing like water, inexorable like a red tide feeling ice melt before her, feeling only emptiness where push had been. Gleeful, anticipating victory. Waiting over. Binding to come. The hundred years plan fulfilled. The thing in the tree gone, dead, dying or too weak even to bother eating. The territory reclaimed. Ahead was satisfaction. Those screams again to be his every night for ever and a day and more, for always. Redness, redness, the forest full of redness, right up to the tree. The bad willow that had housed the thing. To be chopped, no torn down, burnt with acids perhaps. They would do it, their first job in servitude. To tame the wild, to punish the wilfulness.

At the foot of the tree he stopped sensing she was back. The night before she had gone, he knew, he'd felt it. So she hadn't defected completely, hadn't stayed. Well all the better. He would hang her up as a warning. A promise. How lovely was fear. How powerful. So little to do. One drop of fearfulness was worth a whole Armageddon. Let them do it themselves, frighten themselves to impotence and death. First the fear, then the squabbles, then the taking sides, the rows, the spite, the rules, the religion of it. Then weakened and turned against each other he'd have them. By then some would be for him and do his work themselves. Painless. He'd get them without a single scar. Just by showing the dead creature. He'd fling it broken and oozing at them then he'd hang it up for all to see. At the foot of the tree he stopped and looked up. Calling it, calling silently, at last they'd meet, be together. She was so weak he could even touch the tree. Scratch its precious bark and she would do nothing.

He began to pull at the lower branches, pulling and pushing with all his strength. With all his great, pleased, red strength, making the old tree move and sway, shaking the branches, arms around the trunk as if by some great brute force he could lift it like a cabbage, and pull it clean out of the ground. And from the tops, the sound of the birds dislodged, displeased, flapping and screaming; and the tops themselves, twigs snapping and cracking and splintering. And lower a moaning, a terrible noise of regret.

At the foot of the tree some sticky. Those ice buns he knew. The creature was dripping to death. Faint filaments of sticky touched him and clung. Faint filaments floated down, gossamer ice and sugar like dandelion clocks in slow summer heat. Brushing them off he paused in his uprooting and listened for the sad sounds that filled him so with pleasure. For a moment they keened high and low, banshee-like lifting birds from spurs into the icy air to be frozen. On and on went the sobbing and down and down came the silver fragments. As the noise grew and filled the air the sticky fell faster in concert. Filaments thickened to string, touched and clung. Touched and stuck. Stuck to his lovely red, touched and tore. Tough all of a sudden, tougher than he knew. With his fingers now he pulled at it; but as he pulled his fingers stuck and the skin fell to lesions. And he knew all of a sudden as the keening broke and he heard a whisper, '*Mister Knowitall.*'

Now twisting and ripping the cloak, his lovely red cloak, was gone in strips, bubbling to threads before his eyes. But poison, he thought in a second's clarity between glue and pain, poison is my art. All they have is kissing and holding. He had a flash of knowing more and looking up to see long grey fingers, strong, and a bitter lilac mouth. Tired green eyes. Oh so tired, he could weep as that tiredness flooded him, seeing death and fading so near.

But naked he was still red, a match for any green and grey. Even hog-tied with string and poison he could still bring her down. With the power of the red he embraced the trunk once more and through ripped skin and poisoned flesh and torn wood he advanced; up the trunk. Now his noise in its turn filled the forest. His anger welling and roaring, his rage and pain cracking seeds and souring roots. Up, up he came, tearing at the tree, pulling at it for lever and support. In a notch he spied the creature crouched waiting for him, as ever death, the final lover. Though there was something else. A flash, a glint, a spark of white fire. The gem, his gem white and red, a touch of his crimson glue still on the post. But in her fingers not in her ear. It was made for her, for her long felty ears. So it had not been misdelivered. But why wasn't she wearing it, a thing of such great beauty?

He never knew the answer for the weakened Nella missed his ear, where any proper ear stud, even a poison one, should go. She caught him full in the front of his upper lip. Legs tightly wrapped, remembering old Nell, she stabbed him with it through his lip well into his upper gum. And then I fell into a sweet true sleep.

All through the long winter Nella hid, clutching her pendant, not believing it was still there. Not believing more was to come. She was glad of course that he was gone but a deep sadness filled her still. The bead meant continuation. More of it to come. Was it for her or other Nellas or for the groundlings? She wept a little not caring who might hear. She was tired and lonely and it was still winter. No groundlings sighs and no ice buns. No more stolen sweetness or dream drugged loving. She felt a little guilty about that. It had not been a proper thing to do. And now she was being punished by this feeling of aloneness when she should be feeling triumph. All through that long winter, with no one to praise her, missing me her old friend, she grumped and felt sorry for herself, falling in and out of sleep and dreaming. Waiting, waiting, for the spring.

*****

It was Matty who found him. Ironically. What a strange time that winter had been. I couldn't shake off my dread; people dropped off coming to Eye The Girls, healthy animals got sick and then well with no explanation. A strange time. When Spring finally broke it was as if everyone was convalescing, not just Dream Mistress. We all seemed to be creeping around like sick people. Hashie and I made friends again and couldn't remember why we'd fallen out. That day in the forest, a lot of us were exercising legs and laughter when Matty crept up beside me and Hashie, and as we were walking towards the willow I began to tell her quietly about the Nella. Not about my feelings but about who she was and how she got to be there. I thought the walk would tire us both out. Since the trouble over her stories and the fights, she had come to stay in my room. Too young really to be away from home but too old and too proud to bear what she'd borne. So I had a new roommate. One who kept us both awake at night with her crying.

So we were all tripping along talking about Nella and seeing how winter was dropping beneath the hard earth and spring was poking out. And suddenly she ran ahead.

'Look,' she said, 'look!'

I couldn't see what there was to look at but when we caught up with her there he was. Well dead and frozen stiff. A diamond, my diamond, in his mouth. We didn't touch him and I sent Matty on those fast legs for help. Back they all came being sweet to her now and calling her clever, where before she'd been a liar. She was polite, but I think, not one to forget in a rush.

Of course the thing itself took most of our attention.

59

Some of them had never seen a man before, let alone a frozen stiff, dead one. The air was full of outrage and 'how interesting' as we recognised him and tried to get two and two to make four. But it was himself that was fascinating. Everyone peering at the differences. Arguments about whether he was disgusting or a scientific curiosity. Small children had to be restrained from poking the body with sticks. It was almost like old times when a quarrel was just a quarrel and no one got hurt by it. Then Pook and Delia came up and began to snigger. In fact Pook laughed so hard that she fell over and splintered her elbow and had to have it strapped later. Silly woman, still, laughter being what it was with us, though there hadn't been much that winter, it soon had all of us rolling in the forest aisles, even the interested scientists. That lovely noise must have woke the birds and I'm sure it brought the buds on early.

We threw some leaves on the corpse so it wouldn't frighten anyone until we could get a hole dug and started back home. Hashana and Matty were ahead talking together, and I couldn't resist my old addiction so I dropped out of the gang and crept back like I used to. I didn't bother to hide myself for I hoped she was watching. I wondered what had happened, what terrible battle had taken place. The tree was scarred as if torn by a pick. And remembering my dream again wondered if I'd been part of some kind of war.

Then something happened that I can hardly credit after all my longing. Something so wonderful but so unbelievable that I never told anyone, for who would believe? I was staring at the nest and blowing it a kiss which was silly for it was only an old bird's nest or a squirrel's drey, when my eyes seemed to lose their focus. From the nest's outline a face shimmered in and out of my vision and finally, just for a second, I saw a sweet face with a familiar smiling, lilac mouth and I heard that humming again, humming that was almost like purring. Just for a second, like the promise of Spring, a few leaves that still hung on the tree seemed to be waving like fingers, and then it all vanished like a breath across a mirror. I was frozen to the spot and then I ran.

*****

Later in the dead of night Nella woke to the sound of breaking twigs. For a second she was full of fright again. But a gibbous moon shone down for her to see. A little groundling scrambling up the trunk. At last, she thought, a new one, my sprig. And with a heart full of relief she leant over and down to put a helping hand on the wrist.

At that moment Dortha woke also, but cold. Putting her nose out of the bedclothes she saw the bedroom window wide open once more. Sighing, she slipped out and tippy-toeing across the cold floor to close it and noticed the other bed empty. I'll think about that later, she thought, half asleep, and stumbled back to her bed-cave. The room was too silent, and I knew she'd start tomorrow, all over again looking for a new roommate.

Chapter 5

Breath of Dogs

~ ~ ~ ~ ~

The moment I saw the bones I knew it would make a good story. But I was under oath, so that was that. There was no sense to be got from Ryo; she would never tell what she knew. But you know how things get out, and as well as translating, old Susasima couldn't help herself, and soon everyone was whispering and wondering. I never guessed I'd get to see the cave; a storyteller doesn't go hiking off into the interior for days on end. But I knew if I saw it I would make more sense of it than those pigeon-toed historians. After all who gets paid to make something out of nothing? But truth to tell, I'm nearly no longer Storyteller, and if I'd had any sense I should have found another idea for the competition. I'm still haunted by the sight of those poor little bodies curled up in each other's arms. If only they could have spoken; told us what really happened. And burning books; however did our Lady get away with that?

But I'm getting ahead of myself here.

Which brings me to the dogs. And I don't mean our own silly bunch. When the others arrive each year we are all a little afraid. This year the thunder of their arrival was worse than ever. We heard it from afar and began to take the usual precautions. Stabling the horses, driving the cows and the calves into the farthest pasture and putting the youngest children behind locked doors. A lot of heavy sticks were cut, not that there's been too much trouble or damage in our time. Of course the children made the most fuss. Especially those coming out of childhood who fancied themselves as little brave-hearts. But it doesn't do to be careless.

They burst out of the forest like an explosion of water breaks a dam. Like a stream of flood water they flowed into the town and skidded to some kind of halt outside of Eye The Girls, their uncut nails sparking on the stony paving. Of course they weren't a machine so as the front came to a stop the back was still going, the head not in control of the tail as it were, and then there was confusion and falling over and rolling around. It could have been comical if you didn't know. They snapped and bit at each other for a while until the leader, a great skinny pied beast, brought them to order. He lifted his forefeet on to the matted back of another dog and so, getting himself even bigger and taller, lifted his head and started up a howl that rattled along the length of his long throat. At this the crowd ceased their commotion and all began to circle around their singing lord and to join in. Having got their attention and made them do his bidding he went back to four paws, gave his head a shake and accepted the homage of a long red tongue from the very beast he had used.

Behind them I could seen the distant sky full of commotion where the forest quiet had been disturbed. Rooks and starlings and red water doves all screamed and chattered angrily, flapping and shedding their pretty feathers, black silhouettes against the white sky. So as above, below; the air was as full of noise and movement as the ground. But the commotion of the birds and the dogs outside quietened us to whispers as we crowded together peering from the bar window.

Behind the bar, Big Manjit opened the door to the cellar and called for some help. As she disappeared into the dark with her lantern, one or two, mostly excited youngsters, rushed to help her. It wasn't much of a job to risk a dousing, but its purpose was great if we escaped a few nasty bites.

When the pipe was screwed in place then was the worst danger; a moment when we all held our breath. Long ago, some, who'd not calculated on the strength of the creatures and reckoned with too much human arrogance that a wave of a big cudgel would do the trick, actually lost their lives, were torn to pieces before their very homes. One year when the door had not been oiled and it was thrust open too noisily the dogs had taken fright and rushed the Bar. They say the Bar Mistress had had her cheek bitten off and one young thing lost a hand. Each year we learn something new. I wondered what it would be this time. So carefully on the oiled hinges of expectation the door was inched open. I took this duty as someone who knows its importance. Also of course, since my tongue is my tool and not my other extremities it doesn't matter so much if a Storyteller gets bitten, especially one about to retire.

Slowly, slowly, first I lifted the latch, as quiet as a feather. Carefully, carefully, not letting it drop with its usual clack I eased the weight of the door to me. Heavy, heavy the wood. Cut to keep out the winter blasts, to keep us cosy, to keep us safe. My hand seized up a little; it's a hand that's seen heavy work and light. And other tender and lovely things. Today I held it firm, through the little spasm of nervous muscle. As the wood left its jam the air sucked on the edge as if unwilling to see its partner gone. Normally such a noise, like the intake of breath before an exclamation, is hidden, swallowed by the everyday cries and greetings of the moment. But just then it was enough to make us all jump. And to silence the beasts and turn their curious heads to us. It was a bit of a game, of course; they were all waiting for our next move and we knew what we had to do. But all the same.

'Sorry,' I mouthed, and they shrugged and grimaced in silent sympathy. Big Manjit started a battle with herself to keep her laughter quiet. That's typical of her. She gets the easy job and then finds the mistakes of others amusing. But I got on with it and ignored her. As the gap widened the dogs quietened down.

There was a soft yelping and some baby growling from some untrained puppy or two but mostly what filtered in to us was the irregular chorus of the breath of dogs. Their panting, wheezing, gasping. Their sniffling and snuffling. The click of their teeth and jaws as they opened their wet mouths to yawn.

So I got the door opened wide enough without too much damage and Big Manjit brought the pipe. As I peeped out of the crack I was impressed by what I saw, enough to turn and whisper, 'Hurry, hurry,' to her ladyship. But she had turned away and was on to the next part of the job, making the most of her bulk, doing it slowly, showing us, as if we didn't already know, how important she was. She turned the tap on, and as slow as she had been, the liquid filled the pipe like a snake brought to life until it popped itself outside the door where it had been thrust. For a moment the dogs looked unsure at the brown puddle that spread before them. Some backed away, but when puddle grew to lake and the rich aroma filled the air black noses twitched in memory and soon it was heads down. Funny how all dogs have black noses.

Inside we all breathed a sigh of relief and even felt a pang of sympathy for these creatures who travelled who knows how far. Dusty and dry. Paws cracked and bleeding. Coats filthy and matted.

I wonder whoever first thought of the beer trick? After a while they'd stagger off and sleep for an hour or two, a day of two, and then tiredness gone and with it some of the aggression, they'd let us feed them and even pet them. And then they'd go and probably that'd be the end of it till next time. Probably. When they had slept again the air was full of sighs and dog breath and the little whines of dog dream. They lay where they fell, where it pleased them for they owed to nothing but their top dog. They lay in heaps, in twos and threes, in single solitary sleepings. Their bodies, with their different hues and patterns and spots and stripes heaved in different syncopations; curled or stretched, some feet pattering, paws twitching to the hidden worlds behind the tender lids. Top Dog, mindful of his responsibilities, slept light, lifting a sleep drunken muzzle now and again over his family while they, oblivious to duty, were a mass of sleeping dog.

This mass woke one by one some time later. Stretched, scratched and relieved themselves in the bushes. That would be some clearing up job for some one. Not me though this time. Then they looked around for their next need to be met. To play. Now while you might have some little puppy or two or a few water hounds at your hearth that are your greatest joy to entertain, or who love to entertain you, believe me when I say these creatures were no fun. You know the phrase rough play? It was invented with this crowd in mind. They were their own beasts. No constraining human hand, fair or foul, had touched them. Their own bellies and feet were their trainers. As puppies, in the few months the pack gave to such things, they got a little advice in the shape of teeth and tongue from the bitches who birthed them. Thereafter, nose, eyes and wits kept them with the pack and, if they could keep up, thus alive. So when it came to recreation, to play, they obeyed no rules of our kind. Don't jump up, don't bite, don't yap or whine too insistently, don't race around. They did all those things in a flurry of dust and hide, round and round and round again. They chased anything with any amount of legs; cats, our dogs, horses, spiders, cattle, us, our children. Or they would if we'd been foolish enough to leave our precious tribe at large. They tracked our animals with their noses and finding only shut doors and gates did much leaping and scrabbling of paws. The long nails splintered wood and carved great gouges from lintels and frames. Some leapt at trees perhaps thinking, if thought was there, that dangling apples were a game specially laid on for them. A few over eager leapt so hard they landed themselves in low branches and stood for a while precarious and wobbling, stupefied at their new view of the world.

When the fights started it was time to put a stop. Then we wrapped knees and arms and took our cudgels and pails of water and did our worst. Cold water is a great pacifier and as soon as it hit them, for the most part, they stopped. Then they set up a shaking and a flailing of fur, water spraying far and wide drenching us all. Some of the older beasts seemed almost to wear an expression of glee when we were as wet as they, and at last heads down and stinking some, they padded for the last ritual towards us. Kat with her loving sense was often the first and squatted down with a wide toothed comb and began to work. Of course for them it was more play. They endured the grooming for a while, those of them who trusted human kind, but most soon fell over, paws to heaven and tongues out, demanding caresses and to have bellies rubbed and tickled. After, we would all need the serious ministrations of a bathhouse ourselves.

Meanwhile it was quietening to see the savage beasts tamed for a few hours. Kat loved those dogs who came to her. She minded not even the biting insects that jumped on her, but stayed long after we and many of the beasts had gone to sleep. She had some salve which she had made up and tended wounds and scratches as if she were a nurse at a battlefield. When it was dark Big Manjit called her and she left them. But all the days they hung around, wild, half-tamed or growling suspicious and she went to most of them at one time or another with her little pots of herb smelling stuff and that wide-toothed comb.

Big Manjit and Kat were lovers. Kat. A woman I dare not look at. She had four fingers on her right hand from a terrible accident and was reputed by the women she'd partnered of old, to be a fabulous lover because of it. Jokes would abound; but not when Big Manjit was serving. And I never looked at her anymore. Once I'd never stopped and my life was on hold with dreaming. She noticed and smiled and her unmatched eyes that gave her name had beckoned and she'd flashed her smooth white hands at me, but I'd hesitated. I wavered between what was and what I longed for, what I desired and what I might get and the moment went. She never asked twice. Even if she had, now she was with Big M. and that was that. Not that I was frightened of Big M. but I never cared to be a piece on the side of anyone's plate. So I never looked into those strange murky green eyes anymore even when she teased me with a smile and I avoided all thought of her carved mouth, and especially all thoughts of her four-fingered right hand.

It was Kat who found the little black dog. In the aftermath when they'd all gone and she was helping with that clearing up. It was by an old furry oak in a far meadow that she found him. After several hours the dog was still there and not to be shooed away. Kat said she heard stories of this thing happening before, long ago. The dog pack sailing down from the hills and leaving a pup to be cared for till the next year. And woe betide those who didn't. Though maybe she made the whole thing up. Perhaps she was baby-thinking and a puppy-dog would take the edge off it. Not that it was much of a sweet thing; untrained, gangly, ears a mess and with bad breath. I thought Big Manjit would never have it, but Kat took it back and who knows what was said. It became Big M.'s dog so she sorted it out. Got a few bites on the way, I bet, but when Big M. says do this it gets done and the creature didn't stand a chance. She soon had it clean and dosed and trained. Dog took to it and her like it had been meant. Just swapped one top dog for another, you might say. Not that Big M. looks like a dog; though you might think she was a little heavy on the jaw. And the hips. Dog settled down just fine. Followed them both around and started putting on flesh and looking content. Guess if you got fed by hand and washed and stroked and petted anyone would put on flesh. Lucky dog.

But then one thing led to another as is the way and it was Dog who found the bodies. The bigger Dog got with all the food and loving the more active he became, if that were possible. After a while they hitched him to a small cart and he began to pay his way as a working animal. Which meant that like all other working creatures he got time off. But unlike the cattle he didn't want to laze in the shadow of the orchard or go galloping round the meadows like the horses. He wanted to go running. And Kat loved to run.

Two trips round the perimeter soon became the snack before the main course. And where before Kat would hang out with Big M. on Bar nights or stay home and do things, soon she was off with Dog running in the forest. They'd be gone often for long stretches of time. Then just as Big M. was getting restive and bad tempered they'd both return and flop panting and hot into the Bar and demand water and wine. Then Kat would tell us of the clever things Dog had done; the ditches he'd leaped, the nutpigs he'd faced and seen off; and the strange things she had seen, night moths the size of bathawks, birds whose song was a rattle and a squeak, huge boulders covered with strange carvings; and always how far they'd gone this time and how far they would go next. I got tired just thinking about all the exercise they did. It seemed to me as Dog got bigger Kat got thinner. Then one night they returned with tales of the terrible find. Two bodies gone to bones lying inside a cave, more bones at the cave mouth of a big dog. After she told what they had found she looked down at Dog who looked back at her and hit his pointed muzzle onto her knee. She seemed so small as to be hardly there, but Dog looked pleased enough with himself. Perhaps being dog he knew what he would find and took Kat there. Perhaps his pack had always known and we were simply following their purpose.

A little while or so after all this was happening the Lady Ryo began her seizures and we were all bid to watch out for her that she did herself no damage. And to record her words if there were any. Though this was an irksome duty and dangerous work for oneself, not preserving the Lady's body from harm, but that being a Seer she saw. There are no secrets from such a person. And thinking of mine I worried, when the duty fell to my turn, that I might give too much of myself away. I dare say everyone felt like this. I expect she keeps her counsel. No one would trust her else, would they?

My chief fault is that I think first of myself and when it came to it the task was both better and worse that I'd thought. It was just past midday when she began and I was feeling more hungry than watchful. But since she had thrown herself down on the stones where we were sitting I could hardly get up and leave her, so I took her hand and held it while she flexed and writhed. I felt sorry that we'd sat were we had, for I knew she'd have some bruises the next day if she didn't get to the Apothecary. And slowly she became still and my heart too. It is no easy thing to witness and I waited to hear what she would say. She propped herself onto her elbow and smiled at me a little and wiped her mouth. Then she sat up and smoothed her hair.

'Well, Storyteller,' she said. 'That was as good as one of yours.' And despite her words, she shivered as if to throw it off.

'It's no joy to feel the running of another time and world in my blood. To know I have again to witness things I can never touch or alter.'

She had a pack with her and now she opened it and drew out a fine selection of tasty things. Is she cook as well, I thought? Or does some loyal friend keep her supplied like this. The good smells of warm bread and pickle made me swallow and lick my lips and she smiled and pushed some towards me.

'I'm not ready to eat,' she said, 'but I can see you are.'

I made the usual polite refusal but she frowned at this so I did what she said. As I was eating as slowly as I could, for politeness sake, she began to speak, in a strange blank voice.

'It was dark because it was dark. No candle, nor fire, and cold. Bitterly, dourly cold. This I could tell was not to be one of the pleasant times. A voice screamed unremittingly in anger, somewhere. A hollow sound that moved from far to near and then away again. And a tramping of boots on stone. Inside the dark I was breathing fast but lightly, as silently as I could. I was heavy with fear and I was tiny, longing for someone and knowing my tears must be shed in silence. Only a second, and then the boots, and I was heavy with something else. Before I could know what it was a chink of light appears and through a dusty glass orange light picks out moving shapes of metal helmets. In long regular formations moving forward like wind across a dark cornfield, and a rocking left and right, hypnotising. My hand at the edge of this window, a dry bony hand, not old, and it was a curtain being pulled back. But this fear was sickening and I wanted to come out but I couldn't, as I never can. And then I dropped the curtain and the feet and the screaming fade away and I feel again the other heaviness. And though there was anxiety, there was a kind of triumph and my hand falls to my waist and I feel my thick belly and I reach to my aching legs to rub and rub. And I believe that I was happy.

My eyes are sharper to the dark now and I can make out my reflection in the windowpane. A thin drawn face. I am sitting on a bed by a curtained window. I make lamplight from a switch, begin to write and as I gather up the quilt around me for the cold I hear another sound outside the window. Softer this time. A kind of pattering and a quick panting. There is no fear and I thought her braver than I, though maybe she didn't know what it was. Paw marks cut deeply into the frozen snow on the sill could have told her if she'd wanted to look. Certainly she should have recognised the long plaintive howling and have felt fear. But she yawns and putting down the book and her pen reaches out for the switch on the lamp. But even before her fingers touched it she is gone, switched off and I am here on the hot rock once more with you.'

It's not often someone transfixes me with a story. But the bread lay half eaten and as she reached for a share I found that it was I who couldn't eat.

'Is that the end?' I said. But she looked at me as if I was mad. 'The end of the story.' My job makes me persistent about details.

'There's no end,' she said, obviously straining for patience, 'it's not a story like you tell. It's a life being lived.'

I thought it a most unsatisfactory tale, though. And I told her, too, though I was respectful. She simply nodded.

'Whose life did you see? When was it?'

'I'm not sure.' she said, 'Maybe this world. Maybe not.'

That got me thinking. She was invading my territory now.

'All worlds are the same. Innocence suffers. The powerful are greedy.'

This was getting too deep. I snatched some bread, hungry now.

'Sometimes I think I see my own life. As though in a mirror reflected.' She was half talking to me, half to herself; almost drowsy, her voice hypnotic. Then suddenly she turned sharply to me, eyes awake, and said, almost crossly, 'How did you wheedle all that out of me? I hope I don't hear it at story time one night.'

Well, I thought that was uncalled for; all I did was listen and ask a few questions. But I remembered her position as

Treasure and tried to soothe her.

'Lady,' I said, 'I know what a secret is.'

And this time she smiled.

Then later, when I was with my friends, pretending nothing much had happened, the Lady Ryo herself did me a favour. She would travel to the cave and is allowed, of course, where others are not. So great is her devotion to the One who sends her visions, so she says, that only seeing the cave itself and the bodies will allow her to translate properly. This is what she has told the council and this is what she believes. I think some do not but she is so great a community treasure and has undoubtedly suffered much over the years to serve us and her gift, that she may have and do anything she wants. Trouble is, that while she is much revered and not permitted to go alone for the harm that she may do herself, too many are afraid of her gift and stay away from her. I, however afraid, was as desperate as she to see what I would see that I offered to sacrifice my spare time to her needs. I was given much credit for my act of social responsibility. And a long lecture from the Chief Archivist about what, how and when. And an even longer one about how-not and when-never.

Before we went a bunch of trackers sat us down and gave us a talk about the dangers we might see and the equipment we might need. I was sorry that their concern didn't extend to offering to come with us. The Lady is delicate, and Hashana, the Carrier, is off somewhere carrying, so I was to be the mule. This part I didn't anticipate though I sensed the Lady did. Not that she spoke to me or looked at me then but her lips were smiling just a little as they packed the bags and strapped some of them on me. Then I became aware of what it might mean to be with one who sees and hoped she stuck to her visions and hoped again she didn't look too closely at me. In the end we both had seen things. But that's to come.

When we struck out on that first day there was a small crowd to send us off. Not exactly cheering but cheerful enough. Kat was there and Big Manjit who thought it a huge joke.

'Bring us a new story, Storyteller,' she said, splitting her sides. Though I couldn't see what was so funny. Telling stories was nearly no longer my job. I'm sick to the gills with fables and I determined to find the truth this time and who better from this community. So, Big Manjit, stick to your bar and your beer and your belly and leave me alone. Anyway she threw a packet of sweet jellies at me for the ride.

'You'll need these.'

She's all heart, that one. Kat was looking very trim and Big M. obviously thought so too as she put her arm round Kat's slight frame. I had no time to think about that since the Lady Ryo was waiting for me to help her into the pony seat. I gave her my hands for the job and wondered after, why she is thought so frail. No lightweight, though she flew well enough into the saddle and we were off. My pony was a bonny creature called Tork, that I like to ride whenever the occasion demands and she's available. Brown as a nut and just as sweet. We know each other and she's kind to me. The Lady was riding Watervole, bigger than Tork, and just as reliable. No leaping over brooks or fallen trees; I remembered the instructions.

At midday we were well into the wood and it was a welcome change from the bustle of home. Trees grew stronger and mightier the further in we rode.

But always a dapple of light followed us as we crunched over the soft forest floor. I was hard put to be the sensible leader of this expedition. At every step there was something to see, something to admire and wonder at. How the birds tried to get us to sing their songs; how the tree rats threw nuts at us, how the trees themselves made faces as we passed, watched us with subtle eyes and waved us on with smooth and slender limbs. In a sparse clearing we halted, the hot sun above our head and before I could help her down the Lady had dismounted, tied Watervole to a sapling and rearranged her dusty robes. I watched her as she laid her hands on an oak and a stone at its root. I hadn't realised she was so observant and I felt obliged to do the same although I'm no believer and hadn't prayed or blessed since I lived with my mother. But under her eye I thought it politic.

After our pack meal we dozed and it felt good to be there with two fine ponies munching the green herb, a great lady softly snoring and no need to summon up my energies for a smoky night of tale telling. I felt at peace, as though I was doing what I should be doing and all was right in the world. And I thought that giving up my trade mightn't be so bad after all. Then all of a sudden it changed; was it before the Lady began to mutter and turn in her sleep? I wasn't sure, but I felt a restlessness now in that green place. A creeping sense that where before there had been space filled only with green leaves and trees, now that space was filled. The ponies were alert, poised and snorting. The air was both less and heavier, and pulsed silently as if being breathed by a great animal.

Remembering my duty I woke the Lady which was more than I would normally have dared and had us both back on the ponies and on our way before you could say 'what if?' She made no complaint that I had spoilt her dream but obeyed me like a child. A pale one at that. But even then as we rode fast trotting clip-clop away with Watervole and Tork, ears laid back and nostrils flaring, I thought I wasn't the only one who could sense a running and a pattering that hadn't been there before. After a while all four of us sweating and stinking to scare the birds, cantered into a dusty common where the forest thinned and the ponies' hooves struck stone. Both the Lady and I slowed as if we had agreed to and the ponies arranged themselves head to head with heaving sides. The Lady was smiling at me. I'd never seen her so disarrayed. With red cheeks from the exercise she looked like any one else.

'Were you afraid, too?' She asked.

'The Lady afraid!'

'Why not?' she said, 'Am I not the same as you?'

'But, My Lady,'

'Will you not call me Ryo? There's no need for etiquette here, surely.'

'If you want me to. Ryo.'

It felt very daring and I'd better not do it at home.

'No,' she said. 'It'll be fitting. We are, after all, of the same age class, aren't we?'

And I had to admit there had been a little girl in my pigtail class who always sat at the back, who was quiet and had few friends. I didn't now like to remember that I had been one of her tormentors. And I remembered too the times we'd been angry with her for doing what we now praised her for.

'Yes, Ryo,' I said, 'I think I can remember you.'

She looked thoughtful for a moment and then smiled at me. 'It's those times,' she said, 'that design our futures.'

I knew I was red now. I couldn't look at her. 'I'm sorry, Ryo, for how I teased you then. Will you forgive me?'

She shook her head. 'I'm not the Holy Maker, I cannot give forgiveness, you must forgive yourself. Anyway, what does forgiveness mean? Only that you give up hoping that the past will change. And I did that years ago.'

'Oh, my Lady.'

'Don't grovel, Storyteller, must I command you to call me Ryo? The title Lady is meaningless here.'

'Like Storyteller.'

'Exactly. So let us be friends, now.'

And she stretched across the gap between the horses and kissed me. I nearly fell off my pony and she laughed out loud like a girl.

'So now you will tell me your name, Storyteller.'

My name. It had been so long since it had been used by anyone who had kissed me and laughed with me that I'd got out of the habit of thinking of it. I was called Meriam after my great grandmother's grandmother's, mother's sister. I rarely wanted to think about the fragments of story that surrounded that name. I thought about them only when I wanted to cry. Another tale of one who survived a monstrous state.

'My name is Meriam,' I said, and she paused and something flickered across her face as though she was cold. I know each job has its bad side but just then I was glad I made up stories for mine and didn't have to live them.

We had made good time for the sun was on the dim and we had only another short ride till we found the cave. At least that's what the map said. According to our instructions we were to visit in daylight only so as not to disturb the remains. There was a series of caves and the archivists had left bedrolls and a weather cover in one of them. So on we went. Ryo and Meriam. Who would have thought it. That would make a good story that no one would believe, how only one day away from civilisation could turn two stuffy middle-aged women into red cheeked girls; one of whom at least was now concealing a fast beating heart and a racing mind. So on we went and I tried not to keep looking at Ryo and noticing things about her that I hadn't noticed before when the cloak of her nobility and mystery was tight about her. She was my age but she looked quite different from me or any of our age group. She was both older and younger. She had a look of innocence as if she had been constantly surprised by things and yet her face was lined. Her hair was pulled back and I swear it had been coloured. Her eyes were a bright blue and with her dark skin they were like a knife in your soul. I wouldn't say she was pretty; beautiful maybe, although some might call her plain.

We reached the caves only just in time, and thank the Maker that they faced the sun, for I'd been too busy not paying attention to think about lighting torches. We tethered our poor old ponies to a group of trees near some horse-tasty mickleberry bushes and began the scramble up the tight incline to the caves. It was only a short way though steep. But the little rocks beneath our feet made it twice as long. After I'd fallen three times and three times cursed in terms not usually considered suitable for the ears of the Lady Ryo, she stopped laughing and took her own bag and hoisted it on her own back. Then we made some headway pulling each other along and heaving each other over awkward boulders. I never dreamed that this job of aiding the Lady Ryo would entail me shoving her from behind with both hands on her noble bottom.

Of course we made our way first thing to see the bone cave. And there they were the two of them curled together in death. Two young things. And the bones were not just old, even I could see they were ancient. From another time. I was transfixed. Later in the weather cave we realised how tired we were. I sank onto a bed and was trying to remember which pack the lighting tackle was in when the cave lit up and there was Ryo standing like a queen holding one of the lamps above her looking around and then down at me. She smiled and shook her head.

'My gift has its practical applications,' she said.

And I thought that she and I were a little alike. I know I was really only a bar worker despite the position I'd achieved, and she was a great Lady but we both could make a little magic when it was needed. But if I'd known what the night would bring and what we would find; if I'd known the danger that was waiting and the destruction, the blood and the tears, I wouldn't have felt so happy just then sitting in the glow of her light. But I didn't and we ate a little and fell onto the beds and before my wild mind could possess me I sank gratefully into slumber to the sweet sound of another's soft breathing.

*****

Valerie's Day Book
Dear Babies,

Today I heard there are two of you. It was quite a shock but the Doc says you are both well and I hope you are already learning to like each other though not as much as you will come to love me, your mother. I thought of writing this letter just in case we are parted by accident and you would not know your history. You should know that you have not just one mother and one father who have brought you into being, but many others on whom your lives have depended.

You may never meet these wonderful people, whose names I may not tell you, but it was they who decided that you would be born and live in freedom. We live in a difficult world, my babies. A long time ago you would have lived with your parents together in harmony and all would have rejoiced in the family. But present times are not like that. Our Blessed Republic has taken over the raising of its children, and mother and father are disregarded. That in itself isn't such a bad thing if what they taught the children was for their own good and not to fill the factories and swell the ranks of the Forces. Everything I write here is dangerous, for the Box knows everything, and so my letter will be hidden until we are free. I am an active member of one of the Cells for Freedom, at least I was until you began to grow in my inside. Since then I have been hidden in a secret place with someone else doing my job. Your mother was a communications officer, one of the best, risking and daring for the sake of liberty and independence for all people. When I speak of people, I could be sad for most people live their lives as if the loss of their freedom were nothing. As if the Mai Day celebrations that we have this week truly reflect the ancient day of workers' triumph. The noise all day was unbearable because I was shut up here with my belly growing large. Outside they were letting off bombers and firecrackers; shouting and singing and street dancing, plus the usual chasings and beatings. And a few criminals and wild dogs shot by the Forces for the glory of the Blessed Republic which does nothing for us if we may not be who we are, say what we want to say or go wherever we want to go.

If the plans my friends have put into action go well you will be born in fresh air away from the daily sound of marching, and the crash of gun butts on stone. I will not say where for even I am not sure but I dream of a high mountain pasture with green fields and grazing cattle. I have many dreams, my babies, some about your dear father, Yves, who cannot be with me just now. And some others that frighten me. I hope they are not prophetic; just idle crazy dreams. In one there is a child shut in a dark cupboard. Her mother is outside and the Forces, only it isn't quite them, drag her away. I don't think I am the child but still I see my mother through a crack in the wood and I am behind the heavy coats and she hasn't said goodbye and I know I must be silent and I am terrified in the dark. After this dream I wake crying and it was like someone else was crying not me. Other strange things happen to me which never did when I was working at my dials. A wild dog comes to my window. I suppose I should be afraid but he is so thin and his eyes are a beautiful clear yellow. Yesterday I opened the window even though it had begun to snow and threw him some bread which he gobbled up straight away. The others would be furious to think I was squandering the food they brought me on a wild animal. But, dear babies, I will blame it on you if they criticise me. I'll say you made me too hungry and I ate it all up.

I do have one good friend. My new doctor friend. At first I thought she was stupid. But I think all this work is new to her and she is still afraid. She is a little older than I am but seems much younger. She has only seen what disease and sickness can do to us; I've seen and heard what human kind can do and that's much worse.

Sometimes I think I feel someone else in this room. I twist around fast but there's never anyone there. How could there be? Perhaps it is an angel come to visit you. Of course I shouldn't speak of angels as we were taught as children that they don't exist. We are creatures of flesh and blood and belong to the Republic and the Box, when we die we return to the ground to fertilise it. A good enough thing to do. But I have read other things in a book that Doc has and when you are grown I will tell you and you can see what you think.

Even though we do not believe in angels it seems there are witches who must be caught and destroyed. Every so often the Newscast has another tale of a witch and her spawn. Usually they report that the child flew away on a broomstick, or that the mother ate the child. Isn't it strange that witches have so many children. We must thank the Blessed Republic for saving us from such women who are occultists and cannibals.

To stop me brooding I have been teaching myself to knit which will be useful when we escape as long as there are some sheep to hand. But I think you will soon grow up strong to help me wherever we end up because today you have been kicking so hard I think you have a ball in there.

Soon we shall go and one day when I have taught you to read I will give you this letter. Meanwhile I shall hide it for the Blessed Republic marches on in its steel capped boots and the Box has eyes in every wall.

From your loving, soon to be mother.   Valerie.

*****

In the night I was woken by the sound of a wolf. 'Ahoo. Ahoo. Ahooo,' it went. A terrible noise like the torment of the damned. And near. And I was alone. The full moon shone straight into the cave and onto the empty bedroll where Lady Ryo had slept. I was bolt upright and completely awake with all the possibilities racing through my mind. Suddenly sick with the idea of the loss of my beautiful charge. Not to mention my responsibility. I crawled on all fours, as quiet a tracker as I could be and edged my head out of the cave. No wolf, but the noise still ricocheted round the hollow walls of the cave. It seemed to be coming from the cave of the bones where I had been forbidden to go outside the hours of daylight. I stood up and knew that everything was changed. That this was no nice little overnight stay in the wilderness. That bird song, and tree-rat tricks were not the point. This was not what I had been trained to. Or born for, for that matter. Or maybe I had. Maybe all the stories I had told, the pictures I had translated from my head to the ears of others were the training. If they weren't, my life had been a waste of time. For I was alone with the Lady Ryo and she was trancing bad.

At the edge of that cave so full of history the Lady was writhing on top of a pile of disarrayed bones. Her hands were beating on the rock floor and blood was flowing from them and from her head. In moonlight blood is black. Her howling echoed across the incline and beyond. From out of nowhere, away in the unknown distance I heard the sound of an echoing response. Over the uncharted mountains other creatures heard her and spoke. Were they reassuring her? Did they say, 'Wake sister, you have dreamed that dream too long?' Or did they cry, 'We are coming!' I dithered. What should I do. They said it was dangerous to the Lady not to mention bad luck to wake her from a trance. But I was sure the echoes were growing louder. If she had disturbed the precious remains I didn't want our bodies, especially I'm afraid, mine, to be offered as compensation. I was about to touch her when Tork or maybe Watervole, obviously my allies in fear, gave a great scream of apprehension and Ryo's cries stopped like a gate being shut. For a moment there was a long silence while wide-eyed she stared at me, uncomprehending. Then I took a step forward, she saw her blood and we both began to cry. The great Lady began to sob like a child and forgetting all my instructions I crunched over bones and splinters of bones to sit with her in my arms while she wept. And sitting there I felt all the pains I'd forgotten return to me there mingled with hers and the people of her dream. We all met then in that terrible bone cave, and hardship and loss and betrayal belonged to us all. All my failures, all that I could have been, all the destroyed hopes of great ambitions, all the harsh realities that scar and torment. Her pain and suffering was the greater for I could sense she held it for other worlds, but none the less my heart opened then and I let out things that I'd not thought of for years and things I'd never known I had to cry over. The moon had the grace to leave us and as she went and darkness embraced us we settled down two living among some dead to sleep together, as they say, the sleep of the dead. It was a fine sleep.

Just after sunrise when the light beat on my eyelids as though there was some urgency, the first thing I saw was a pile of books. They were high up in the rock on a ledge. They were undisturbed and covered with a pall of web and dust. I wondered if the archivists had even seen them. I suppose they had. My storyteller heart was pounding so loudly at the thought of them that Ryo woke. Immediately she eyes flew to where mine were gawping and we both struggled to be the first to stand near them.

'We daren't,' I said. 'We mustn't.'

But Ryo smiled, slitting her eyes at me like a lizard,

reminding me that she was a Treasure and could what she would, and usually did.

'They will not correct me,' she said as I lifted her up in my arms to reach for them.

That moment will be forever in my memory. The patter of bone fragments falling from us. The feel of her body under my hands. The smell of hot sleep in her and the smell of the ancient dust as it flew down from her fingers over us both. A baptism of complicity. Would that we had left well alone. Would that I'd dragged her sobbing body and my own back to the permitted cave. Would that... As I put her down I could hardly stop myself from snatching them from her. After all, she had no need of them. I can't see the unknowable realities that she makes truth from. I need all the help I can get. All the help I can to invent truths for others to make into reality. You will say, and you are right, that my term as Storyteller is over. But remember for how long it had been my trade. It can't be cast off by the tearing up of a contract. Anyway, with the end of such a long term comes the responsibility to the young chicks who take my place; these books should belong to them. And I was consumed with a terrible curiosity. Of course she knew. And handed me one. It was a day book such as many of us keep. Small and thick and full of loose papers. But we needed Susasima's skills. I could not read it, except to see that it was very old and passions of different variety had altered the writing at different places. I put it safely in my pocket. The other book was much bigger and printed. Its binding had been wonderful once. Ridged leather, smoothly tanned and still some gold letters embossed on the spine. Ryo stood there reading, did anyone know she had that skill? But as she turned over the lace pages, which fluttered like innocent flower petals, the minute script like pollen, a frown grew between her brows the like of which I'd never seen. She began to tut and mutter and breathe between her teeth a sibilance that grew as she turned pages faster and faster until before my eyes I could swear she was turning into a great writhing snake. I had never seen such anger. Suddenly she ceased and with blank eyes she grasped the book, and began to try to tear it asunder.

For a second I could only stand and stare in horror. This was what they meant by the danger of Lady Ryo. Then coming to my senses I reached for the book and called to her, 'Ryo, no! No more! Haven't we done enough damage?'

But she was in full, flaming flood. Her eyes flashed at me like lanterns and as she struggled to tear the precious book she glanced down to where one of the skulls lay, and our oh so frail Lady Treasure gave it a good kick with her foot. It spun to an outcrop on the cave wall as sure as the ball in a champion game flies to the mark, but this ball smashed to pieces and the only applause was my cry of horror. Then, with a public criticism hovering over me, I leapt to defend my duty and reputation. Under both our hands the book did remarkably well I think. We tore pages it's true and her wounds re-opened and they got a little stained, but nothing a good paper maker couldn't put right, given time and a fat fee. And I could see that coming from my wages not the Lady's. But still I grappled. And so did she. We bared our teeth at each other and growled. We pulled and shoved and pulled and shoved and thrust each other up against the cave wall for leverage. As we fought we argued.

'This is dangerous.'

'How can words be dangerous?'

'Meriam, Meriam, how can you ask that. You of all people.'

'Give it to me, Ryo. I must take it back!'

'No, I won't have you take back lies to infect our innocent! I am the Lady Ryo.'

And we started up again, she calling on the Faithful Watcher, Elle Hamoon! Elle Hamoon! Round and round the cave we banged, trampling the bones worse each minute. In my head flashed all the gory story fights I'd made up; all the wounds I described to make them gasp. It wasn't like what I'd imagined. My knee grazing on rock, her nails in my flesh, her strong hands squeezing and twisting and bending, her sharp teeth on my wrist; it made me know what body pain was. And as I did the same to her I thought, this is sacrilege, what am I doing? And there was blood though whether it was hers or mine I didn't know or care. Then finally we fell out of the cave into the morning sunlight and suddenly the warmth of the sun and the soft whickering of the ponies and tang of their dung rising up to us seemed like a spell. Or rather broke a spell. And we both stopped and Ryo let me have the book while she closed her eyes to the bright blessing light, and I knew she was saying the morning prayer for after a bad night. So I left her to it and went to where we'd put our packs and took out some biscuits and fruit and laid them on a clean plate for her. And I wrapped the terrible book in a cloth and put it in my pack and went out again and picked a mickleberry blossom and put it on her plate.

*****

Valerie's Day Book

How strange to find this letter after all these years. I can hardly bear to read what I wrote. Was that really me? Iris persuaded me to take some time to write what has happened since. She said the children have so little sense of history, either theirs or ours, and it may help them. When I get time to teach them to read. Just a few lines then to fill in the details between when I wrote it and now.

How hard it was, how I could never have managed without her. She has been everything to me — friend, physician, mother and more. I was a silly little girl who would have put the children's lives at risk and died myself through sheer ignorance. I thought the revolution was all and my job with the radio made me valuable. I was soon proved wrong. They brought me here when I was nearly due. That was some journey. I was torn many ways, by leaving all that I knew, even if it was bad, and fear of what was to come in a strange place where I knew nothing and no one. Now I think of those others, men, women and children who'd been saved by the Railway, and I'd just thought of it as part of the machine I helped run and hardly given a thought to what it meant. The Doc, as I still called her, then left me when I recovered from the birth and I managed well enough with poor Jaqui and Derick. At last it's safe to give the names. And who was the one who became section leader after Yves? Brian, Bran something like that. Bjorn, dear Bjorn. How could I forget? Their names should be carved into my flesh. All that they did.

Anyway, to continue the story. Bjorn and the others came with supplies every week and helped with the work when I had collapsed in sadness and exhaustion. I had thought twelve hours on the dials hard work till I had two babies. And more important they brought me good humour. And I think they were glad to come for their own sakes. Each week they seemed to grow more thin and drawn and we played with how it would work, the three of us. Building more shelter. Food. How we would run our lives and one week I was sure that they would. That was one week too late. They never came again. After six weeks I had gone from despair to madness to neglecting you babies and back to madness when Iris arrived. She collapsed and was silent for three days. I shall never know how I did what I did. The babies, winter coming on, a sick woman. I opened her doctor's bag and chose any bottle to use on her. Fortune must have been at my side for Iris picked up and recovered.

It seems that Yves was never dead, but in their hands all that time. They must have worked on him all those months and he never gave them anything till the end. We waited to be found but they never came. So the plot was a success though it claimed the lives of nearly the whole team. And to go on without them was the worst thing. Just to look at the children and imagine. All our work, all the politics; but what good is that when everyone is dead.

The babies are grown now. Six years. Those first hard years full of deprivation and work. Survival is no joke. But now the beauty of this place is a joy and it's no longer so hard or perhaps it is but I just don't notice. Ou and Lou are not like the children of my time. Sometimes I wonder if to deprive them of a childhood is cruel, for my Ou and Lou work alongside us each with their tasks. I named them Orlando, for Yves' father, and Leonora, for my mother. But Ou and Lou is what they called each other when they first began to speak and couldn't manage long words. And when they think I'm not listening they call each other Oumou and Loumou. Well twins, they have their own secret life.

And the dogs. My yellow-eyed friend from town appeared one day much like Iris. Starving and bloody. He healed and now he too works for a living. Once a season he runs off but he always comes back. One time he brought a crowd of friends but they didn't like the discipline and left. I thought he would go with them but he didn't. We must have something. He is a beautiful old creature.

Winter is coming. Then we work little. We sleep. Not much food. Mostly grain, onion skins and old tubers. Then we have time for stories and Ou and Lou ask questions I can't answer. The meaning of life. The meaning of work. Who are we? Where did we come from? Why do they want to know such things? Surely it's enough that we live and we are safe. They're all fired up for adventure and who knows what. I tell them to like what we have. I tell them about the old days and they listen as if it was a fairy story and not about the bloody death of people who saved them.

Spring again as ever. Except for the passing of Yellow-Eyes. He was old and these last years, had slowed down. I could not have been sadder if it had been one of the twins. It was as if we had both lost the only witness to the old life and now only our memory stood between those days and oblivion. Ou and Lou have gone off looking for him. I don't think I have explained the concept of death to them very well. Iris and I dug the grave in stages. He is buried at the edge where he used to sit and watch the valley below. There is an earthy patch so it was not too arduous. We started to lay a cairn on top. Ou and Lou can add theirs later.

They were gone several days and came back with a puppy. They found it they say, and that is all they say. It is a strange looking black creature half wolf, half hound, with eyes like dishes. They are very strange, but in all else it is just a puppy and it stays outside until it learns not to wet in here. At least that's the rule but there's much rustling and creaking of doors and tip-toeing that goes on either side of bed time. I pretend I'm a little deaf. Dogs must sleep with their owners. That's a known fact that can't be disputed.

One more thing in this history, since Ou and Lou were in my belly. I should write it down before I forget but what are the words for such strangeness. Magic? Or holiness? There is a holy book here, from Iris's old life. Inside there's a list of her family going back to another time. She wanted to burn it when we waited to be found but its stories were strange and I loved to read about the god figure and how he worked. We never had that. We believed first in the Box and then not in the Box, but in Freedom. And then those strange things happened when I waited for the birth. I remember dreaming about a dark place of hiding and when I was alone up here at the beginning there were many things in my dreams. A lost child. Pain that wasn't mine. One about a child with its eye to a chink of light.

I don't know why I felt so connected to those dreams. As if someone was dreaming me. After the babies came they stopped. I was too tired for dreams then, I suppose. But then a different strangeness came upon me and I began to feel that the babes in me were more than what they seemed. But I think all mothers feel that, don't they? I see something of this in the children. I know they speak without words to each other. Sometimes I forget they are two. Sometimes I think I have only one child. Iris tells me not to be so silly but I've seen her looking at them too. They are ours but not ours. But isn't that as it should be? We are the guardians of our children not their possessors. But that doesn't quite answer the question of their strangeness. Loumou used to ask me about the ghosts. I could only say what ghosts?

Chapter 6

The Competition

~ ~ ~ ~ ~

They'll all start the same way, I bet. 'This is the story of Oumou and Loumou.' And why not? It's what I'd do. But now the first part of my retirement is to sit and listen to all the youngsters trying their luck. Ready to step into my shoes. Now we'll see; after all the complaints. 'Can't hear.' 'That was too short.' 'That was too long.' They've been practising in corners for months. Jen even asked me for my tricks of the trade. I said to her, 'There are no tricks, girl.' That upset her - 'girl'. No tricks, only the careful artistry and skills of a craft polished by years of practise and study. Not to mention a certain natural talent. I remember my first time, so long ago. I had apprenticed myself to Touraine who must be the greatest Storyteller of all time though she's all but forgotten now. Holy Watcher, I'm sounding like a grandmother already!

In part, all the excitement is due to Susasima's indiscretion. So much for her Oath of Silence. The College of Archivists has called her to a council; she's surely whispered her way out of a job. What amazes me, is that they wanted the translation fast, so she only had them for a few days. But the details I'd had whispered in my ear just couldn't have been made up. I should know. The rumours

93

ran round the community like fire in straw. Books, Bones, Bible. Everyone had an explanation, everyone guessed another solution, didn't matter who they were, farmer or baker; never mind that it's someone's trade. So I thought, why not? It's not really breaking an oath; I'm bringing a little up-to-dateness to the exercise. And there'll be points for a smooth handover. None of that blocking that's got so popular in the last few years. Let them work together, that'll sort the gifted from the fakes. And who knows, in the competition some young mind will be bound to catch the mysterious wisps of verity that the cosmos secretly collects. There's two days to go. Dancer Moe's first on the list. Wants to be called Storyteller Moe, I don't doubt. Perhaps her young ears will be sharp enough to hear the voices of the past, as history whispers its secrets into the void.

Ryo, Lady Ryo, has the true story, of that I'm sure. But her mouth is shut fast. And who am I to complain if that? The Archivists are cursing the damage that wolves did to the precious remains in the bone cave. And if one story comes out it would surely bring the other with it in a whole avalanche of trouble. And who would that land on? Who cares about truth, anyway? It's not what matters. No one wants lessons at Eye The Girls, they want entertaining.

*****

Dancer Moe's Story

The two young things were playing. Or working, whatever, as you like. You decide. If they scarcely knew there was a difference then why would you care. They were together and pleased to be together. So like each other, you hardly noticed at this age that one was a boy and the other a girl The sky was blue, of course, and the grass green and the sound in the air was the sound of the wind and the trees and the birds. Time passed and hunger told them to stop. They had their lunch in a little box waiting in the bushes. They ate. They drank. They pulled down their trousers, lifted their blouses and relieved themselves in a proper place like they'd been told. Perhaps they laughed at each other. At the teapot spout and the smiley mouth. And wondered for the hundredth time why and how and what. Then with a breeze cold on their bare bums they pulled up clothes and dabbled hands in a stream. Like they'd been told and got on with whatever it was they were doing. Playing or working. Working or playing.

Then suddenly, or perhaps it was gradually, a change began to occur. At first they didn't notice how the sky darkened as if a huge bird had lent its shadow to the picture. A great arm of dark covered the sky so the grass went from emerald to forest and the sunny air became cold and still as if the trees were waiting and the birds, too apprehensive to open their beaks. At first they noticed nothing, being self-involved in the centre of their little world as healthy young things are. But the chill brought up bumps on the flesh of their arms and their legs and then they noticed and looked up. Without a word, since they knew each other's thoughts anyway without speech, they moved together for comfort and protection and with those great round eyes that are lost with the end of childhood they too waited. Unknowing. This was to be one of those moments that change lives. For many, day flows into day and action into action, there are no deciding moments. Such lives are safe, unaware, uneventful. Full of small wonders and pains. For those who inhabit such karmic clothes the steps up the ladder are slow and purposeful. They must earn the right to find the broken rung that will fling them into the abyss of drama. For Oumou and Loumou this was their broken rung day. After this nothing would be the same. Not life, not love, not work or play. And how young they were, scarcely out of the egg. Certainly not old enough to bear what was coming round the corner.

Coming with a rumble and the sound of spattering scree. Coming with a purposeful thunder with the rhythm of hundreds of scratching feet and swishing tails. With the thump of pounding hearts and heaving lungs and thrashing ears and lolloping tongues. Before whatever was coming came while only the sound of it filled the air, while only the stench of it swept ahead like a bugle call, the little lost dog that I haven't yet mentioned, set up a howling and a wailing so energetically that its joint owners looked at it with surprised eyebrows for it was so quiet a dog usually that you hardly noticed it. It had been there all along with the children, hardly noticeable rummaging in the bushes, chasing its own quiet little tail and its own quiet little shadow and mostly sleeping. Who'd even seen it? Not you. Nor I, till now. When it had bellied up to them eleven or twelve months ago with its saucer eyes, then it had made a big noise.

'Please take me in,' it had whined quite clearly. That done, it was a very silent creature. Till now. But then it is a peak moment and dogs notice these things. They like to mark things. Corners, trees, momentous occasions.

'Shush,' the twins yelled together.

And the little thing shushed itself and as if its own special moment had arrived it pointed with its nose at what was coming. Good that it was a Pointer and not a puppy Collie. What was coming would defy all rounding up and not be pleased at having its ankles nipped. What was coming was a cloud of dust that bellowed and belched like smoke from the mouth of a monster.

But the monster stopped a little distance before the twins and the dust slowly settled returning to earth where it belonged but not before inhabiting hair and eyes and noses of those big-eyed children. After they had recovered from the spell of coughing they saw through the settling dust eyes looking back at them. How many? Fifty. A hundred. Two hundred. No one was counting. First there were eyes, then noses, then the heaving dust-covered bodies of a dog pack. Then as if with one mind they suddenly shook themselves and once more dust rose and fell leaving dog hide cleaner and children dirtier and choking again.

After a while there fell not dust, but denser, a silence when each party assessed the other. And for each, something was not quite as it should be; what they saw and smelt didn't quite match up to what they knew. On the one hand dogs were friend, dogs were fun, dogs were warm and floppy and sometimes wet and silly. But here were dogs too many, with eyes too mean and wild. With tongues that knew more than licking noses and salt off legs. Here were creatures that didn't know the lash or the leash or a full belly. Here were creatures that were many parts of a pack, and the many that was at once one. On the other hand, or paw perhaps, here were the two legs that were such a risk. The two legs from whose long-clawed paw came fire and rock and heavy stick. Two legs, whose hard voice threatened 'Gercher', and 'Getarafear' as they hailed the air with painful darts. And yet these were small. They sniffed at their youth. Two. And they stuck shoulder to shoulder as if one. And their eyes were very mild like the eyes of unschooled puppies.

The pack padded one step forward. And another. No darts filled the air. There was a twitching of fur and fleas and heads lifted. Little lost one gave a warning snort, though to whom is not known. All eyes swivelled to him and under the glare of so much attention he sprang up wagged his tail and trotted nearer to the pack. Twins, who knew each other's mind like their own called as one, 'Koby!' which was his little lost name. And Koby gave his obedient - I hear and I obey, yap, and sat down again. Then it began.

From the centre of the pack heaved Chief Dog. Black and brown brindle. Heavy jowls, overhung jaw. A few scars on his greying muzzle and an old wicked slash, badly healed on his rump. Not so big, not so cruel. Just Chief. He fixed little Koby with veiled eyes, one blue and one grey and called him.

'Come now', he said. 'It's time. We've come for you. You are ours, leave these two legs and return to your kind. Say farewell sweetly, but say farewell and come'.

And he turned and shouldered his way back into the body of dogs and it was as if he was never there, as if he had been devoured. In his place stepped a younger, smaller, high strutting black and white mutt. Whose eyes were as bright and shiny as fever and just said, 'Now. We mean now.'

Koby, entranced by the pack and high on command lifted up his skinny little rump but before he could take a step Loumou herself stepped up to Fever-Eyes and said, 'No!' in a high squeaky, nervous voice. It was over before it had begun. Fever-Eyes growled and lowered his muzzle, snarling. The girl backed, Fever advanced showing teeth, and the boy picked up his potato hoe - so it had been work after all - and as the dog sprang, brought it into a collision course with the creature's head. Sharpened metal cracked bone and without a sound the dog dropped to the ground motionless. Another silence. Another stillness.

Out of that crowd of creatures, human and canine that day, only the two children knew nothing of death. Even little Koby, whose bloodstained body had been dragged by the maw of his dog aunt from the belly of his dying bitch mother, knew corpse when he smelt it. Especially dog corpse. In that second Koby was puppy no more. He stood on his two back legs and licked one last time the two children who had been his companions for that nurturing year and he too vanished into the dog body.

They didn't seem to move. Had they moved? Silently with no malice they surrounded the killer. Blood on the hoe, such a little blood, it seeped into the ground and the eyes that had glittered so brightly were filmed like oil on water. Body cooled fast. No more the sleek muscled beauty. There had been life, then it was gone too fast. No time to say wait, or sorry, or I didn't mean to. But still the boy found himself in the centre of a great ring of dusty dogs. His sister was no longer there. He could feel her no longer, though he heard her away somewhere crying, howling impotent, invisible. The dogs were quite calm. It was reasonable after all. He too was no longer a child. But someone upon whom fate had laid a heavy burden of responsibility. He could quite see their point and they in their turn understood that it had been love and duty and not malice that had felled one of them. But he had reparation to make. He wished though, something; that he had time for one last, something, but he couldn't quite focus on what it was. And the pack grew closer, their breath heavier. And one dog dragged itself towards him. Old, she was old. She would be joining Fever-Eyes sooner than later, she said, and it was beholden upon her to do this last thing for her pack. Her old bald coat was stretched across her thin ribs, her white muzzle trembled and her mouth frothed a little from her toothless gums. And as she came the boy sank to his feet and sat on the cold ground shivering. Old lady dog came closer sniffed him and sat half across his legs. Seemingly not content with this proximity to the human she shifted and shufted until she leaned fully on him with all her weight, her nose inches from his. She sighed and thumped her tail and turned her head once to her pack and then back to him.

And then what happened? Well nothing much, seemingly. The pack snuck closer, creeping low and shuffling like dogs do when they've been banished from in front of the warm fire and their bodies are blocking the warmth but then after a while they're back with a careful look, smaller this time and you pretend not to notice because you are master and they are hound and your word goes. So before he knew it the boy was lying propped up on the hot damp body of a great grey creature who seemed to be a cross of several matings and very pleased to be so too. He leaned back and could feel the smart tump of the dog's heart under the smooth svelte muscle. He could smell dog all around him sweet and musky, the smell of dog sweat and grass and earth and shit. He was drowsy now and hot under the weight of Old Lady. Then she heaved herself up, her front paws soon over his shoulders, her muzzle under his chin. Way in the distance some time away it seemed his name was called, 'Oumou, Oumou'. Too faint now to remember who that was, who was calling. A tie was being loosened, his mind was heaving slowly, and he yawned again and again. Then Old lady lifted her head and a high whine erupted from deep in her. She lifted her old head and gave a howl as hollow as an empty beach, and suddenly all but his back rest were on their four feet and their panting came rhythmically in unison like a husky chant. And she, Old Lady wise one, who knew the ways of the pack and knew how the pack must be to work, looked down at the child and taking a great gulp of air into her frail body caught the boy's eyes and expelled the air in small rib-rippling puffs onto his face and down his open mouth. Then he knew, a part of his old self knew and he struggled to stand on two feet.

But it was too late. Old Lady had done her duty, got off his legs and flopped down onto the ground. Not so the rest. They sat and watched. At first little happened just a darkening of the skin. Then an itching, an unbearable itching at his mouth; all over. Scratching, he scratched at the small bumps growing, and the hairs that emerged, with sharp fingernails. Sharp, sharper, sharpest. At the same time at his rump he knew a strange sensation, not one he had ever had before, as if...as if there was another part of him to move. Turning round he tried to see behind him and the circle of dogs made him a space. Round and round he went, slow at first and then faster trying to catch whatever it was on his back. And it suddenly seemed easier, more efficient to flop down and do it on all fours. And it was so funny, so very, very funny to be able to do this. More fun than he'd ever had with. . .Who? No one. No one had ever let him chase his tail like this and he went round faster and faster and faster in the widening circle of his family yelling in a strange voice that wasn't his but that was so much better than his old one. And they were yelping encouragement, and Old Lady was nodding approvingly and telling him to make as much noise as he felt like making because right now was a celebration, a re-birth. One had gone and one was come. He had no debt anymore. The past was over. He had found his home.

They found her later wet-eyed on the ground shuddering

with spent emotion clutching her brother's scarf. The red one he wore to keep off the sun. Of him there was no trace. But the ground was torn up as if a great many animals had been chasing around. Eventually some weeks later Loumou told them what she had witnessed. Her mother's first reaction was to administer a thorough spanking for telling lies about something so serious. But there was something about the girl now, so she didn't. Anyway there certainly was blood on the potato hoe which held up her story. A few years later when she was fifteen the girl left. She said she would bring her brother back or not return. It was a strained parting. In fact they never did see each other again, though Loumou kept her promise.

*****

Well this was very good; Dancer has more than promise. A very good try. To start is always the worst. If you are selfish and don't leave a good ending you can lose your friends and the sympathy of the crowd. But this was a good ending, complete in itself but with plenty of places to go. She really caught the dogs; clever of her to use our life and make it story.

Now that Afaf. Not so young as some of them. You could tell she's sick with nerves; bitten half her fingers away. This is her second try. She was in the final three last season. Many supporters here today; all nodding to her like berries on a bush. As if nodding ever helped once you're facing them all.

*****

Afaf's Story of the Court of King Dogg

'Who is your father?'

'Who is my father?'

King Dogg waited imperious but a little impatient, not being one given to repeating himself. My father. Father, she thought. Indeed there is no father than this for me. He means the end of my journey. And knew enough that, supplicant and stranger, she should not correct his speech.

'Great King,' she said at his feet. 'I have come so far to find you in your beautiful Palace of the Three Spires and know you have what I must have back, in the clutch of your hand. So I know there is no father than this. No father than you.'

And looking up she saw the eyebrows of the King shoot up into his tawny hairline while at his side his Queen's lips quivered like two little dancing worms.

King Dogg leaned forward nodding and smiling.

'Good, good.' He said. 'But today I do not favour smarm. Today I want truth. Your mother and your father? Your parents. Who are they?'

Loumou must answer. This she knew. And fast. But how?

'King,' she said. 'I have not come to wrath you. But I know not how to give you your answer. Is this a puzzle for me? My parents. My brother and I left behind us our dear mothers. We had but mother and mother.'

Mother and mother! And she heard behind her the whole crowd snatch in such a breath as to empty the whole hall of air. That was not the right answer, she could tell. In fact she suspected it was more than not right. What she had said had the echo of spade on earth and of deep hole. The King's reddening face held no clues and the Queen looked not at her but at her royal Lord. Over her shoulder most faces were covered with hands or sleeves or fans. Yet she saw some who were more stunned than shocked. Stunned and thinking about it.

'Not such a bad idea,' came from one girl's eyes in a face mottled green and yellow like a cabbage. Then with a roar and clank the King rose and pushed past her into the shivering crowd of his courtiers. Reaching among them he pulled some towards her.

'This,' he yelled, pushing a man towards her, 'is a father. And this,' screeching now, 'is a mother.'

Now it was the turn of a woman to stumble her feet in her long robe.

'And this,' he said grabbing the girl with the bruises, 'is their child. That is a family.'

And the girl with shrinking face and closed eyes fell under the royal shove into the man whose fixed scared eyes were only upon the royal anger, and his child would have fallen but for Loumou who caught her by the shoulders. And for a second they looked into each other's eyes and saw their own and each other's lives mingled. And the girl's eyes became wet and Loumou let her dry them on her shoulder.

Then amidst the swirls of anger Loumou felt a wave of coolness and soft hands pulled her away from the girl. The coolness was the Queen.

'Now Lord.'

Her eyes over Loumou's head looked at his Majesty.

'Enough anger, dear Lord. Her ways are not ours. She is young and can learn.'

And leaving Loumou she went to the King taking his arm with little calming, patting movements. It seemed to work and the anger sizzled out of him like a pricked omelette.

'Very well. My Queen has interceded for you and I will let her. I don't know what you want from us and I won't hear it until you hear me. Return when you know the meaning and value of the word father.'

He leaned forward again softer now he knew what to do.

'Be off now. It will do you good one way or another.'

All through the years while Loumou was growing up, between the time her brother had disappeared and when she was old enough to leave, she grew tall and healthy enough and after a while forgot the brutal details of that day. But in her heart there was a purpose that waited for its own time, and this was determined by a wonderful vision. Now the moon herself had had some finger in this, for when it was young and thin Loumou would be fresh and happy, but when it was big and round Loumou would know her brother again and be with him, though she couldn't tell how or where. One night when she was a few days from her fifteenth year under the flower of the big round moon Loumou fell into her fit and lay in a hot huddle with her brother, the dog. They played and spoke together about all that had happened to them since they had been parted and about their deep love for each other. Oumou absolved his sister for her part in his fate but said the debt he had incurred was nearly paid and the time ready for her to fetch him. And though she felt she was in heaven to know she would soon be with him, part of her strained to know where he was, for rescuing Oumou from the spell could not be done in dream but was a task that must be done in the real world. As she lay in her bed that night it seemed to her that the moon's beam coming through the window had a special intensity about it. Creeping from her bed with her brother's teeth on her ankle she peered through the window. Day was breaking and the moon was fading and she felt the faintness that heralded an end to her brother's stay. But leaning on the sill she saw briefly but clearly a beautiful palace perched on the side of a mountain whose peak was split into three. She counted the three peaks and saw three spires of a palace, and as the sun chased the moon away completely she was no longer able to hold onto this world and fainted into darkness with her brother's mournful whining in her ears.

As she turned away from King Dogg and his Royal Queen the crowd parted, their robes swishing and shushing on the hard floor like the sound of the tide on a hard beach. The great door opened with its sad creaking and somewhere in the darkness outside she heard the sound of dogs and knew that somewhere in the beautiful Palace someone waited for her to return. As the door began to close behind her Loumou was filled with desolation. When she had found the Palace of the Three Spires she had thought the long journey over. She had thought that soon, soon, she would find her brother and take him home. Her new task sat on her shoulders a heavy weight that sank into her sad heart. Then behind her came the sound of silk snagging on wood and she heard a thin voice call.

'Girl!'

And turning round saw a figure silhouetted in a sliver of bright light.

*****

Afaf. Did you like the way she did it! Started softly so we had to strain a little; a teacher in the little girls' school, so I expect she learnt that trick there. It was a good beginning and she made us laugh with the King and the Queen. Left an easy ending to pick up. I think she gets points for that and for the strong characters and the voices, which she did really well. I bet the little pigtails love her. She's had lots of practice, you can tell. Babs next.

The youngest competitor. Dortha's daughter. She's a pasture farmer now; so Babs never has much time, in the summer days at least, for bar visits. You could see why she'd want a change of job.

*****

Bab's Story

When Leonora, for that was her name, knelt by Orlando, her dog-brother, the girl from the Court wept tears down her green and yellow face. She'd taken Leonora the back way, always the best where there are guards in question. They had gone walking carefully, of course, but without hiding. Walking straight and firm as if they had some permission or it was an errand they were on. In the stables the dog Orlando had begun to howl before they had got even three lengths from the place and when the girl from the Court lifted the latch to open the door he flung himself on his sister and the two of them fell to the floor gasping and weeping with a terrible joy. And the girl from the court stood in the shadows watching Leonora's back as she had promised she would do; her part of the bargain.

'I knew who you were from your eyes,' she'd said. 'That you were a kin to that strange beast. And I smelt it on you too, when you were close to me in the court. It was a dangerous smell of something other, of wildness, of another place and time. And I know that you were why it had been saved. Many a time they had nearly shot the beast for its strangeness. For it only just being a dog. Sometimes when the moon was on the turn its howling was like a child's cry and the whole place, Court and kitchen and cloister was up in arms not able to bear the sound of it. But every time they took a gun to it the gun broke, or the guard took ill, or a war broke out, and every time the creature was saved. The King keeps it for he says it's charmed, but he never pets it, and no one dares say he fears it. But he is King Dogg and all dogs are his, and he will need working on but nothing is impossible. And there in the Court I envied you. The freedom you had to come and go. If I show you what you want, will you show me the way to leave? My family will never miss me. My father will find another punch-bag and my mother will be glad never to feel ashamed to set eyes on me. I will be your servant if you want and watch your back. I'll bring some of my father's gelt and we can live well, and when we've spent it all I'll sing for our supper and do other things that will pay, and you'll see all will be well.'

In the stables once they had got over the weeping part they got down to the rest of it. How to get all out safely, the first part of which had to do with the subject of fathers. Now having lived for several years at Court, Orlando knew about them and had got quite fond of his, for as a dog who had no real bitch to call on he had been all at sea at first in his new life. Hadn't known how to do a thing right. And while he was good-natured enough to take a good bit of joshing, after a while of not knowing and being nipped and roughed up as part of it, his good nature had begun to desert him. At that point he found a father. Another lone dog, not old but older and certainly much wiser that he. This was Brown Boldo, and Orlando quickly learned from him all that he knew. Now this wasn't everything a dog should know but it was enough. So when Leonora began to complain about the fathering she'd seen, how strict fathers were and how they used their tallness to make girls do their will, Orlando put her right.

'....remember,' said Leonora, 'our two mothers, how sweet they were? And how strong? And how they brought us up and trained us out of our childishness. How could a father do that?'

'...a father can be strong and growl when you misbehave.'

'Well,' said Leonora, 'that was just like mother Valli, our first mother. Remember how sad she was when we misbehaved and she would have us be good?'

'...a father can carry you when you are tired and can run no further.'

'Well,' said Leonora, 'that was just like mother Iris, our second mother. Remember how tall she was and how she could carry both of us when we were little, one on each arm?'

'...a father can teach you to catch sticks.'

'Well,' said Leonora, 'you've forgotten the games we used to play with mother Valli. She had a hundred ways of making us run and when we were tired, another hundred for making us laugh.'

'...a father can teach you to catch fish with your tail.'

'Well,' said Leonora, 'you've forgotten the times we used to go fishing with mother Iris. Remember how we'd sometimes bring home enough fish for weeks and enough to dry for the cold weather?'

'...a father will let you go grubby all day long and go to sleep without cleaning yourself.'

'Oh,' said Leonora, for she had nothing to say to that. She

knew going to bed dirty was something neither of her mothers would ever have put up with nor, she suspected, would any mother anywhere in this world or that. She was persuaded. And though Orlando didn't have as much experience as he thought, he had had some sort of a father, while she had only observed them from afar. But she privately thought that dog-fathering would probably change somewhat if dogs became men.

Later, after some instruction from the girl from the Court, Loumou was before the King once more. He sat ready for a fight with both hands on his silken hips, while the Queen by his side had a mind-how-you-go-little-girls look on her royal face. Now Leonora if she had learnt anything while she had been on the road had learned, eventually, when to hold her tongue and when to keep her mouth sweet. So she looked up at him, fitted a suitable expression onto her face and lowered both her eyes and her head. She didn't see his satisfied smirk but she felt it and she said, 'Royal father, I have learned much, thanks to your wise instruction. I have learned the value of fathers. How they are strong and kind, how they care for their young, how they play with them, how they are less fussy and particular than mothers. I see now that I am who I am because I had no father. That I came here on one small mission, but under the spell of your goodness I was entranced by the example of you, the Royal Father to your people, who are your children.'

There she waited to give him a chance but it seemed this time he would hear smarm.

'I am grateful,' she said, rubbing it in even further, 'for you putting me right.'

And lifting her head she saw him sink back into his fat cushions with a sharp puff of air and a smile for the whole room. That was the other thing she'd found, that top people, like dogs, can take any amount of flattery and not even notice it. His Queen, however, was quite a different person. She opened her mouth to speak, to reprimand, Leonora felt, but King Dogg held up his hand.

'Later, bitch dear,' he said without looking at her. 'Didn't you hear, she has enough mothers already?'

Then instead of holding on to her luck Leonora nearly went too far.

'One thing, Royal Father, that puzzles me.' And he gave a benevolent nod to allow her to continue. 'Why is it that some fathers paint the faces of their daughters yellow and green?'

King Dogg leapt up and growled as good as his name.

'I didn't say bad fathers!' he yelled, and stood staring down at her. 'It's time for you to be on your way. Now what did you want and don't think I'm in any kind of a mood to grant you much.'

'It's just a runaway dog, royal King.'

'Just a dog! There's no such thing as just a dog. All hounds are mine. This is the Court of King Dogg.'

So they stood there glaring at each other for a while. Leonora had got no further with her planning and couldn't think how to move forward to what she would have. She was about to lose her mind and her mild manner with it, when the girl with the cabbage face who had been her friend all this time, fell on her knees and burst into tears. The Mighty Father, stepped down off his dais and bent to her lifting her up and even wiped her tears with his own eye-cloth, for he was a compassionate man at heart.

'Oh dear King,' she sobbed, 'let the beast go. It is the possessed one that has needed shooting. This rude girl's father is sick near to death since his ungrateful hound ran off and came to our pack. You know how cursed it is and she will be doing us all a blessing if you allow her to take it home with her. If it remains here on our happy land its curse may infect us all and bring misery.'

Leonora thought they were pretty good lies especially since most of her curses and misery seemed to come from the back of her father's hand.

'I'm sure the dog is full of a dangerous spirit,' she went on. 'Indeed, King, I heard it speak like a boy'.

At that Leonora too fell down and sobbed, in case the Royal Brain thought about that and concluded it might be a good thing to have a talking dog about the place. But the Royal Brain was obviously more concerned with the sight of two weeping girls at his feet.

'Take it, take it,' he said.

And swirling on his heels he left the room. His Queen followed more slowly and paused near the two figures on the floor. She didn't actually look at them but Leonora was sure she heard the words,

'Good show, little girls, good show.'

*****

That story really wound it up well; and smooth, with the way she picked up the tone and the voices of Afaf's like a runner in a stick race. Confident too; but what about the boy-dog getting back his shape? She ducked that. But Dancer had done it earlier; I suppose she felt she'd lose marks for copying. No satisfactory solution to that problem, I fear. If it had been me I'd have had the dog becoming a boy again by moonlight or some such thing. And what about poor old Brown Boldo?

Still the story had promise. 'Good show, little girls, good show.' Very funny. Who'd have thought it; a farmer's daughter with that sort of a gift. And what a bonny girl. Ruddy and golden. Watching her I suddenly thought of lying in the sun and getting brown. That's no way to go. Start thinking about the right things will you, woman. Faithful Watcher, when will I grow up!

It had been a cold, wet miserable day when we began the competition. But for Winners Day which was also my last it was one of those wonderful blue sky, blustery days. My favourite weather. There was a big crowd, and at first I couldn't tell whether the held-in grins and whispers were for me or for the things to come. I was nervous imagining that my worth and all the years I had put in would be forgotten, or worse, rushed over in the excitement of the moment. But no, I had my day, as they say. They made a big speech and said things I liked to hear and all the young storytellers who were waiting to jump into my shoes looked suitably respectful and grateful, though there was a sense of restlessness and I hoped I wouldn't be cut down in the rush to welcome my successor. Big M. was the surprise because she made the biggest speech and handed me a gift. It was a carving of a tree; very fine and detailed. Must have cost a handful of hours. Round its roots were words to remind me of the event and what had already been said. I think I blushed and for once I didn't have much to say. That made everyone laugh. Then Kat stepped up and kissed my cheek and gave me a paper and Big M. just watched her with some kind of a smile on her face. The paper said I had free bar privileges until the day of my death. Well, that was a thing.

Then it was my turn to say things and to put the

competitors out of their misery. I'd given it a deal of thought, but it wasn't as easy as I hoped with one clear winner. In the end I took the cowards way out and declared a dead heat. Dragging it out gives the whole event a bad name though. When I won it I won it outright, no competition. That was the old days though. We knew how to tell a story. Now it will go to a vote and they'll have to wait at least another five days while that's sorted out and everyone will be cross with me. Of course, finally I did my goodbye story and thank my luck it was so easy. I remember when Touraine did hers, I'd been such a cleverness that she was hard put to find something that I hadn't tidied up already. But this lot had left a lot of loose ends and thus gave me a chance to go out shining. Perhaps it was another of Bab's generosities. It was the dog called Brown Boldo that called me, so I began with a growl and that made them all sit up and listen.

*****

Storyteller Last Story

It was a sad day for me when Sister arrived. Mypup was a big dog now and would do what he would do. I could teach him no more but we were good companions despite what the rest said.

'He will leave you,' they said.

'He isn't one of us.'

'When the debt is paid he will be gone.'

And I knew it, though you don't turn away friendship just because you can peep into the future. So when I smell her coming I knew it was time, that she had come for Mypup. They were from the same litter you could tell just by looking at them, though I nearly chumped my chops to see in truth what I knew; that Sister had only two legs and no tail that I could see. But it was a sweet thing to see them together and strange to hear them converse. And I was not the only one to think this for Sister had brought another with her. It was Little Cabbage. She come here often for hiding in the straw. Though it's a lonely game she plays with no other two-leg to play with her. She has soft hands and knows how to touch a dog.

There was a problem, for getting into dog hide is easier than getting out. Old Lady had long since made bone and no one yet to fill her place, so what to do? I thought and thought and nothing made me sadder than a dog who should be a boy trying to unpick his belly and gnaw off his tail. So I began to sing the saddest song I know and a few of the others joined in. We are having a good old chorus with excellent harmonies and no one interrupting with boot or harsh shouting. Then Sister and Mypup join in while Little Cabbage pull up the straw like she were in her bed. All the time I keep my eye on Mypup and Sister and suddenly she take him by his scruff and pull his muzzle to her face. They stare eye to eye and she take in great gulp of air that strain the strings of her covering. They still stare and Mypup open his maw and she chuck the breath down his throat. Not good habit to take breath from two legs. It often stink. Mypup coughs and choke and shake his head like a wasp stung his nose and then he sit plop down again in front of her. Sister do this two more times. And then Mypup make my eyes bulge. He begin to shake his pelt like it was wet; he shake and shake until he is a whirr in the air but nothing comes off, not hair nor whisker, not tuft nor tail. And from his throat, I think it was his throat, there come a noise most un-hound like. Like he would once make long ago when he was alone and not knowing how to be dog. A cry like a two leg pup. Most affecting. The cry grow and grow like he's straining to push a turnip sized turd and it just won't come. And suddenly Little Cabbage leap up and began to dance. I think, what's she doing? Little lady, this is Mypup's moment sit down and attend. When you grown with pups of your own you can tell of this terrible moment and they will listen with big eyes. But she streak across the stable floor brushing the straw away and reaches the door as it burst open. I know the shadow I see, it is Tom, the stable master. Then he yells,

'What's going on in here, you dogs? What's that noise?'

And then he sees Little Cabbage and forgets the noise and I know he thinks of doing something with her that makes four legs where we make eight. And she is more clever that I ever saw. She goes push, pull with him; yes, no; me Lady, me Wanton till he is as dizzy as me watching Mypup. And he follows her somewhere into the dark outside and I look for Mypup but he's gone. My little friend is gone and in the straw is a dirt pale two-leg who is growling a little and crying like a puppy. I give him a sniff and know it was Mypup but his scent is fading fast. He is weak as he was when he first came to us and shivering. In the corner high on a fixing Tom leaves some coverings so I bark for Sister and point my nose to them.

'What a clever dog,' she says, which is my due, but she doesn't say sorry for taking what has been mine all this time. But she's not a dog so how can she help herself. They all need looking after. Mypup is soon trying a new voice and getting on to two legs which is not so easy as falling onto four. But after a while he is up and stretching his pale new body.

Now when he came to us he was a young thing but years

have passed and a grown dog becomes a grown boy. Sister shoves the covering at him and hides her face and they make a new noise together as he covers his soft hide. Little Cabbage comes back, 'What's the joke?' she says and then her eyes bulge too.

'Meet my brother,' says Sister.

'You must go,' Little Cabbage is breathing hard, 'someone's coming.'

But before anything happens, one more time the stable door flies open. This time it's Lord Fist who is reason Little Cabbage hide here. It's a bad day he found her hideout. He see Little Cabbage and his arm is ready in the air as the bad word ready on his lip.

'Where the dogdoo have you been!'

And the arm with his big fist on the end begins to come down. Now I am angry, for Little Cabbage has done well. So I shoot under legs and plant myself before him with my tail on her skirt. I beat it twice and hope she knows the code, which she might not, but means all is well. Then I let him see my front teeth and make a gentle warning.

'You, stupid dog.'

More bad word. So then I put up my bristles and show my back teeth too. I don't need to do big growl for he's not silly. He sees my meaning and backs off.

'You still here?' he says to Sister. 'Take your damn hound and go. We don't want your kind around here.'

He doesn't even see Mypup, and turns and puts his shoulder to the door as if something was its fault and not his. Very bad behaviour. A dog like that would be banished from any pack I know. Then they all embrace and open the stable door and go into the dark outside. And I jump up my forelegs on to the he who was Mypup; he look at me hard and soft, and there is water on his face. He needs a good grooming. Then they go. Mypup and Sister gone away, so I plop my rump on to the floor and think, what next. Suddenly a cloud like Dogg Lady best blanket pushes me to the floor. It is Little Cabbage all over me, so I give her a good wash and it seems I might have another pup after all. Then we trot into the dark after the others. Little Cabbage is bumping everything, so straight away I have to take charge. I don't have much training with two-legs but they're not so different I think. As long as she doesn't put me on a string.

*****

At the end they all went 'Aaah,' as I knew they would and I got up and went home. Another night I'd use my special bar privileges. That night I was dog-tired and no joke. There was no moon as I stumbled back. I had the feeling that some pitied me for the end of my life. So they thought. I was full of ideas. A good long rest to start with. And it started that very night. Then I might take a journey. Visiting. Babs and her friends were whispering about Arkady. Why shouldn't I go there one day? Then I thought of tired dogs and deep sleep. Deep, dreamless sleep. That was the plan. And so it was I believe, until dawn when a stone hit my window with a terrible clank. There was another, and another, and pretend as I would, sleep slid away.

'Meri!' a voice cried softly. And I heard Tork whicker as if to call me too. Dragging myself to the window I peered out and in the rising sun could not believe my eyes. Was this to be another prize? Or a consolation for my lost youth? There, fresh as the dew and lovely as herself, stood Kat with an impatient smile on her face.

'Come,' she said, not bothering to whisper, while Tork stamped in the cold. And she beckoned to me. Come. She didn't have to tell me twice.

You will laugh at me, as she did. Kat. For it wasn't what I thought. Though she'd wakened me so suddenly I could hardly be expected to decipher what was real from what was dreams of the night. She put me on Tork behind her and we went off at a steady pace into the forest. As we drew near the famous tree I could smell the smell of smoke and burning. And soon we were coughing. There was a fire and a thick veil of smoke slowly folded and unfolded upon the vision of Lady Ryo.

'Meriam,' she cried and I dismounted. 'Meriam, help me.'

I turned to speak to Kat but the smoke coiled on empty air. And Ryo and I were alone with the dying heart of a dismal fire. In the midst of the charcoal was a sight that made my stinging eyes leap from my head. In the midst of small and steady flames was a blackened shape.

'What have you done!'

What had she done? The books had been safe in the Archivists' keeping. They had been handed over; been snatched from me by hungry hands with barely a thanks for your labours. The Lady Ryo and I had parted still friends though with much changed in that tie. Then straightway the competition took my attention and Ryo and our journey had been swept from my mind. Now it was back.

'Now you are retired what will you do?'

'What have you done, Lady?'

'Ryo. You called me Ryo, before.'

'That book. We could have learned things from it.'

'Indeed we could.'

'Now we'll never know the truth.'

'Which truth? There is no truth, Meriam. Only memory. Only story. This book is full of story not truth.'

'And you know which is which.'

'And you a Storyteller?'

'Those are fables.'

'This too. Fables and lies. You haven't read it.'

So I stopped fighting her and said, 'Well tell me then,' and she said,

'It speaks of a Divine Retribution, that women are evil, that the Holy Maker is a man.'

'You said it was only a story, Ryo.'

'There is no only, Meriam.'

This, so quiet I could hardly hear it above the crackling of fire with its teeth into something solid. And I thought of the cave where this was nearly done then.

'We fought like this before, Meriam, help me now.'

I believed she had never ever said these words. They stuck to her lips like fluff.

Her face was struggling to be calm as she held that day book out to me, that she'd given me at the cave of bones. It was bulkier now, each page had another inserted. I knew this was the writing that had been with Susasima for translation, that she had whispered to a friend. It was written in her neat script and was scarred with water splashes so it was smudged and the words danced under my eyes with the flames contortions. But I still could read it. Part of a letter. Part of a dream and it reminded me of that other story I'd heard from Ryo, when we went to the caves. When I took the book, open from Ryo's hands, my heart beat fast with the thought that at last I would know the truth. But what I strained to read in the flickering light of that dying fire was nothing but the history of a disturbed and lonely woman. Another story of oppressive times. A lost cause. It seemed like our own history. And it was cheering to think that she had been saved. That was some happy truth; yet some of that story was not to be pondered upon. Ryo was crying like a child. I tried not to think about the bones of the two little bodies we'd destroyed and I don't claim to any gift like our Treasure, but I knew why she was crying. So I did what you do but it took some time before she stopped. As I stroked her shoulders, I could hear her telling me, all that time ago, those things in secret about two worlds reflecting each other. She'd obviously been wrong about it happening in another world; it had been in ours all the time. Then, for some reason, I started to wonder about her mother's history. But I didn't put that to her. Some stories are best left unfinished.

I said to her if I felt anything it was for the dog. That made her smile.. Was it the same, the one in the letter as the one in the cave? Perhaps it was even a wolf. Those bones now are so mixed no faithful hound could be closer to his charges. And the big book? Was she was right about it? If it was all story, we're never short of those. That night I gave it a kick for her and it crumbled and little bits of it lifted, black lace, and floated away like slow flying insects. The dying fire was still hot and for a moment I remembered summer and how you can look into the dark forest and see them, those slow flying things, hovering like dust in the air, lit up by a long finger of sunlight as it breaks through the hot forest roof.

Chapter 7

Book Learning

~ ~ ~ ~ ~

You start with a blank screen, a white landscape, vast and empty. You know it's been blasted by the fires of war. You expect it to be black but it isn't. Once it was, long ago. Long ago at first when the air was full of bitter clouds and poisonous flecks that adhered to skin. Don't dare to brush them off, pull them off, not if you love your body. Better the scars, ugly raised shiny lumps, than the infection of torn skin. And the dark crusts of cinder what were they? Life. Everything that had been; trees, gardens, houses, shops, schools, car parks, national monuments, animals, children. All blackened and crisp. But that passed. Everything passes one day. See the light landscape. The pale horizon, the soft, dusty undulations of earth that once were hills. Volcanoes were never so cruel. After those destructions seeds sprouted in countable years. This land still waits.

The white landscape stretches as far as the eye can see. As far as the watering eye can bear to look. The bright, white sky yawns to meet the bright white land. But you are experienced, you notice features. Your hand is raised to shade the hot glare from your fading blue or weak brown eyes. Through glare masks even more can be seen. Left, the whiteness rises slowly, inexorably, to jagged heights of glistening rock whose incandescence you could confuse with the blazing glory of cruel Sol. But even there is shadow. In clefts and valleys, in crevasses and craters, shadow, and at a certain time of day a blessed cool. To the right, like pillars of an old temple or the bodies of vengeful, guardian warriors, stand erect as signposts the remains of mighty trees. Bleached long ago by time as much as terrible events, they reach blunt fingers to heaven as if reminding, remembering.

A light wind lifts the dust like spray into dry surf and drops it with a careless hissing on a track that winds in arabesques, and oxbow curves. From the horizon it is a barely noticeable dotting which grows, slow as breath, broadening itself to a broken and patched highway, dangerous with its potholes as a mountainside in winter. There at the beginning something moves. An ant perhaps, if they still exist. A weary, slow, discouraged ant. One that plods weighed down with trouble and hunger, no doubt. Weighed down with its purpose to become more than insect. Time passes. Sol moves and ant is bird. Bird flutters now and hops. Is it the flutter of feathers or cloth? A length of rag waves and hop is limp, and bird grows to a figure in the landscape. Creep crawl, weary, sometimes visible, sometimes vanishing in waves of shimmering heat, sometimes gone behind the hot curve of the highway the figure makes its cruel way on.

The wind lifts the hem of the robe and the figure pulls down the scarf over a dry, sunburnt face. Heavy dusty boots kick the shingle under foot, stamp over the dust more quickly than at first appeared. *Kick, stamp, limp. Kick, stamp, limp.* A pack, half cloth, half skin, holds the approaching figure upright and as Sol moves towards the frontier and readies herself to cross the border to the other place where she makes hell, the shadow of the figure lengthens and the wind blows more kindly without teasing the darkening dirt.

This is Ash, whose secret name is a little like that in some languages.

The trek across the white plains was never made lightly. No one walked there unless there was no other way to go. You were at least safe. So flat and empty, if you knew how to see through the heat there was always plenty of time to defend yourself against Bandits. At a push simply lying down and playing dead worked. And if you were seen, by the time any Bandit worth the name came close you would be dead, or as near to it as makes no odds. Of course there were certain other skills, tricks of the trade. Survival was an art; a profession. Ash had made this trip many times.

This woman, whose name is known, why does she fit herself into this dreadful landscape? She could hardly tell you herself just now. Though doubtless she knew well enough when she started. Did she say to herself that she was too old, or old enough to push her luck yet again? Though how old that was, no one was sure, least of all her. At her age, whatever it was, most women were dead; those few who led the kind of life she did. The others in the far forests, whose life while hard is not as dangerous, lasted longer. Just. The World is still a cantankerous mistress who loves and tortures and scarcely knows the difference. Who treats all those who step across her surface with care and contempt in equal measure. As Ash well knows. *Kick, stamp, limp.*

With an empty mind she focuses all energy into the business at hand. That of crossing this waste land. This crystalline desert. All senses vigilant. Eyes under the covering scarf alert for the tricks of heat. Ears awake. And those sensitive parts of her shoulders and shoulder blades, do you know those parts I mean? Perhaps not, our lives are cushioned now and too noisy. Those extensions of her eyes and ears that would be the first to warn her of anything, anything that was out of kilter, out of the ordinary, they lay quiet now and ready under the weight of her pale robe.

And on she goes never permitting herself to daydream of the pleasantness of those far forests. Of the women who work the land there, in the various little hamlets; Arkady, Paradise, Full Mountain. Who look after themselves and their own, fight their enemies, have parties in the forests and by the rivers at any given excuse, and drink beer at night in their crazy bars and hotels. She blanks them and the tears shed at her departure. Silly tears. Tears are silly in this place. All moisture should be retained.

Loss of moisture is a luxury that cannot be afforded now. She lives just now in the place in her head just behind her eyebrows. There, where it is both dense and clear. Where focus is easiest and sometimes blue. It is a place of intensity that can be relied upon not to betray her. There, she can attend to both the now and the near future, both moments of potential danger. The dangers of the now are obvious. Of the near future, partly known but always tricky and changing like quicksand, she is wary. On a good day all would be well; all communication satisfactory and profitable for both sides. But on a bad day, who knows? In the past there'd been some sharp moments where a quick retreat and a few tricks of her own had seemed advisable. But, Boys were like that, even the older ones. Unreliable. Could be loving and sweet and sometimes funny. But get them on the wrong day and all of it turned like water to ice; petty, arguing, spiteful. And big. Hanoon knows how they get that way living as they do. On that diet. You wouldn't feed it to a pig. But big they were, with heavy flapping limbs and no sense of the space around them, nor of course, of the differences between women and men. Except that one, when it was needed. But the hero of this moment, Ash, uses all the skills of any statesmen; diplomacy, bribery, fear and flattery. And some illusions that you might call spells, which again are just the common currency of those in the business. But it didn't mean that simple caution was to be abandoned. The business relationship might at any moment be terminated to her detriment and she knew, if she allowed herself to remember, that Carrier and Sage could at any time become Slave and Slut.

Behind her are the unseen forests, the glittering mountains and the pointing trees. Before her, beyond the long winding trail under her feet, *kick, stamp, limp*, like a smudge on a hand drawn line the horizon betrays a small blemish. This, it seems, is where she is heading. And as those shining mountains fall and fade behind her, this small thing grows and takes on meaning. More mountains. If you want to call them that. And you will need to know about them. How people long dead must have made some effort to control and contain an overflowing world. Grown over millennia from daily deposits of trash and filth and waste, these mountains, the detritus of those tragic people and the treasure of this time, are called today The Mountains of Morn, for the sad story their debris tells. Of governments and people alike responsible, and many of both destroyed on their appalling slopes. Silt, wind and pollen did the rest and if you were interested in such things, and certainly some are, the strangest growths and creatures spawn themselves here. Some, good meat and drink. Not all.

These rocks do not glitter and gleam. And any shining light she sees means her approach is observed. And welcome she hopes. As if in anticipation she shifts her pack carefully. It would not do to break anything so near to the goal. Seeing her alone, they would know her cargo is in her pack this time and not in a skinny half grown, ill-prepared girl, plodding with her, sweating and fearful of the necessary ordeal to come. Today, babies and Boys are in full supply in their right places, both behind and before, and those who need any of that kind of assistance are either not yet ready or can't afford it.

When she arrives, she thinks happily, it'll not be the Body Hut this day, with it's gaudy decorations, old odours and responsibilities of instruction, but the plain, peaceful simplicity of the Visiting Hut. Let's hope, she allows herself to think, that the Boys are concerned with other things and have forgotten women's bodies, for the time being.

From his nook in the hillside at Los Withall, the boy with the glasses smiled and waved. He knew he was too far away to be seen, but he couldn't help himself. The sight of those long robes, even at this distance, brought to him such an indescribable sensation of something wonderful barely remembered, that was full of longing and sweetness and regret. And all this in a second or two of forbidden self-reflection. He shook it off and obedient to his training put the glasses to his eyes once more to double check. The figure was nearer. It was the Sage. He hardly dared think her name let alone say it to himself. And it was exciting even if she was alone. What did she have in her pack? Sweet things? Bottles that stank and sang? Coloured pictures that cast spells? He sighed. He loved to think like this. Wastefully and amusefully. But he got up slowly and stretched long cramped legs and reached for the rattle wire and gave it a good shake.

It made a satisfactory noise and woke that lazy Lug on the hitch below. Ratisbon waited until he'd rubbed his eyes and stretched too and looked up and then with his body and hands made the shapes and signs that said, 'Important, wonderful visitor approaches two hundred stretches go tell, quick.'

Lazy Lug looked across the plains but he didn't have the glasses. 'Who, who?' he signed, but Ratisbon pretended not to see and flipped the straps of the glasses in a casual yet official way and continued to watch the Sage's progress. Lug was the Runner, Ratts was Crow, that's how it was, the natural order of things. Runners got to go places but Crows knew things first. At Los Withall, there was tight order. Ratts kept to himself his opinion that with his legs he was certainly a better Runner than Lug. But what did he know. When he was an Elder he'd see it different no doubt, as he'd often been told; and there were some very definite advantages to being Crow. If you could keep awake.

Sage's arrival was not the thunderbolt for everyone else that it was for Ratisbon. The after meal siesta was not terminated for just anybody unless of course they were somebody special. And a woman was scarcely an anybody let alone a somebody, and certainly not a somebody special. Some grumbling ensued and several bed partners put their respective heads under the cushions and made out deafness, body business or just plain disobedience. Trumpeter soon sorted them out. Sage Ash was a sort of exception to the anybody/somebody rule. She made wary. There were stories of her powers; tales of spells, of bodies loosing potency, of fights going sour, eyes losing their keen. She was always shown some respect, if grudging. Like touching wood, just in case.

A dish of hot meat was put before her. Her gorge rose. But this was a moment of ceremony and diplomacy; of acknowledgement not delectation. She picked up the fork and regarded it. This soft shiny metal had once been valuable; she let her admiration show. She knew her appreciation did them honour. The meat was more difficult, but duty was a mistress she'd played with many a time in this neighbourhood. She chewed and nodded her head and smiled with her mouth closed. They waited till she swallowed. She waved the fork above the dish, 'Great hunter,' she said and stuck the fork in again. As she put another lump of the steaming flesh in her mouth a buzz of pleasure went round the watching crowd. And her words echoed as if she was in a hollow valley; ' ... great hunter,' 'great hunter,' 'great hunter ...' Some of the young boys fell onto the earth laughing and hitting each other with glee. Some took invisible bows and shot each other and one or two fell like wounded animals groaning and clutching invisible wounds. The older men laughed as well at her flattery and cuffed the nearest boy to hide their pleasure. They scratched grimy heads and felt their arms as if to check the state of those muscles responsible for the name of 'great hunter'. She ate it all and when the dish was empty a pattering of stamping applause went round the group watching. Unsophisticated they might seem, but still they knew the difference between gatherers and hunters. Later they'd look the other way. She was always popular with the dogs.

Her public gift to them was a story she'd picked up somewhere. All, without exception, gathered. Crow and Runner too and a gang of sweaty hunters who had heard somehow of her arrival and sat blood-caked and exhausted ready to nap if the tale got too boring. Fat chance, Ash grinned to herself. As she waited to begin, the noise of fifty or so men and boys grew to a deafening level. She knew of old 'quiet, please' wouldn't work, so standing as tall as she could she pointed dramatically into their midst.

'Great hunter,' she yelled. And the stage was hers. 'Great hunter, she repeated, and turning her finger to herself, and lowering her voice to a hoarse whisper, she said, 'great storyteller.' Again her words were like echoes as they tripped from mouth to mouth, 'great storyteller,' 'great storyteller'. And one by one they sat or stooped, bony legs thrust before them or grimy knees pointing to the sky. Triples sat entwined, propping each other up in rest as they did in work. One or two, too old for the athletics of bending, leant on a staff or against the wall of a hut. There was Crow with his smiling face. Crow and Runner, she remembered from last time; both story addicts. They were young, but she couldn't remember them from the forest. Perhaps someone else had brought them or they were older than they looked. She hoped so. Pretty Green had the power to keep young boys awake at night too long.

She began quietly in the patois they used, improvising and translating as she went along and she heard again the phenomena that she'd noticed before. How at moments like this of communal attention and gathering, there seemed to be only one breath between them. One great inhalation and one soft sigh as air was expelled. As if they were some strange breed of creature who breathed together, for each other, as one.

'One time, far away,' she said, 'was boy. Live in hole down by river of mud. Mud suck and squeeze, suck and squeeze all the day, and night-time too. One day, boy find eye sleeping on mud. Eye shut and quiet like fat baby. Boy like but boy not take.'

And there were nods of approval for her boy hero. Warriors were to be cautious; that was the rule. Danger lurked for the unwary. She smiled an acknowledgement and went on.

'Maybe eye bite or scream like baby if him take, so boy start to go. Then eye blink and smile but boy say, "No, eye, I go now." But eye start cry, so him take and hold in hand, and him and eye be like brothers. So boy carry him to hole down by river of mud. Mud still suck and squeeze, suck and squeeze all the day, and night-time too.'

Response was mixed. Old hands wore a smirk of expectation while some of the youngsters like Ratisbon, the Crow, his smile gone now, and Lug, seemed half-hypnotised with the drug of imagination. Those two were leaning on each other and staring almost cross-eyed at her. She lowered her voice.

'Come night, boy tired. Him curl in mud hole for sleep. Him hear mud go suck and squeeze, suck and squeeze but sleep run off and slow, slow him see green, green glow. Him think death come visit. Then him see eye. Eye green. Eye blink and smile, eye look him long, long. Him boy's eye stuck to green eye, all night long.

Come sun-up, boy weary and dry and boy go out. There him see river of mud. Mud slurp and churn, slurp and churn, like demon fall in, and him see shape wrestle to get out. Boy feel cold and chill. Shape lift him mud arm and point him mud finger at him mud head. Moon-quiet all round. River stop flow. Mud shape voice come high and low. "Where eye? Who got eye? Where my pretty green?" '

The sweet story was turning bad. The harsh high voice she used startled the two boys out of their pleasant lethargy.

Now she had them.

'Boy sick with fear and run back to hole. Him still not sleep so him stick him head from hole to peep. Mud shape waiting with arm lift up. Now him finger go point at boy. Him say two time, "Where eye? Who got eye? Where my pretty green?" Boy stuck, no move. Shape finger grow long, long, long. Point come near, near, near. Mud shape say three time, "Where eye? Who got eye? Where my pretty green?" '

She paused a long pause and then, '*You got it!*' At this the crowd erupted with noise and movement. Elders who had heard such nonsense often enough in their lives shook their heads and looked at her in amusement. Mid aged men laughed and slapped each other and cried 'You got it!' in each other's faces. But the younger lads made the most noise. They whooped and danced and leaped at each other making eerie noises, trying to frighten each other.

But Little Lug stood up in his full four feet of height to her, saying, 'Me hate you, Sage. Now me fright all night.'

And his friend Ratisbon, towering over him, tugging his arm, whispering,

'Lug, you man soon. I not let fright get you. Me stay you night.' But Lug was not to be so easily persuaded.

'You stay, you not stay. Lug, boy now. Boys get fright. You wait, Sage, wait me man. I give you big wallop. I get whip. Then you get fright.'

Ash knew better than to smile. When they had lived with the women, such moments were easily dealt with in comfort and reassurances. Here that currency lost something in the exchange. Without doubt Ratisbon would comfort Lug and chase away his fears, but Lug's approaching manhood weighed heavily on him. An older man slapped him on the back of his legs.

'You give Sage good mouth. She tell good story. You fright all yours, not she.'

And Ratisbon put his arm over Lug's shoulder and they wheeled off towards the huts.

There was a smile on Tula's mouth as he watched the two boys go, and turning back to Ash his smile broadened. They looked at each other; Ash had been coming here a long time. She'd brought many boys, wiped their tears and left them to a strange new life and watched them grow to men, and men to Elders. When Tula had first seen her she'd been little older than Ratts. The old man sighed and turned and looked, but the two boys were no longer there.

'Ah,' he said, 'silly boys.'

The smile spread to Ash, 'Tula, you old fraud, don't say you've forgotten young love.'

And Tula put a finger on his lips, 'Ssh. Elders not do love, them too old and wise.'

And they both began to giggle like the young selves they had been remembering. Pulling himself together and replacing the Wise Elder on his face, he gestured with his head.

'Come. Time for deal. New find. Very pretty thing.'

The hut Tula had built for himself was a simple affair, and small compared to the dormitories the boys of Los Withall lived in. But it had one great advantage; that of privacy. Of course when you're young that's not something to worry you. But when the active side of life begins to shrink, other aspects open up and for those, peace and quiet can be an essential ingredient. Some Elders, the politicians and statesmen remain in the hubbub of the communal life; how else can they get elected. But Tula and his kind, thinkers and seers, and some of the crafts men and musicians claimed that right of solitude once the optimum age had arrived. Ash entered carefully. Such invitations were rarely issued. Age confers privilege, she thought to herself. And something to do with him losing two of his triple as well. Not anything to be spoken about. And stooping to enter the dark hut she felt stiffness in her back and her legs from the long trek and the punishing weight of the pack. Time to think about retirement. Tula turned to her.

'You me body?' he said hesitantly.

Her mouth flew open and she stared at him speechless.

'No? No head hefty. Me just think, maybe.'

And again laughter flew between them. Men were the same whatever age, wherever you found them. Would he do it here, or go to the Body Hut? Surely not that.

'You keep shush, Ash. Them think Elder not do body. But sometime me remember.'

The conventions of this place were often beyond her even when she thought she'd learned it all.

'The pretty thing, Tula? That's all I'm here for.'

Often the things that were found were, if not useless, then unusable and beyond trade. Petrified rubber, crumbling foam, metal things so twisted and rusted that they'd not be worth the effort of packing. It was only when things had been abandoned in boxes that they stood a chance of being salvageable. Nearly everything else had disintegrated, which had been the original intention, surely. Boxes and cases were the treasure field. But not every box was fruitful; some were dangerous. Tula's own brother had flown fifty feet in the air in an explosion and come down to be impaled on a spike of some kind. He'd not lasted long, even though Ash had been visiting at the time with her bag. No medicine cures a hole in the back. Another box had held little soft cloth trays full of glittering stones. There'd been a fight over them, but after six months the strands had mostly been given to the little boys as bribes, or hung on hut walls to catch the light. One of the most useful boxes Ash could remember, had been full of metal pots and pans. She paid a high price for those but had got a considerable return on them by the end of her travels that year. Not to mention a bad back. Boxes of coloured pencils were her favourite; light, easily packable, and a very desirable commodity in every community. There was usually a use for everything in good condition, though she remembered a collection of artificial limbs that had taxed even her ingenious mind. She'd refused them and kicked herself when they'd turned up some time later as a bizarre kind of irrigation system that straddled the plain like the remains of a slaughter. Sometimes it took a leap of imagination that was beyond her. Desperate lives took desperate measures. The Elders were convinced that Bandit attacks had slackened off since. A nice soup, they said.

But those were all by the way; keeping her in beer money, as it were. Things to be transacted that were a duty. You could hardly fly in the face of Hanoon and reject her casual generosity. But Ash's real mission, her job, her obsession, was to find those other precious objects. The market was small and particular and bore no repetition. Each one must be fresh, a new one, preferably on the list of the lost. And how frail they were. What grief she felt, grief that was in no way connected to her pocket, but a true sense of loss when, on lifting one, it crumbled in her hands, fragile and brittle as old leaves. How she felt like weeping to see them lifting from their covers and floating off, brown and translucent in the breeze. How strange to have such value now when in the past they must have been throw away, items to be used and abandoned. Ash could never really understand. How unlike them we are.

In the darkness of the hut she couldn't see much. Lighting up time wasn't for a few hours yet. She propped the door open and heard rather than saw her old friend drag a large wood trunk. Her heart began to beat fast when she realised what sort of box it was. The best. Not a commercial packing box. This was one of the valuable ones; one that had been used by an individual and had packed within it who knows what fabulous things. Tula beckoned her closer smiling at her expression.

'Very good, eh?' She nodded.

He hooked his strong old fingers under the edge of the lid and heaved. The lid responded, opening slowly with a shriek of ancient metal. It opened further and she peered in. Hardly anything in it. Disappointment flooded her.

'Oh, Tula.' she said.

But he held up his hand like a teacher, making her wait. He reached in to the shadowy depths of the box with both his arms and when he straightened up and turned to her, he held before him a soft, long bundle which hung across his arms like an offering in a sacrifice.

In the glimmering light of the hut the thing shone somehow, as if it were lit from within. Ash put out a finger and touched its soft sheen. Rough and ragged, her finger caught on the surface and she jumped back as if she had been bitten. 'Oh, Tula,' she said again, this time in awe. Whatever was it? Suddenly, like the magician he was, he flipped the bundle in the air, unravelling it until lengths of pale shining frothed around his body. Then letting it billow to the ground he handed to her a large thin, red book that had been hidden in its heart.

'Very pretty, this,' he said proudly. 'Very strange.'

And he stepped over the white shining thing to take her to the light of the door.

'But, Tula,' she said, confused.

Which was the pretty thing? The book in his hands or that lovely piece of cloth on the floor? Impatiently he took her wrist and opened the book. It was indeed a Pretty Thing. And, nearly perfect. Little spotting, no damp. Its edges crisp and the gold intact. Each page a riot of colour. Patches and shapes outlined in fine dark lines and all surrounded in blue.

'Maps'. Worth a fortune.

'Maps?' he repeated.

'These are places in the old world, Tula. Like the charts you draw for the hunters.'

He turned his head looking at the maps from all angles. Then he nodded and slammed the book shut. The old world was a sore subject for those who had time to dwell on it.

Opening her pack it was time to bargain. He knew, of course, the value of the book to her and her clients. He knew, of course, what she carried. Once more they smiled at each other and she laid out most of what she had brought. For Tula and those others, once orphans of the forest, she made good deals. And they knew it; even those who had forgotten, those who resented her presence. They were all someone's son and for the sake of some unknown mother, she did them well. Tula picked up each bottle in turn reading the glyph on its label. He nodded and gathered them all to him and passed her the book.

'And that?' she said, pointing to the white cloth.

'Oh, him too. Yes. You give maps their coat.' And he scrunched it up and threw it over to her. Then Lantern came in with light and she hurriedly stuffed the pale thing into her pack before he could change his mind.

'Woman thing,' he said softly. 'Not bother us.'

That night, in the shadows of the Visiting Hut, Ash took the pale cloth from her pack easing it out slowly and carefully. Such a thing she had never seen, only heard about from old stories and rumour. Holding it against her as she sat crouched on the floor, the flickering light of the wall sconces caught the sheen of the thing and at once it seemed alive. She rose slowly and it fell against her billowing to her feet as she stood, and a thread of ancient scent caught in her throat. Weren't such robes worn for Hender Festing, ceremonies hundreds of times ago, when women and men were together and pledged vows to be a twosome for so long as they both dwelt on this earth? What would the archivists pay to get hold of this pretty thing? With one worn hand Ash smoothed the glimmering cloth and felt its cool warmth. It was tucked and fluted and sewn with flowers of the self same colour as the base material. How strange, she thought, to go to that trouble and not sew colour. But there were so many taboos about colour, she couldn't remember them all now. So many rules of a dead age, and she was no historian. How thin they were, she thought. This could hardly fit a child. Perhaps the woman had been ill, perhaps — but before she could take off on any flight of fantasy, a knocking at the hut door broke her thoughts and she turned to see the skinny face of Ratisbon peering in.

'Sage? Me come?'

'Ratisbon,' she said, 'What's up?'

'Me have word for you. Let me in.'

'Just for a moment then.'

And the door swung open with a thump and the boy bent

his head and came into the hut.

As the door clumped shut behind him it pushed a breath of air into the room flickering the light which spilled onto the robe. He stopped in his tracks, eyes wide at the swirling cloth which his entrance and her turning had set once more in motion.

'Well?' she said, but he said nothing only continuing to stare.

'Wake up, Ratts.'

And she began to fold the dress. Ratisbon held out his hands and shaking his head said, 'No. Make big again.'

'You're not sick, are you? Tula has the medicine now, not me.'

As she spoke she folded and patted the cloth smaller and smaller, but it didn't seem to want to be made small; as if it had spent so long cramped and unenjoyed that now it would not be tamed. Ratts crept forward as lengths of the robe slipped from her containing fingers and swung out towards him with a sigh. Again, putting out his hand, Ratts touched the cloth as she had at first done, tentatively and tenderly. Like hers, his fingers caught on the smooth surface and he too jumped back as she had done. She smiled and he said, 'What wild thing, this?'

She let him take the robe from her and his fingers convulsed the cloth as if he was kneading dough. She watched him and he lifted the bundled cloth to his face his nose twitching as he too caught the fragrance of the past. But as he started to rub its smoothness on his boy's face she grabbed it from him frowning.

'No, Ratts,' she said. Look.' And both of them looked down on the patch where his face had been, now stained with dirt and sweat.

'Oh, bad,' he said. 'Bad Ratts to make mud spot.'

And he looked at Ash.

'Ratts, bad with himself. You too?'

Ash sighed, what could you do?

'No, Ratts. I'm not bad with you. It make sweet again, soon. Now what did you want? I'm tired, I have to sleep.'

Ratisbon, pulled himself up to his full height, his head scraping the rafters. 'Ratisbon comes with Lug word. Him full of grief at temper. Him never wallop you, you him great Sage Mother. Him put him head under pillow till you say you love him still.'

Again Ash hid the smile.

'You tell Lug, I always love him and he can take the pillow off his head. All you boys are my babies.'

And even in the gloom of the dying light she could see Ratts stand a little straighter and feel his widening grin.

'You too, Ratts. But enough talk of love. You both men soon, and then no more love-mother talk, eh?'

Slumping now, the duty was done for his friend, and perhaps also with the thought of the privations and privileges to come, he nodded.

'No more love-talk soon. Sure thing.'

And before he slipped out of the hut he patted the hend fest robe once more.

'This, love-talk thing too, for sure.'

And he was gone. How did he know that? A seer or a thinker in the making? Let's hope. And she put the robe in her pack and took the book of maps instead. Too dark now to see, she stroked its cover and touched its pages feeling their contrasts. The strong roughness of the woven cover. The cold smoothness of the wide paper inside. Tomorrow this pretty thing would be on its way to the Library, and she'd soon be on her way back home to Paradise.

Curse the boy, curse the boy. Curse the Boys. It was worse than she expected. How could she make her usual time dragging him along? In this the most dangerous stretch. They know that. Her pack held only the light robe and the book. And, of course, a few unspecified rations for emergencies. She tried not to stride, tried to empathise with the boy's distress and pain. But really he only had himself to blame. Hanoon knows, he knew the rules. Animals were irreplaceable. Boys they could get. And she remembered now all the times he'd appeared a bit different. And how she'd secretly cheered him on. Now that damn difference was her problem. How could she have refused. And little Lug. She put that thought away from her. Think about that later. She saw him smile at his friend as Ratts' hands and feet were untied. What a brave thing he'd done. Ratts would know it one day. When he was properly grown. If he ever made it. If they both ever made it. She gave a cursory look behind to see if he was keeping up. He wasn't. Too far behind and slumped on the earth sobbing again.

Her heart softened and she turned towards the boy on the ground.

'You're wasting your wet, Ratisbon,' and he looked up with a frown on his face.

'That wild thing kill me, Sage. That wild thing call me sweet and now me done.'

'You call me Ash, now. Not think of trouble now. And you get up and we keep walking. Soon we eat and drink. Then we make a hole and we sleep.'

'Hole? Like demon hole?' He began to shake.

'Ratts, that was a story. Not true.'

'Not true? But Lug fright all night long,' and remembering his lost friend he began to sob again.

'Ratts, if you make such a noise the Bandits will hear you and come and kill us both.'

Ratisbon dried his eyes on his sleeve and the sobs became the heaving shudders that signal exhaustion. He's picking up, she thought. Too young, despite his size, to have to face the choice of death twice in one day. Who knows what life has in store. Yesterday he was just another boy thinking about his manhood tests. Today he was a disgraced émigré. Some hand.

'Maybe Lug follow soon?' he said setting his feet to match her steps.

'No, Ratts. No more Lug.'

She wasn't going to encourage this stupidity. Lug was gone. The old life too. He'd know that as soon as he could think straight. Though what in damnation am I going to do with him. There weren't too many Boys' communities in this part of the world. Maybe Bandits would be the answer. She'd be meat and bones in one Sol's turn. But Ratts, with any luck, would just be slave. It'd be a start. Many a great Bandy leader had started from less.

A rumbling at her side was life triumphing over tragedy.

'Ratts belly groaning. Big empty.'

Great; a whining baby, now. Tula had, in his capacity as Wise Elder, overruled the Punishment Council and she'd walked away with enough food and water to get them to the Library. Ratts carried this. Which was appropriate enough, considering.

'That's called hunger, Ratts.'

'Hunger?'

'New word. Put in head box for later.'

Let him think of that. Anything other than the terrible scene that had woken her this morning.

From flat on her back as she opened her eyes she knew something was up. Silence was not a normal occurrence in any Boys' camp. Young or old, Boys were a noisy lot. Chattering to each other every moment, shouting orders if they had authority, laughing, grunting. Noise was a form of communication for them in a way it never was for women. A woman sharpening a stick might chat to a neighbour, but if a Boy did it he became the effort and his grunt expressed the action. From faraway the noise he made told his Gang Father that he was busy as instructed and working hard. That morning's silence hung over her like a shot bird about to plummet, and she lay for a minute wondering. Outside, she pushed herself to the edge of the crowd to the gate of the stockade. There in the distance lay two bodies; flat on the sand, spread and tied. Ratts and Lug.

She listened to the low stunned gossip around her. Whispering, unusual. In the early morning while it was still a little dark, instead of watching from their guard post the Boys had been arseing around. Several valuable animals had been Bandit-snatched and this is how the Fathers dealt with it. Punishment and warning. Very effective; very memorable, that sight. Everyone would work hard for several months; forswearing forbidden pleasures until the vision faded. Until the bones were scattered and became part of the landscape. Already high up one or two scavengers hovered. One of the boys was moaning.

A face in the crowd grimaced at her and a low growl rumbled at her back. Without a flicker she was ready. Her fingers poised for the knife in her boot. From nowhere, for no mouth moved, she heard a soft, 'Bad magic.' The speaker, whoever he was, was right. To lose potential warriors before their full flowering was an economic and tactical disaster. She fully understood. She also fully understood that someone had to take the blame. And it came, 'Sage magic.'

'She no Sage. She witch.'

'We get you witch.'

Time to do something. Returning whisper for whisper, threat for threat.

'Not before you hair fall out. You prick swell, blister and be nought. You suffer needles in the skin. You piss be full of sand, you arse run red, you sap dry, you. . . '

The pressing crowd evaporated. She turned sharply away and fell against Tula. He held her wrist to stop her falling, and holding onto it pulled her with him into his hut.

'This you job.'

She didn't quite understand at first. A wave of anger sheeting up at the ambiguity of the patois.

'What the Hanoon are you saying now.'

He held his hand up as if to ward her off.

'Ssh, Ash. Sage. You hear me now.'

And he told her what had happened. Bandits wait to raid just before a team changed when the night watchers are exhausted and near to sleep.

'We not boys,' Tula said, 'we smart warriors, plenty clever over rotten Bandys. We change watch before daybreak. So fresh eyes cover end of dark with new wake.'

But that night as they were taking over the watch Lug was too full of Ash's remark about love and Ratts too engrossed in the white robe. Just for the few minutes it took. Gossiping instead of watching. Chattering, a little inattention and the beasts were gone. An hour later the loss was discovered by one of the herdsmen who called the alarm. An hour after that the boys were off the hill, standing before the council for trial and on their backs as dawn broke.

Ash found herself weeping. The innocence of life here hid a starkness that she didn't often see.

'They're just boys,' she said. 'One mistake.'

But she knew what he'd say, and he knew it.

'This you job,' he repeated.

And suddenly there was a deeper meaning in his words.

'What d'you mean?'

'You take one?'

'One of the boys?'

'You weak, feeble woman,' he said.

And as she laughed he held up a hand again. He touched his ear and she knew she must listen.

'Bandys you danger. Most like they kill you. No spare man here. But them boy not useful now. I get one off if you take far away.'

She knew he was powerful and could do more or less what he wanted. Old and brave, he had served the community for a long while. And stayed alive. That alone conferred privilege.

'Yes,' she said. 'Of course. I demand an escort.'

And he looked down and blinked away a glimmer of wet. Warriors never wept. That was a sign of their status.

'Which?'

She had to choose? And as she had looked into his old eyes she could only think about the words, 'This you job'. The patois always sounded like the stumblings of ignorant, ill-educated children, but suddenly she knew, and with that knowledge a jolt of realisation about her own pride shot through her, knew the subtlety and double meaning of his words. He'd waited for her to realise that he was blaming her for upsetting the boys equilibrium but also offering her the task of making amends.

'Why not two?'

'Food only belong one.' Ah, economics. She understood.

'You choose.' she said, and he smiled. Not calling her a coward as well as everything else.

*****

Cuspangel stood at the window, eyes straining to the horizon. For days there'd been that uncomfortable feeling of expectation. Something coming. Once it had been them and Cuss imagined Isidore standing here, watching as they approached. Remembering; their wariness of the place, their dread after that other terrible journey. There had been altogether too many journeys. They should have simply stood still and survived somehow, anyhow. All that they saw and learned on that second trek. They'd thought their own escape proved something but it seemed that the Box was just one manifestation of a much bigger ague. For a second Cuss remembered The Mountains of Morn. Remembered the terror of seeing so much destroyed and disintegrated that was familiar, and yet obviously so very ancient. Remembered how no one they met could tell them exactly what or when it had happened, let alone why. We can never go back. They had said that often enough. Soon the destruction of the world they had left would be a half forgotten story. Rena said it should all be written down so it wouldn't be forgotten. Another job undone. Cuss sighed and wiped the window.

Now little dots half seen in the distance. Something coming ? No, just dirt? Another sigh. In ten years the plastic had deteriorated dreadfully. When they'd arrived the windows had been new, almost. That's the trouble with plastic, Rena always said. One day they'd get some good old-fashioned glass. Ten years ago they were just passing through. Now look at them. Isidore came in putting on his apron.

'Hungry?' he said, as he began to gather to him all the bits and pieces he needed to make the evening meal.

'Rena in the book-stack?' Cuss asked, knowing the answer.

'Yes,' said the old man sniffing a bunch of herbs.

'Hope they've got something good. I'm a bit short on pencils. Any signs yet?'

Cuss swung round away from the window, skirt swinging.

'What d'you mean?' Snapping.

The old man raised an eyebrow at Cuss and tutted.

'No, not yet.'

And Cuss flung back some grey curls and strode out of the kitchen slamming the door.

In the dark, slightly fragrant air of the book-stack, a slender, long haired woman of about thirty seasons is bent over an open book. The fine yellow paper ruffles as Cuss wrenches open the door.

'Rena!'

'What's up?'

Cuss insinuates her tall curvaceous body past the door, coming to where Rena sits busy. Leaning over her, peering at the pages of the book.

'What's that?'

'Just more stuff,' she says, leaning back into another body. Cuss brushes a kiss on Rena's hair.

'Are they here yet?'

'For goodness sake, everyone round here knows what I'm thinking before I do!'

'Well are they?'

'Am I that transparent?'

'Yes, you are. Devil to be with until something arrives.'

'Maybe soon. It feels like it. Dor's doing supper. Looks like he's getting ready for an army.'

'Good job Le Duk was just here.'

'But we don't want to use everything up on the off chance do we?'

'Have faith, Cuspangel. In our cook at least, if not yourself.'

Cuss moved away screwing up a face at her. Rena laughs, but the sound is drowned in the banging of the book-stack door, and Cuss returns to the warmth of the kitchen where the Librarian smells of garlic.

*****

Light was fading fast and the evening stars were beginning to light the sky. Too much light. Didn't need so much to finish this hole. Big enough for her was easy to make, but one big enough for the two of them needed more energy than she wanted to give. Now his wrists were recovering Ratts seemed determined to pull his weight. It was good to stride along with only the lightest pack because a lanky strong boy carried the heavy one. It was good to have someone to talk to, to curse when things went wrong. But if they didn't hurry she'd be blaming him for ending up in a Bandy's pot. No real satisfaction in that, she thought. Finally it was dug and banked and they were snug inside with the opening tarpaulined safely under the heavy gold of a full moon. And she'd been right. The old ears never let her down.

'You magic ear,' Ratts whispered as they heard the Bandits thundering past.

Thundering past was good, she thought to herself. Thundering over, not so good. Thundering over could mean thundering in, shrieking and cursing and coming face to face with a mean-faced Bandit with filed teeth. She'd always been lucky. Hanoon saving her for a crotchety old age, she hoped, and not a nasty death. In the speckled gloom under the tarp Ratts face was wrinkled up.

'Bandy's fall in, they kill then?'

'Ssh.'

She was saved from having to answer. She pointed to her ear and Ratts looked up. The sound of more of them. The walking wounded? Those who couldn't ride? Those whose animals and machines had died on them or those whose wings were still sprouting? This lot were nearer this time. And being stragglers made them more dangerous, more uptight and kill ready. But the tarp was a good one. The best. Worth several months wages.

'Let us be invisible, Hanoon, dearest Watcher. Watch over us,' she prayed. Ratts turned his head and opened his mouth. She frowned threateningly and stealthily took his wrist in her hand. Was she containing him or comforting herself? Shit if I know, she thought. The stragglers limped off into the distance, the ground over their head resounding to the thump of their feet, and something else? A crutch? A shoot iron butt? She didn't care to look. Let them go until the ground is still, she could hear her old teacher's voice, and then wait longer. Wait some more and then some more, but don't go to sleep. Snoring is a dead give away. A few crumbs of earth ran like ants down the side of the pit. Her heart contracted. A little scrabbling sound at the edge of the tarp. She dropped Ratts wrist and reached for a handful of dirt and the knife. The edge lifted. Glancing at the boy she saw that his nose was wrinkling and he was smiling as if he could smell something good. Before she could stop him he stood up his head poking a dent in the tarp, his arms reaching up as if to a lover. 'Oh Hanoon!' she groaned and prepared to die.

Sudden cool air and gold light on her face and the sound of gabbling happy voices. Before she could open her eyes something heavy fell on her, and Ratts was laughing.

'I don't believe it,' she said. 'I don't believe it. Where have you come from? How did you. '

But she was cut off. Ratts face beaming in the moonlight.

'Ratts say he come. Ratts know more, more, more. Sage no good.'

He had his arms round a ragged and emaciated Lug.

'Now we triple. Lug, Ratts, Sage.'

But Lug was asleep and couldn't be asked for his opinion. As she clambered out of the pit, Ash saw the slave branding on his shoulder. What had happened back there? She didn't like to think. Sleep now. And wrapping herself in a corner of the tarp, her exhaustion swept her away to a beautiful dark place.

She woke with a slice of dough cake thrust under her nose and Ratts happy face above her. How were they to manage? Food, drink, another boy to worry about. And she felt exhausted again as if she hadn't slept at all. A little voice beside her said.

'Lug not eat. Lug belly always full.'

And turning her head she looked and saw Lug. His face expecting the worst. She softened and put out her hand to him.

'Lug, great warrior. Him run from Bandys?'

He nodded and said, 'Runner legs do Lug good job,' and she saw his eyes flicker from her face to the cake and back again several times. Even a week with the Bandits would teach him more about food rationing than a month of manhood school. She broke a bit off and gave it to him.

'You must be strong for the trek.'

And he gulped it down with no quarrel. When he had finished he told her what had happened. The Bandits had returned the next night presumably hoping for the same carelessness. The Boys were ready, but the Bandys were just out of reach of the arrows. A couple of them had got close enough to cut Lug off his stakes and drag him away. He'd be a strong enough prize when he had mended. And in the middle of his story with a pleased smirk he produced Ratts' spyglasses from his baggy rags.

'My glass,' yelled Ratts with glee holding out his hand for them. But his friend pulled them away to his grubby chest.

'My glass now. Tula give, in dark. Him wrap in pocket.'

A look of amazement crossed Ratts' face followed by a hardening of his jaw.

'Lug,' he said warningly.

That's all I need, thought Ash, a fight on my hands.

'Ash, Elder,'she said. 'Ash hold glass,' and wrenching the glasses from Lug, glowered at the pair while her brain whirled with what she'd heard. So who'd blown that back at the huts? And Tula, he had had a hand in Lug's escape too.

'So then what did you do?'

'Me walk special slow behind Bandy. Me so bad, sun popping skin on rack, them not whip. Them say dead slave no slave. Me get little food, drink. Shade in sunny day. Them soon forget Lug and Lug spy you in glass. One day Lug lay down dead. Them kick some but Lug good and dead. So them leave to lammers but no lammers come, Lug not true dead, him make like dead.'

And his little face split in pleasure at his own cleverness. Ash shook her head at the sheer miracle of it. At the boy's tenacity and cleverness. Ratts was weeping again.

'Ratts! Don't waste wet.'

Both she and Lug at the same time. A chorus. Then laughter. They'd manage.

Ratts beamed at Lug. 'Lug true man now. True brave man.'

Ash nodded. You had to agree with the boy. True bravery.

Somehow they managed to go with more speed. Three went faster than two in good spirits and excitement at what was ahead. And ahead was that strange three who called themselves family. After she'd told them that a mother and father and a child lived together and that the child was a girl and grown up at that, they were silent for a long while. The rest would have to wait. It was too complicated and no amount of explaining would help. Boys were not good with irony. But books they'd heard of and one evening when Sol was taking her time to lie down Ash got out the book of maps to show them. Ratts instructed Lug on the finer points of her merchandise.

'We not put smelly skin on this thing, Lug. Dirty make bad bargain.'

And she looked at him remembering his delight before the pale robe had started the trouble.

But as she turned to the place in the book where there were more words than maps Lug surprised them again. He licked a grubby finger and wiped it clean on his rags and pointing to the top of the page he slowly read,

'M. A. P of ...' and stopped and looked at Ash a little dazed. She looked back not knowing what to say. Then slowly rose and with the same finger he carefully traced three letters in the sand. They spelled Lud. No matter that one was up side down, it was without doubt his name.

'Where did you learn that, little Lug?' she asked. Still dazed with his unexpected visitation, Lug shook his head.

'Long ago,' he said, 'in dark place. There was she. Like Ash.'

What rebellious woman had tried to teach the child to read so young? What misplaced kindness? It was forbidden to teach boys anything from the normal education programme and for good reason. What good would it do in the huts? But here was one with some knowledge above his station. Well, as things turned out it could be useful. He and Ratts had their heads together being careful not to make the pages dirty. Lug now was master and Ratts the student.

'You look here. Word tell story. You read words. See?'

'Me no read,' said Ratts. Was Lug stupid? But Lug was not a teacher to give up.

'See little mark,' and both their heads craned nearer in the dim light.

'It word?' said Ratts.

'No. Little marks inside word like seed in fruit. See that mark say B.'

'How say? No mouth.'

'Scratch on earth say dog near.'

Ratts nodded. That was obvious.

Lug's finger moved on. 'That mark say R. Like Ratts.'

'Ratts? In book? Where? Show!' And delighted his shining face lifted to Ash.

'Ratts in book. Ratts name in book! Read more.' But Lug shut the book with a soft thud and held it out to Ash.

'Some pretty hefty,' he said, and Ratts didn't insist.

'Book word tell good stories,' and the boys eyed each other warily. Ash packed the book away. Somewhere in her body she felt uneasy. Did this change things? What was changed? The order of things. The hierarchy they'd established? Maybe at the Library, Ash thought to herself. But the thought petered out. Maybe what at the Library? They might not even be welcome. It might be full of Bandits. Making plans for other people was a thankless task. Feeling responsible for two homeless boys was a thankless task too.

*****

Three of them, the Mother, the Father and a child stand close, as families do every once in a while. Standing close, touching easily at shoulder, elbow, arm, hip. Perhaps with a hand on a shoulder or an arm round a waist. Such ease, such trust, such familiarity. This is how it often was, in the old days. In the far distant old days that we have learned about. Then they often lived as triples. But not like those of the Boys. These triples had always two Elders of equal authority, one of either sex and to it they added, by different means, a third called The Child, also of either sex. This formed what was called, as you all know, The Family, and was bound by rules, convention and practices that were sacrosanct and invariable. Those who defied the conventions and disciplines of that order were exiled and often punished. The idea of family that we have is both like and unlike those of that time.

This family stood looking out of the window. Before them, a garden filled with edible plants. An old tool stuck in the dark crumbling soil. Beyond the garden, scattered trees, maybe some fruiting nearby, and then a field with unkempt grasses waving their loose heads in a breeze, and raggedy broad leaved flowering plants whose silken petals float on a mote laden air. And just a little way beyond, where a patch of low green bushes sway and bob in that same wind, a glimpse of water; a lake or a pool or a stream glinting like a mirror. Sol shone down, gently here as if this were a place she loved to bless not punish.

At the window there is no clear view. The panorama is so full. Full of the blessing of earth's bounty, full of colour, full of movement. As the wind blows the leaves into the air it seems as if figures in the landscape move in and out, together and apart as though dancing. Are there three figures? Or is it one, seen and not seen and then seen somewhere else over and over again?

'Someone's coming.'

'Bandys?'

'Don't think so.'

'Is it Ash?'

'Maybe.'

'Le Duk wouldn't like his spoils wasted on Sages.'

'They're gone for a bit. How will they know?'

'It is. I knew it. It's Ash.'

Cuspangel turned away from Rena and Isidore and opening the heavy door stood waiting, a welcoming smile on a face lined by the years and framed in curling faded hair. In the undulating distance the figure of the Sage waved and a question rolled over in the air to Cuspangel.

'Bandys?'

'Gone.'

Cuss signed back and saw Ash turn slightly in the fading

light. Suddenly from nowhere, a second figure materialised and then a third.

The two boys watched as Cuss embraced Ash for a long time. The two held each other, long arms wrapped, heads resting, eyes closed. They watched serious, and remembering in some part of themselves a past life where this was not so unfamiliar. Catching each others' glance, and embarrassed as men should be at this sort of thing, one banged the other with a bony elbow and putting grimy hands to their mouths they pretended to stifle their giggles. Ratts drew in a sharp breath and pinched Ash's arm.

'That Mother?' Lug was not so sure.

'Mother have brown hair. She white hair Elder.'

Ash shook her head. It was going to be difficult.

'You two've got a lot to learn.'

Pulling away from her friend she introduced them.

'This is Ratts and Lug. We've been travelling together.'

At this both boys frowned. Her tact did not mitigate her lack of protocol.

Standing very tall they glared at Ash, and Ratts said, 'I, Ratisbon, Crow.'

And the other, 'I, Lug. Runner.'

Both glasses and legs proclaimed them no liars at that and Cuss, straight faced, bowed, held out strong hands and said, 'We welcome you, Crow and Runner.'

At this, mollified, but not before giving the Sage a little nod that said at least someone here knows how to behave, they each took a proffered hand, to be swept surprised, and somewhat horrified, into a hard, tight embrace. The three close together, Ratts and Lug looked at each other through the tumbling hair of their captor and knew something they had not known before. This person who held them was not what she seemed, but a Warrior attacks only after mature deliberation, good conference and if danger threatens. Here seemed to be safety. The other thing could be excavated later, if found not to be a mistake. They pulled away abruptly. Behind was a Father and a Daughter. The Father spoke in a gruff manly tone pulling them into a low dark room full of warmth and steam and the smell of food. The boys smiled and relaxed. The Daughter simply waved a hand at the boys before she too was swept into Ash's arms. They were at least equal numbers.

The boys sat on low stools to eat while the rest lounged around the central table eating and talking. The boys heard their sad story retold and for a moment looked up from their bread and their bowls to see themselves reflected in sudden tender regard. In those eyes they remembered another past; the Elders, the Fathers, the Brothers. Gone now for a moment's mistake. The future was a shiver of unknown and they returned to the hot food. That night in the light of the moon they lay on hard mattresses and spoke in the old way with their fingers about many things. About the meaning of the strange woman, the chance of sanctuary. The Daughter. They tried to estimate their worth to this place and its people. If the place could only support one of them; which one? What would the life with the Sage be in terms of survival? But they were only boys, they knew little. Finally as day ran out of light their fingers ran out of talk and they slept, each one visited in their dreams by Tula, old Wise Elder, who may do what he liked, but still risked much to save them.

That night in the light of that same moon, plus a lantern or two, Ash brought out her prize. The book of maps. With its index, its mysterious categories, its rainfall gauges, its population estimates, climate graphs, its interpretation of structure, the sedimentary and igneous rocks, the geological cycles. Gondwana Land, Laurentia, Baltica, Angara. At charts of forest vegetation, unreadable; at densities of population, unimaginable; at the green of natural vegetation, unendurable. Isidore said, 'I had forgotten that an Atlas was more than maps. I had one like this, though not so grand, when I was a boy in some school or other. Or when I was a teacher. I forget now.'

They waited, but no more came. His grey eyes were unfocused and they knew where he was. Where they all went from time to time. Away, back. To another time, another house, to others who were once family. Lost now. Alive merely as a heart's shadow.

Rena stood up abruptly closing the book with a snap.

'It's valuable. We've waited a long time for one like this. Last year one of Le Duk's men produced a tiny one. It must have been for a child. Anyway it was so disintegrated that we daren't hardly look at it.'

She seemed to run out of things to say and looked down at Isidore dreamily, blankly as if half longing to join him.

'So, what's it worth, Sage?' Cuspangel now, ever practical.

'We've not much left. The Bandys only left us food this time. Not a good bargain. But there's no arguing with them and I think they're feeling the pinch too.'

Ash nodded. Somehow it didn't seem so important; a good deal. What had happened to her? This was not the way to survive.

'It's these boys. I don't know what to do about them. Ratts isn't like the others. He'd never make a Man even if he'd passed the tests. And the other, Lug. Would you believe he can read?'

At this, Isidore sprang to life making them all jump.

'Holy Mary! How could…?'

'That's what I thought. He can't do much; just his name and some letters.'

'A miracle, a miracle. What can we do with this?'

'Calm down, Dor, you'll have him reading you bedtime stories next. He's still a wild boy. He hardly knows which way to hold a book. It's the other one that has the promise.'

They looked at her, Sage, and she blushed.

Days later, as the rest of the household prepared in their various ways for the evening, Lug lay laughing softly to himself in the library. What a place it was; he would never finish seeing all of it. Stretching high above him they squashed against each other, some in cases that fit them perfectly, in light or dark wood, and metal. Some were on open racks built, he could see, from strips of wood laid on square edge, red stones. So many books. He remembered books from before, but none of those had been like these. They had been small and thin and full of brightness. These were mostly very big; some half as big as himself. He imagined, for a moment, what it would be if they all fell on him. Surely he would die under the weight of them all. Some were rich and strong and winked gold down their sides, while others seemed no more than a bundle of torn papers that you might kick aside for the fun of it. Just to see them leap in the air and then float silently down. But the old Father would teach him better. Teach him book manners, then he would be very wise like the Father. Like Fathers should be.

He was stretched out on his back, head resting on folded arms, eyes on a trophy pinned to a board. Or maybe he thought, not trophy. Maybe gift or prize. The list of words in his head-box multiplied by the day, though most remained in there never slipping onto his lips. But his ears were the busiest part of him and at night he fell into deep slumber where, in another world, he conversed fluently, easily with the Father while a crowd of awed faces of bandies and triples and Elder Tula smiled and nodded and bowed to him. The trophy reminded him of his time with the Bandits. Old, with some of its feathers bent and dusty, none the less, once it had the power to terrify. But now look at it; and where was the owner? Dead or useless with a lost wing. And here was Lug, laziness unpunished, not dead. And certainly not useless. All day yesterday he had helped the Daughter put papers into important heaps. Some on one heap, some on another. And by the end of the day what at its beginning had looked to be a task both thankless and indecipherable had begun to make a little sense. He had gained much praise when he had started to recognise some of the pattern of the sorting. Certain coloured papers belonged in one pile. Others with a feel to them of their own in another and then to his immense pleasure words began to signal themselves. Not understood as meanings but as shapes and sizes and densities. Like sorting herb leaves and grain, his fingers understood before his head did. And the Daughter noticed and smiled and nodded to him and spoke to him as if he was a Man, not still a boy.

Ratts too was being useful. His glasses once more in his possession, he had without being asked taken up a post of Crow. What he did best. In the night, fingers flashing by the moon or tip to tip at darkside they had decided to make themselves indispensable. That was not the word used but that is what was meant. Good place home, only so long we have place. Work they were used to and knew what happened to those who shirked; who better? A ladder got Ratts to the roof but not before he'd mended the broken rungs. The roof was more exposed than his old place on the hillside but he liked it. The house was a palace of comfort and friendliness, but for some reason he felt an indefinable sense of insecurity that made him restless and unsure. Somewhere in the library was probably a book and had he been able to read it, this would have reassured him that his feeling had a name and was perfectly normal. Why would he not feel alienated living as he did on the charity of strangers? He put from him the picture of Tula's wet eyes at the trial. And he kept watch remembering his training, remembering the tricks Bandies used; how they slip under and over sight using the rays of the sun to hide them; how they cover each other; disguise themselves as birds and even play rhythmic, hypnotic games deflecting sunlight off their shining feathers in sleep inducing patterns. A good Crow is ready and wily at all times. And here where no triples or Fathers or Elders could see him, Crow did his best. As invisible as he could be on the strange unprotected roof, he turned with Sol; against her; watching with no regular pattern; using his eyes, his glass and the same senses in his shoulder blades that all his people used; attentive as he never was on the old Mountains of Morn. Too late he regretted that sad day. His dreams of Tula were full of regret and sorrow, and his dreams of his old life were about breathing together in the old way.

Ash was waiting. For what she didn't know. Like Ratisbon, she had a terrible itch of discontent and dreaded its easing. For what could be about to happen. No more damn events, she thought. Enough has happened to me for a lifetime. It's time I retired.

'Come home with me, Rena.'

'I'm needed here.'

'If you're thinking of Cuss. . . '

'Well I am.'

'Cuss has a place.'

'And Grandpa?'

'Him too. You can't go on living in this place.'

'The book-stack. . . '

'Damn the book-stack. It's just an excuse. It's ruining your life.'

'Ruining my eyes.'

'You don't owe anyone anything.'

'No but I'm part of a balance here. If I go the whole thing falls down like a pack of cards. '

It was the same conversation they always had, every year when Ash came. About balance and survival; about tending the garden, tending the library, tending visiting Bandys. Since the arrival of the two boys life had become a little easier. Crow, bored with his self-appointed task with nothing happening had drifted to garden work with Cuss. A set of young strong muscles halved Cuss's work, as Lug in the library had Rena's. One evening around the table eating their meal Lug sighed and signed to his friend. Ratts frowned, shook his head and bent over his plate ferociously. Ash smiled and the old man began a conversation with himself on the many signed languages that existed.

'Of course, we know little about most of them since they are of themselves languages of secrecy that will not be recorded.'

'This one was something to do with meat or lack of it,' said Ash grimly to her plate. The boys looked at her and she shrugged at them.

'It's time to think about returning,' she said simply.

'We banished,' said Lug. 'No can return now. It too late to find triple.'

'Two no good for huts,' agreed Ratts. 'We two. All boy turn Men with triple.'

'Well,' said Ash, 'you'd better find a third'.

There was a long silence and Cuspangel rose, collecting plates in a sudden crash of noise.

'Why can't they stay? We can do with help around here.'

'They can't because they won't. In the end they'll go. In the end you all have to leave here. It's time, Cuss, and you know it. This hand to mouth stuff can't go on. You all have a place and you need to find it.'

In the library a fire was burning in a huge grate. The weather was changing and this was the first fire of the new season and thus was big. Rationing came later. The firelight flickered on Rena's long hair as she knelt putting sticks into the flames, poking them in between glowing embers, watching them catch light, letting the incendiary sparks fall on to her, never flinching.

'How frightened I once was of flames,' she said, more to herself than to Isidore, who was somewhere wandering between the stacks. He suddenly emerged clutching a large old book whose cover, once strong enough to hold tight all it knew, now gave itself away in easy crumbs.

'I was remembering before, Dor, how strange to be thinking of that now. Now we're both so safe.'

'This is what we need,' he said and pulled up a stool next to her. She took the book in her hands but it was so heavy that if fell into her lap like a big baby.

She read its title, 'The Book of Common Prayer and Service of Holy Matrimony. What do we need this for?' she said looking into a face suffused with an expression that she didn't recognise.

'Lug,' he said. 'That boy is coming along in leaps and bounds. Already he uses verbs. Not correctly yet of course. But soon. And speech is a facile kind of communication in some situations, Rena. You've been alone for too long. You can help me to keep him here.'

They looked at each other; he in hope, she in bewilderment fast turning to something else.

'This old book. You love old ceremonies. We could do it. This one. You could use that robe Ash brought. He'll soon grow. It used to happen like that, Rena, many, many histories ago. There'd be a Hand Fasting to secure a dynasty and one of the couple would have to wait a few years for the other to mature.'

He smiled a nervous, fluttering smile as Rena clutching the Book of Common Prayer rose slowly to her full height.

Leaning over until her face was close to his she said, 'You know about me. I could never do that.' The voice rising with every syllable to a screech. In the firelight the two faced each other, their flickering shadows parroting the drama that hung between them.

'Rena,' he implored 'This is my life. My books. It's important. We are preserving the past. For posterity. For your children.'

'I don't want children'.

Again the high strained sound, and she lifts the book high into the air, he gasps, reaching for it now high above him and she dashes it into the flames.

'No, no,' he screams, scrabbling at hot coals. 'That's the only copy,' and tears running down his face, his fingertips blister as he snatches the book and smacks the sparks from it before dry paper and crumbling leather catch light and sink into the impenetrable glowing mass.

Ash and Cuss put them both to bed and sat by the fire in silence watching the dull shape of the book smouldering on the stone floor.

'It's beginning to unravel, isn't it?' Cuss said. 'You always said it would.'

For several days Ratts worked alone. Morning, midday and evening he'd climb to the roof and watch, returning to the gardens only when he felt that dust puffs on the horizon were just sand storms and that birds in the sky had beaks not sharp teeth. This was the time of the year when the harvest was slackening off. Most of the work of gathering was over and past. On his own Ratts could clear and tidy; clip and burn. Solitude was a novelty and one he both relished for that novelty and dreaded for its meaning. At night in the kitchen he sat close to the beautiful Mother and told her all he had done for her that day. And she didn't disappoint him. She smiled and praised and gave him his tasks for the following day. And the following day he did what he had been told and pondered on her mystery. She was, and yet she was not. But what his senses told him he could not understand.

Sometimes in the night when he and Lug had finished their talking and Lug had rolled away from him and slept, Ratisbon would get up and, wrapped in a bed sheet, would wander around the house. At each door he would pause and listen and sniff. Each room with its different occupants felt and sounded different. In the Mother and Father's room where Father's smell was so strong there was often a duet of soft and sometimes not so soft snoring that made him smile. He imagined the Mother and the Father wrapped together in their couple embrace and wondered how different it was from what he and Lug might do. At Rena's room there was the sense of the unknown. Here the smell of female was strongest for Ash shared this room with Daughter. Although he had wandered many stretches with the Sage, still Ratisbon did not really know her. As he did not really know any of the Fathers back at the huts. You knew them but could never know them. At the door of this room there were fewer snores, sometimes sighs as if someone struggled in dream. Sighs and groans and unknown rustlings.

A few days after The Book of Common Prayer was saved from the fire two things happened. Dreadful things. Dreadful small things which led, as small things often do, to dreadful big things. Dread. Do you know that feeling? Of looking back and remembering something so awful you did that it doesn't bear thinking about? Or perhaps it's so awful that you can't quite remember it. Perhaps you have been responsible for the death of someone, or worse, the death of many. But it's been forgotten; you've thrust it away into the recesses of your mind and all that remains is the terrible feeling of dread and responsibility. Perhaps even, it happened in a past life. Or perhaps it never happened at all and it's just part of the way you punish yourself for existing. This was the feeling that had been creeping upon Ash for all the months she had stayed away from Paradise. Since the burning of the book it had intensified unbearably and she often sat with Crow on the roof watching and waiting. Then one evening the first thing happened; Lug and Ratts had a fight. In itself that was not unusual. They often scrapped; wrestled, testing themselves against the other's strength. In the Huts it was one of the few permitted body contacts of the daylight hours and many sports and games were built around it. Wrestling, jousting with sticks, frog leaping, slap-shoving and so on. And indeed when an argument could not be settled by dispute agreement, or be reconciled by Elders then a proper fight was set up. For this there were rules, stand-ins and fight organisers and a proper time, place and set of witnesses were arranged. The rightness of a point of view could never be decided as a result of a casual scrap or beating up. That was not justice. But on the evening of which I speak no such structure was in place.

It started innocently enough. Ratts and Lug were enjoying a conversation at the midday break, they'd had many times about Mothers and Fathers. Especially about Mothers. Ratts never talked about Lug's mother to him, and Lug tactfully avoided mentioning her. Since coming to the Library it had become obvious that she had done something remarkable in teaching her child to read. Remarkable, special, loving. Something that marked her love for him in a way that Ratts' mother had not. It was as if there was a wall where she had written on it for all to see the words, *I love my child.* But here they were talking about the idea of mothering, how Ash did it, how Rena did it. But when Ratts began to speak about Cuss's mothering skills Lug fell silent and his mouth twisted into a snake of a smile. He looked away, but Ratts pulled his face to him and looked into the eyes of his friend.

'Cuss best Mother. Cuss sweet and make good.'

But Lug shook his head and shrugged. Then he nodded. 'Cuss good Mother and make good.'

But something was wrong with that. With the way he said it. Ratts stood up and towering over his friend he glowered. 'What you say now?' he demanded. 'What you say of Cuss Mother?'

Getting up to face his friend, though broad and stocky, Lug was still a good hand and a half shorter. They glared at each other not knowing what to do. They had been banished from the huts before they'd been taught the skills to deal with this situation. Suddenly tired of tact, Lug let it out, what Ratts had known from the start and had put into the far reaches of his head and heart. Lug said the unthinkable.

'How Cuss Mother? Mother do cook, not Father. This family not good. Only Daughter do Daughter job. Cuss not Mother. Mother is woman.' More glaring and Ratts began to tremble with emotion.

Again Lug. 'You know. You smell him, too. Long time now since we come.'

And as the second dreadful thing flew high overhead, Ratts threw the first punch.

*****

It was a special day and not merely because of the weather. The sky was blue, true, and the down draft excellent, and there were some calm shelter pockets for the buds who were on their first flights. But more important it was a day of celebration in the calendar even though no one knew exactly what it was they were celebrating. Some said it was the time of the season for celebrating the last of the bright disc, when the air was beginning to cool and the cold change about to arrive. Some said it was a day to rejoice in the compatibility of difference in their tribe and some said it was something to do with wings. Perhaps the day when the first set had been grafted on to the back of some Bandit ancestor. This made others angry. It depended what you chose to believe; that the noble race of Bandit birds had always been creatures of flight or that they were descendants of some experiment in the dim, distant past. Most professed the former despite family and friends on the ground; those with hooves. It depended on who you were talking to really, and hooved kin thought very differently about most things. One thing was certain, it always paid to agree with someone stronger, unless you felt like a blood fight.

In the air the winged ones swooped and cackled and butted each other with glee. One or two had brought nose pipes and drums and were blasting out a hypnotic, insistent song. One or two were in ecstasy sharpening each other's teeth mid air. Their wings wrapped around each other they plummeted until the very last moment then broke from the other screeching with pleasure and delight and spiralled up like pollen on the breeze. On the ground the hooved ones held each other's hands and cantered in circles occasionally stopping to scratch each other or lick the sweat off a panting bud. The buds about to be Bandits leaped and fluttered, leaped and fluttered endlessly frustrated, endlessly unhappy as only unformed buds can be. And the slaves too had been told to take it easy today.

It was a convenient tribe to be born to whatever your form. Speed on the ground and in the air made for success in many ventures. Especially kidnap, theft and slaughter; the essentials of all creatures with no fixed home. And even now the celebration was not just a piece of random idleness. As they cantered, as they swooped, gradually mile by mile they approached a goal. Even pleasure could be profitable. For many years they had been coming here, to this smaller tribe who were very small and seemed never to produce young. Yet they were, on account of status and learning and courage, acknowledged as equals. Different, but equal.

When they'd first swooped down many, many seasons ago now, they'd found only one creature who wasn't worth the effort of killing, and certainly was too old for slavery. The next season, expecting to roost in the empty ruins of the building and peck over the creature's bones, they'd been astonished to find two more. Younger. As they'd approached with ropes, clacking their teeth in fair warning, the taller of the two creatures had begun to dance in time to the noise and to make its own noise with its mouth. At first they'd fallen back in surprise that there was no fear, and then they'd been entranced. The creature undulated with grace and liquidity and the strange languorous humming noise put them into a trance. Some of them, both Wing and Hoof had joined in dancing and butting delighted that a blood fight had turned out this way until all of them had fallen in a sweating exhausted heap. The second smaller creature who had shown some fear flung food at them and cowered at the edge of the place with the older one. But since they obviously belonged together that one too was given courtesy not fight. After that they'd made a point of coming at any celebration time to that place with the dancing one. Over time the dances had grown shorter but they knew each other better and the dances grew sweeter for it. On one occasion there'd been no food to offer so after that the tribe brought their own and it became a stop off, a resting place to clean wounds and sleep, as well as a place to have joy. And sometimes they brought things that caught their fancy that they could carry; ropes, bits of carved wood, old machines, a rut pig. It was a matter for wonder that they had no young or any slave. The older one did strange work with signs and letters in the building sometimes alone and sometimes with the small one. The big dancing creature worked outside and was sometimes helped by the small one. And they didn't want slaves, though many were offered and it was easy to see how a slave would like the life. Their feet wouldn't bleed much there. They were very strange but if you weren't in fight trim then other creatures were to be allowed their ways, whatever they were.

From the air two boys fighting looked at first like two anythings. Two ants, two voles, two rut pigs. Until closer it seemed that the little tribe they visited had actually produced two more of its kind. But closer still, it became obvious that one at least must be a runaway. Celebration became quickly conference. This was indeed a good slave to survive without protection. And smart; no one had realised exactly how smart. The slave had been dead the last time anyone had seen it. Messages to the ground halted the charge towards the objective and swooping down the Bandits of the air gathered like a conference of winged warriors, which is of course what they were. And soon Hoof and Wing hunkered, forgetting the specialness of this day, to consider the next move.

So when it came she was ready. And ready too for the relief it brought. The immediate calm and sense of rightness. She met them half way with the library nestling behind its walls at her back, and the wide expanse of the hills before her; like a cloud of insects they were everywhere. Those who were in the air flew low, whirring and clacking, the dying sun reflected on shining teeth; those on the ground leaping and trumpeting in triumph. She could hardly see the two boys. Curses on them, she thought, and the day I ever got involved. Was there ever a couple who needed so much rescuing? Ratts for once was not crying; perhaps he was past it. Wrists tied he was at least on his own two feet, though not likely to remain so much longer, she thought, held as he was between two of the most powerful Hoof Bandits. At first she couldn't make out where Lug was in all the flurry and dust and movement. Limbs, she had never seen so many limbs; so many strong muscles oiled with sweat and grease, so many moving thighs and haunches, chests and breasts, so many bellies flat and round, hairy and shaved. And she realised that in all the years of her dealing with these people she had always met them on her ground, or at least at the library where it was human territory; where air was a separate space simply to be breathed and not used as a dimension for living and being. They were always either in motion in the air at a distance or quieter, still. How different they were in their own territory where they acknowledged nothing and no one over them. They were uncontrollably themselves and their power was terrifying. Then she saw Lug. He was bound in something tight, chest to ankle and looked like a carpet flung round the sinewed shoulders of a full breasted, crop haired female. She was riding in the company of other females who laughed as they galloped some of them clucking and cooing at the bouncing boy.

Ash let out a piercing whistle which she knew would hardly be heard in the hubbub. But from above she was seen and soon, before they were upon her engulfing her, they focused and gradually slowed, seeming to stumble and tumble to a halt. Then they were around her, breathing hard, coughing and spitting, with the dust settling, telling her of the recapture of their runaway. When she did not offer the expected smile and applause they gathered closer readying themselves for offence. Dealing with Bandits was no easy matter. She knew she was safe physically. Probably. She knew they would never kill her. Rough her up a bit, maybe.

But death, no. None the less, their size and enormous physicality could be overwhelming. She remembered the first time, when she was a young sprout. Out in the desert, disobeying her trainer, how afraid she'd been. They'd come out of nowhere, hovered and trotted around her as if sniffing her. That time they'd not spoken, just looked her over and then taken off again in a rush. She still remembered the silence, how intense the sound of nothing was after their presence and she'd gone home and sat down at her work and not complained again for many months. It had taken several meetings over several years to perfect communication. Language was not the problem. Other things were. They had no one leader, for a start. No one was in charge. Now in theory that's how they did it at places like Paradise and Arkady. But in practise it didn't work like that. There were always leaders. Sometimes benign, just; often benevolent, usually unselfserving. But leaders none the less, if only because of experience. But not with the Bandits. As she thought this she could sense them speaking to each other, mouths still, eyes beetling on her. But she knew that she must deal with not one or two creatures but with the whole lot of them. Still, she tried to be positive. It's as if there was only one, isn't it? And a wave of Bandit smell swept over her and she felt their exhaustion. They're only human. The thought came to her, and she suppressed the nervous laughter that came bubbling up from nowhere.

Let us sit, she motioned. And arranging her robe she sank to the ground. Then she lifted up her hands and clapped the applause they loved so much. As they all sat down with her on the ground Ratts and Lug looked at her. Don't speak to me, she prayed. Stay silent, stay calm, and she flicked her eyes away from them. 'These are bad boys,' she said. And everyone nodded, those nearest Ratts and Lug giving them a few sharp slaps into the bargain.

'Very bad, runaways.'

More nods, more slaps and teeth clacking. I'd better get them out of this she thought; how those teeth did shine even in the gathering dusk.

'Very bad, to run away twice.'

Now puzzlement; she held onto her silence like a rope. Each side waited, eyeing each other. Still no words, and heads turned to each other, eyes shifted, frowns appearing. Hanoon, let my timing be right.

'Runaway first from you, second from me.'

She sat still letting the information sink in. Then uproar. She was Ash, the Sage. They had smelt her powers on that first meeting. And over the years they had used her as she had used them. For survival. Sometimes she had had to turn away from the excesses of their nature. When they killed, when they ate, when they mated. Now she would see. It was, of course Le Duk who spoke for them when they'd calmed down, who passed along the words of the tribe and while he was himself part of the whole he was in his own right one very quarrelsome and dangerous creature. Leaning against a young Hoof, he clacked his beak and the two boys were before her. One flat on his face choking in the dust, the other lolling like a badly cut sapling. Everyone laughed. Ash laughed. And as Ratts drew his brows together in a fury of anger and disbelief she shot him the minutest hint of a wink. For the smallest part of a moment her lash closed on her eye; as if she blinked a fly away or a speck of dust. His brows untangled and she looked away before they were done. Pray wink means to him what it means to us, she thought.

She spent a lot of time arguing with Le Duk and trying to

remember that he was not an individual. That he was not speaking for himself. Back and forth it went. Who had first claim? Whose right should be upheld. They had in the first part created the slave. It didn't exist before their action. That she conceded. They had tended it during a period of initiation. Put value into it while it recovered from wounds that they had not inflicted. Again she conceded. After a pause the Hoof whispered in Le Duk's ear. Then they had a suitable mate for it in their breeding programme and it was part of an inter-connected system that would collapse without it. That it was a poor argument and they all knew it. So she said nothing in words; her mouth and her brow were expressive enough. The Hoof turned away. She kept her best card till last. Who had he run from first? Who had held on to him longest? Who was then the best owner? And...she waited a moment knowing the value of silence...who had made two where only one had been?

This, of course, was her strongest point. Not only the multiplication of the original number, but that they belonged together. That went straight to the centre of all they were and knew. They had never been one. There was no one. They were part of a two. Broken, which she had repaired. And that was the end of it. There was a kind of sigh which ran through the collective body and a lot of nodding and shaking of heads. Le Duk gave a sharp kick to Lug's head and she knew that she'd won. The kick wasn't hard enough, of course, to damage the goods. Reparation was on everyone's mind. A wing spread over Lug's stiff reclining body and a set of young glistening teeth were bared. An exhausted Ratts lifted himself up and Ash grabbed his wrist.

'Calm,' she whispered, 'this is ritual.'

The teeth ripped at the binding and soon Lug was free.

For a long while he lay still as death with his eyes closed and Ratts tensed under her grasp. Then slowly he rolled over until he was face down in the dirt and painfully pushed on his hands till, on his knees one leg at a time, he could stagger upright. A pattering of applause went round the tribe like rain on a drum. Regret. A good slave had been lost this day.

They saw the flames as they drew near to the buildings. Already they had been running, the smell of smoke drawing them towards danger, towards their friends. There was plenty of smoke and soon the terrible crackling sound of fire on wood and paper. Rena was standing, by the well, a wet bucket at her feet. Drenched with well water and tears she turned a face black with soot to them at the sound of their approach. Holding out her arms to Ash she cried, 'Help us, help us'. The bucket was seized and dropped into the well, but what were one or two or even three pairs of hands to do against that force. A westerly wind blew the flames away from them, fanning them none the less to a bright noisy fury.

'Where Cuss? Mister Dor?' Ratts cried over the noise.

Rena pointed; flames beckoned, burning, unapproachable.

'Cuss.' Ratts screamed. 'Cuss, Cuss.'

And Ash fell to her knees and put her brow on the ground. 'Now, if never before, hear us, Great Watcher. Hear us. Show us your power.'

She knocked her head three times on the ground and sat back before the fire.

The others turned and looked believing and disbelieving at the same time. For a while nothing happened but the greedy flames at their meal. Timbers fell with a crash and sparks flew brilliant in the sky. A roaring wind sucked air from them and pushed its might into the raging fury. Second by second this violent thing grew before their eyes like a brilliant monster, its growth unnatural, unkind. Flames were no longer distinguishable. It was a hungry mass of motion, red and black, yellow and blue. Inside itself, unseen explosions crashed sending black emissions of foul smoke, covering them as if to mark them for later. Rena knelt down next to Ash as if joining in the prayers, as if she would wait there forever if it came to it. And then, as if by magic, a shape appeared through the furnace. Like a tall, dark ghost, no human features visible it staggered to them smoking and black. A blackened arm appeared, held out an appealing hand, and it was a burning blanket that fell from the shape, smouldering to the hot earth, revealing a Cuss that no one but Rena had ever seen. Cuss's body, naked and smoke blackened, was well formed and muscled under the dirt. Though what it revealed made the boys turn to each other as if to begin again the fight they had started once before. For though it still clutched several large books to it, the body they saw showed none of the usual signs of maleness, but yet neither was it obviously a woman's. No roundness, no curves, no breast. With the hair singed short, the boys saw that Cuspangel was indeed as Lug had said. Ratts turned away, Lug followed, and Cuspangel fell down on top of the books.

Hanoon made another gift that day, as well she should if her plan was not to be thwarted. She cut her winds and brought unseasonal rain. Later they found Isidore Bascombe, or what was left of him. In due course some of the Bandits returned. Seeing the devastation they were satisfied, once Ash had explained it, with the book of maps as Lug's reparation. It seemed a useful item to those who spent much time in the air; although much time was taken in showing how they worked. The others that Cuss had rescued didn't seem worth the effort. A book with lists of numbers, one with close packed print, another with no words just little raised dots in varying patterns and a volume of plant references. But Ash took them for her pack. You never knew when something could be useful.

No one asked Rena or Cuss directly what had happened. For a start Cuss didn't speak for several days; shelter and food and clothes had to be improvised out of the havoc. Let it not be said that Bandits are all bad. I won't say that they were full of compassion; most probably they had an eye to a future indebtedness. But from their baggage came all manner of goods and soon Cuss's naked body was clothed and his blistered extremities bandaged. Ratts and Lug waited on Cuss night and day. Who knows what they had said to each other, but two and one surely made three, and a ready-made triple had some status or other, in certain places.

Days later, on a bed made from some salvaged thing or other, Cuss lay recovering, with Rena sitting silently by. As he opened his eyes she said, 'History repeats itself.'

He nodded and they looked into the other's eye and saw a smile grow.

'I hope you're not going to stay in bed as long as you did that time.'

Across the shack, Ratts shifted in his sleep, snoring gently. Brother and sister looked at each other and smiled guiltily. Another silence, and then…

'Too many lies, Serena, I'm sick of it. What are we going to do now?'

Before she could answer Ash sat silently down, a question in her eyes. The brother and sister looked at each other. Quickly Rena said, 'It was Dor's own fault. He upset a lantern on some papers. We did what we could.'

And she gestured towards the bandages on Cuspangel's hands. Ash was quiet for a long while not looking at either of them.

'He gave you sanctuary all those years ago.'

'We rescued him from certain death. If we hadn't come along just then... ' Rena broke off.

'He needed us just as we needed him,' said Cuss. 'He was at the end of his tether. He wasn't that old, it was simply that he couldn't survive here alone. We made ourselves useful.'

And Cuss looked away as if remembering. 'In many ways,' he said.

'The thing is,' said Ash, not looking at anything in particular, 'that his skull appears to have split. I suppose that must have happened in the fire. It must have been unbearably hot at the centre.'

'I suppose it must,' and Rena looked at Cuss, but his eyes were closed.

'Isidore was a good man,' Cuspangel said, 'but sometimes there was no talking to him. That damn Library. His books, his papers. Lug. He never saw that people might want different things. Not be able to go along with his plans.'

There was another long silence. Rena said, 'It was his only real weakness.'

'I see,' said Ash.

And she did. Suddenly Lug was there with water for Cuspangel. Already belonging. She looked at Rena.

'Let's leave the boys to sleep, and go and talk about what to do next.'

*****

And then one day, two came. From far away. It was summer

when the light never goes but only dims a little as if to bow in the new day. Some of us had forgotten to sleep that night and were sitting in the garden out of the back of Eye The Girls. And when I saw them I was reminded for some reason of something that had happened long ago. There had been a young woman who was quite remarkable, but she had had some obligations and so she couldn't stay. This time the visitors came from the other direction, slowly as all our guests do, for we are a long walk from anywhere. *Kick, stamp, limp.* As they drew near one lifted an arm and waved. *Kick, stamp, limp.*

'Ash,' I said, and most people woke up from the stupor into which they had sunk.

'Who's that with her?' said another, and a buzz of curiosity ran round our group.

'Is it a boy?'

And we all looked at them coming near to us. Certainly it looked like one. Skinny, grubby, cropped hair; but too old for a boy surely? And then I saw the shirt. Faded, but mine. It had been my favourite; and I found my heart beating too fast and I pushed myself to the front of the crowd, and even though they were some way away she saw me as if she'd been expecting me. 'Noor,' I heard her say. And she smiled.

Chapter 8

Roseen and the Angel

~ ~ ~ ~ ~

How hot it was that day. And how Sol glared down on us. Sweat was in my eyes from the moment I picked up my spade. For weeks the summer heat had been growing so it was any excuse now to stop and stare. High above in the blue air there were specks that day, like dirt kicked up or flecks across the eyeball. Blink, blink, blink and the damned things were still there. From field and forest and fold you could see them; and then someone yelled out that they were angels. Didn't anybody remember? Lady Ren would've. And April-Mae. Oh dear. Oh dear. Angels. They're all too young. It must have been somebody's idea of a joke, but you know how some things can't be called back once they're out. True, I found a feather, after, that wasn't there before, but actually those angels looked to me as if they were flying at each other, stopping short, and then tumbling over and over each other just like starlings fighting for nest space. Very holy. But what would I know, I'm just a gardener not a cleric. So that became the day that angels flew over Paradise. The place was in an uproar. No one could talk of anything else, not archivist, not cook, not hog-girl nor forester. Some children who should have been in school began to whirl about with their arms stretched out going, 'Look at me, look at me, I'm an angel,' and that was altogether the most exciting thing to happen that whole week. Apart from an infestation of carrot blowfly, which I don't suppose would interest anyone except gardeners, and even we were sick of it. So having cricked my neck for a while and got an eyeful of Sol bright so I couldn't see, I went back to my digging.

But that night as I lay down in the dark to sleep I could still see those dancing dots; birds or angels, wheeling and diving, but so high you could scarcely see them. Then pictures of claws and the snatching fingers. Or was that a dream I'd had before? How easy to mix dream and memory; and how irritating.

*****

No angels, Tron and Fremzle would have been pleased to be the subject of another's dream. Why they were so far from their desert skies that day is a mystery only they could unwind; and there would be those who wanted to know, so it had better be a good story. When they had finished wrestling, Tron and Fremzle stretched in flight, balancing on shifting draughts of wind. Here in the air, their true element, they should have been oblivious, but between the silken pads of their claws were crusted slivers of blood and soil. Later, it would take a long, painful session of spit and tear to get rid of that dirt; until they did, they would be two very irritable Bandits. Had they known someone was on the warpath they might have stopped their fighting games and returned speedily and with stealth to their tribe. They might have hidden awhile, or chosen to perform some unlovely task to get back favour. Or even, if they'd thought of it let alone dared to do it, faced him. Gone straight to him and bowed and vowed to behave, never again to cause such worry, to be so careless with the feelings of the others. There'd have been punishment, of course, that same unlovely job; some messy, filthy, heavy task or other, fit only for slaves or bad Bandits, but it would be finished with. And soon. But this time, this time, he was really mad. Having to leave the desert to come to this hot wet place was guaranteed to have him make up a punishment list so long and so convoluted that it might last from dawn to dusk and dawn again for several spins of the sky.

Of course Le Duk didn't know exactly where the two rebels had gone. At first like everyone else he was worried. The tribe was a good size but not so big that it could lose two very easily. His first thought as leader was of enemy activity and he flew straightway over to the nearest Boys place by the Mountains of Morn. And while he could see little of his quarry he knew he himself was spotted and noted. Dangerous stuff. Out of character. Bandits of the air came only at night. Swiftly, silently; did their damage and left. Le Duk prided himself in a clean battle. Nothing unnecessary, either in theft or cruelty. Take only that which is needed, no more. A denuded enemy can be used only once. And certainly never come in daylight as he was doing. Breaking his own rules. He could see below him some Boys, skinny, well muscled and tall. They were mostly dark hued with dirt and weather, dark haired, clad in bright cloth; keen young warriors waving weapons and jumping at him, whooping and calling. A glimmer of amusement warmed his discontent and he swooped down a little, still well out of range, to give them a thrill. Some of them ducked. One or two stood transfixed, gaping with open mouths at him. He knew very well how he looked, how his wings were burnished and his claws gleamed.

Vanity was a bad thing, he always told his band. And quickly ashamed and seeing no signs of his own boys he peaked and was soon a dot too small to be seen. Now where else would those two fools have got to?

Le Duk lay on the wind, his body lifted and held, sweet as a down cushion. He stretched his limbs in the hot draught and let a few loose, itching plumes go, cocking his head he watched them float rocking through the air away from him. Lower and lower, smaller and smaller. He could if he wished race them, swoop beneath them and snatch them back. But he let them go, he didn't care; it was a moment that he allowed himself once or twice. Pretending he was an ordinary Bandit. He thought of his parents. They had had no leader; had needed none. But things were different now. Changed for the better; at least better for them. Once he had been looked after. Now he sometimes felt sire to the whole tribe, all of them, young and old. And these two. Had there ever been such stupid, such bad Bandits? Crossly he thrust them from his mind and felt again the soft caress of the supporting breeze buoying him and touching all his parts. Wind was like that, it got everywhere. Each feather felt warm and clean and flexing his fingers and claws dirt fell away in a shower of powder. Hot wind slipped over his head and into his ears, along his body, his thighs and legs. He rolled over, languorously, and let the heat onto his belly and his neck. How hot the light was up here. What could compare with it? The wind, the air. It was bliss. How good it was to be a flying Bandit. Hoof was good, he knew; how swift they were on the land. But to be Wing was best. To know no constraint of dimension. How would it be if Hoof had feathers and Wing had legs and a tail? The thought made him choke with his own daring; he'd better keep quiet about that idea, leader or not. He knew what was right after all. He flipped over. That was the problem with these two, their mixed blood and their youth; you couldn't expect the same behaviour from them. Suddenly into his musings crept a disturbance. Slight, subtle. What was it? He focused with a sigh; enough enjoyment for now. Back to work. And he shut his eyes concentrating on the new sensation. His beak quivered as his nostrils dilated and his nipples twitched. Ah, so that's what it was. He'd get them now.

The trouble with Fremzle and Tron was not their youth; in fact they were almost over that. Nor, really, their distressing mixed blood. It was simply a matter of a poor match of characteristics. Personalities that should have been kept apart. Le Duk and Barziley Dvek had argued about it often enough. Everything had been tried. Allocating them to different work places, different nests even putting distance between the two. But you can't go on doing that forever. There was a fateful connection between them that eventually everyone acknowledged. Sooner or later the purpose of their attraction would become manifest and then at least everything would be clear. But meanwhile they always went too far. Like now. Fighting, tumbling, then full body contact and then the sex games that always put them in a good humour. In broad daylight out of their own pale. For a moment when Tron had latched onto Fremzle's nipple it had been the start of a perfect coupling. So high, so hot, so heated. But as the strong savour of sex and milk sent them into close-winged rapture Fremzle at least remembered Le Duk somewhere in her watchful back brain. She pulled away rapping her beak on Tron's to snap them out of it, but it was too late. An angry clattering plunged them to a chilly attention as they saw a small dark spot grow all too soon into the wrathful shape of Le Duk.

He grabbed them from underneath, paralysing them and dowsing their waning ardour with a spray of piss. There was no need for words, they could tell he was angry. His strong wings beat demon-like against the heat, bigger than ever, and piss and tears dripped off them evaporating in the chill of his contempt. Eyeing each other, Fremzle and Tron silently blamed the other, then themselves and then each other again.

From the dry hillside beneath, a girl only saw three angels. From the dry hillside beneath, as she rounded up some hogs, stick in hand, she saw her angels fly away into the bright disc in the sky.

Too late he saw the trap. He hadn't even seen it at first. Carrying the two rebels was heavy work for which he had planned some rich payment that they would earn. But Fremzle and Tron whose mother's mother had been a Hoof began to twist and squeal instead of hanging limp and compliant as befitted prisoners on their way to jail. 'Hoof, hoof,' they called, and looking down seeing the captured Bandit his mind went into a whirl. How? Who? The impossibility of it overwhelmed him but he swooped down despite himself to take a better look. But the fallen body was a stuffed hide, and its threshing limbs, tipped with rusted cans that glittered a little like pitiful hooves, were moved by metal threads. Then, all of a sudden, the net was around them and closing fast. In a moment he'd dropped the two and held a gap in the falling net too small for himself. 'Fly, fly,' he screamed and for the first time in their lives they did what they were told without argument. Beating his wings against the terrible ropes, tearing at them with his beak and claws made little difference as he was slowly pulled in. To give them credit, Fremzle and Tron didn't simply abandon him.

Flying at their attackers, weapons before them, snapping and grabbing they were two against ten. 'Fly, fly,' he called again and watched impotent at the unimaginable. He, Le Duk, Master of the Bandits, captured by Boys. Later, he saw that all things had led to this moment. Anger had always been his downfall. He should have simply waited for them to return. Barziley had been right, where else would they go? One day, sooner or later, sheepish and full of lies, they would have returned. He only had himself to blame. He was the one who had shown himself in daylight; giving them the idea. Succumbing to his soft feelings at the expense of his children. How could he ever lift his head again? Who would call him Master, now? He wrapped his gleaming wings around him hiding inside, closing his eyes. He felt the net settle on him tangling into his feathers and he sent his mind into blankness, waiting for what must happen next.

As the net wrapped the creature, holding him like a great hand, a circle of Boys stood around him, unsure now they had a Bandit, what to do next.

*****

In a brown field on a brown hill sat a girl with a stout stick. Smooth and long, it was just the thing for herding swine. Sometimes they were swine, sometimes they were just damned hogs. Today they were her pretty pigs. Red and grey, hairy round their necks with long silken tassels hanging from their rusty ears and tails that twitched and twisted according to their mood. With the help of some rain their sharp little trotters could turn the hardest, most packed field to a mire of mud in no time. Often she drove them to the forest where they were most happy, rutting and rooting under the trees. But today she was doing what she wanted. She loved the heat; loved to feel the fingers of Sol stroke her, bouncing off her dark skin, pressing into her bones. She felt relaxed and easy, in such a good mood as her fingers parted her hair and plaited it. Parted and plaited, the motion hypnotic. Her pretty pigs, and they were pretty today, shining and clean with curling snouts and bright, knowing eyes, were slumped in deep shade under the field's only tree. Soon she'd take them back to the cool of the forest, but not yet. Just for once she needed heat more than she needed to do her job well and the pigs wouldn't tell, she was sure. A sudden snort brought her to attention and a little hog, his tail twirling with excitement, was up on his two hind feet snapping at the air. At something falling to earth. Not leaves, unless they were the golden leaves of the Sol.

And suddenly the path of her life changed. She hadn't known when she woke that morning that it would, nor did she then at that moment of turning. But she lifted her eyes and saw the one who would change it; the angel, dark and beautiful filling the sky. Almost motionless, a miracle of flight; hovering, balancing on the wind; riding it like a horse. His eyes shut, his bronze fingers flexing and retracting in ecstasy. Her hands fell from her hair and in a trance she reached for him, for the beautiful shining vision. Suddenly short of breath, she stumbled to her feet, heart racing. 'Take me with you,' she begged, though not a sound came from her dry mouth.

When he had gone, suddenly, his wings like great cloaks, she felt cold, though the Sol had merely moved sideways, not vanished. But she felt chill and dizzy. She picked up baby pig and held his firm little body to her, burying her face into his small solidity. Then they went, stick and all, back to the forest.

The bee landed on her wrist the moment she took off the gloves. Her skin, if it was like paper and mottled over the blue ridges, was at least warm and alive. She loved how the trusting body moved on her. The legs light, she could feel the little pads gripping and ungripping and its back end tap, tapping on her innocently, as if there wasn't that barbed sting concealed and always ready. She'd been stung many, many times on nearly every part of her body. But the punctures and the pain were a fair exchange for her quiet life with these creatures. The sensation of the bee made her smile and she tipped her head so that her hot breath would not reach the creature. Slowly she lifted her hand nearer her eyes and watched for the thousandth time how the tiny banded fur bristled and glistened and how it balanced on it's two back feet, while it cleaned itself with the front two. Just like a cat, she thought, again for the thousandth time.

The noise of the hives was soothing, a constant soft thunder that rose and fell with their mood and their life. The bees' life was so simple, she thought. No words, no malice, no loss. She sighed a long sigh and the bee feeling the breath on him, kicked off from his soft seat and vanished into the horde milling around his own house. At the other end of the path a colourful figure appeared. Lady Ren, Mistress of the Bees and Keeper of the Hives, tucked her melancholy back into its place and waited. Looking at the sky she smiled. Grey clouds loomed. Rain would quieten them down and unlatch the buds on the butterfly tree that they loved. Butterfly honey was much prized for its superior flavour.

The figure was indistinct, blurred. But Lady Ren knew who it was. It never appeared without seeming to burst on to her consciousness. Others came smoothly and their arrival grew on her slowly, giving her old eyes time to focus until she saw them and recognised them. But with Roseen it wasn't like that. She was a waving, flapping star; immediately Roseen at any distance. Sometimes, especially in wet weather, if the hogs had been particularly hoggish, and Roseen hadn't been particularly concerned with cleanliness, sharper senses than her eyes identified her granddaughter even sooner. Her adopted granddaughter. There had never been any deception about it. Truth was good for both of them. Roseen had agreed about the truth bit as a tiny child but had continued to call her Grandma. What could she do?

'Grandma. Grandma. It's me. How are you?' The voice sang out and a flung of long arms, damp hair and young sweat wrapped around her before her eyes had time to focus. She held her and felt the strength of the girl's youth. Precious moment.

'Did you see the angels? I've come to say goodbye. We're off to the pasture for a while.'

'You and the angels together?'

They laughed without humour. Roseen, for a moment startled by the old woman's uncanny perception, and Rena, because one day a parting like this would be forever.

'No. Me and the hogs. To the high field. How are the bees? Can I take some honey with me?'

Lady Ren hugged the girl again and they sat on the wall together. Every parting was like all the others.

'I'll see you when I get back.'

'If Elle Hamoon wills it.'

And for a moment they were quiet, under the spell of what The Faithful Watcher, did or did not will. In the distance, in a garden surrounded by high walls, someone was digging a hole. From the bee field the hole was a tiny dot and the figure like a doll, which straightened for a moment, turning and stretching. Then it waved a minute hand and Rena lifted her hand in greeting. Roseen knew the gardener must be hot and sweating, the spade heavy and chafing.

'I'm glad I tend hogs,' she said and ducked as a couple of bees arrived to smell her out. 'Perhaps I'll be a beekeeper like you one day. It's so peaceful with the bees.'

Rena smiled at the girl. 'Unless you're chasing an angry swarm up and down a mountain in the rain, or get lost in the forest looking for them in a fog.'

Perhaps the girl would follow her, one day. But not yet. She had a lot of living to do first. You needed patience, delicate patience to serve the bees and handle their coming and goings. And the comings and goings of others.

'Sing me a bee song, Grandma, before I go.'

'I'm not your Grandma. You don't have a Grandma. She's gone. Like your ma. Death is always with us. When you least expect it. Like love. Don't expect easiness.'

She regretted the lecture the moment it had left her mouth. She knew she couldn't protect this beautiful, messy, grubby girl. She had to find out for herself. She slipped a sly look at her granddaughter but she was almost dozing, she didn't look lectured at. Rena felt her leaning against her shoulder as she had done as a child.

'Am I like her?'

'Who?

'My mother.'

How many times would she have to answer this question? 'April-Mae? Yes, of course. Though she washed more often.' Another thing out that should have stayed in, but Roseen ignored it.

'And how did she die?'

This one too must be answered as if it was the first time.

'It was a mistake. She took a wrong turn. Said the wrong thing. Bandits are very different creatures. Not vindictive, just careful. They would have thought that she posed a threat. But she was simply killed, not punished.'

'And you loved her mother.'

Hardly a question. It was an old story. 'Noor? Yes I loved her.'

'She must have been very sad when my mother died.'

'Children should bury their mothers, not the other way round.'

'I'm so lucky that you got to be my Grandma.'

Indeed, the way it happened, everyone was lucky in the end. Particularly Rena. With Ash gone, there were few people to speak for her. Few to be kind about her difference. To understand why she broke the unwritten rule. Leaving Charlie, the last of her family, had been a terrible thing. She'd never been so alone in all her life, until Noor had refused to let her be so. Mary had been her first true love; but one day she realised that her memories of that time and the people in it, were more a memory of a story that had been told over and over, rather than of something tragic that had actually happened to her. So she had found happiness with Noor and April-Mae. And the community had been good to her for a while, especially after April-Mae had been killed. Later, with Noor gone too, she yearned for her brother and found that she would not break with him completely. Things had changed then.

At first this life with the bees, its isolation and distance from everybody, had not felt like the gift they had said it was; it felt like punishment, that she was a contaminant. But of course they had been right, she wasn't like them, however much she'd tried. Learning the rules and the language was not enough; she was still as unlike them as she had been all that time ago when Ash had first brought her. It no longer troubled her. There was Roseen. At least she was one of them. She started up an old song that she knew the bees loved to hear:

'Bees are coming on the wind
In the sky, so don't be shy.
Hives are humming, sweetest din
Don't you laugh, don't you cry.'

And Roseen, on her shoulder, drowsily joined in the cradle song she knew.

'Whisper, whisper, in my ear
All the things you want to hear.
I will tell you in return
Everything you want to learn.'

*****

It had never happened, such a triumphant thing, within the memory of even the oldest one, and so they danced a dance of nobility and pride. They were graceful and strong. They rattled and sang, waving powerful arms and legs and jumping higher than had ever been jumped before. They kicked up dirt and made the ground tremble with their noise. 'Never before, never before,' they sang. Two Elders, sat on a wall watching. Friends since boyhood, tossing off a few of the old finger words, there was no need for speech. They drew a deep breath from rusty lungs at the same time and sighed a deep sigh together. They had in fact seen it before, many times. Memory is short as history is long. The two old heads turned and they looked at each other, eyebrows and lips twitching and turned again back to the dance.

Dance was a new thing, though. Since the coming of their three. And had there been any thanks? There had not. Until Cuspangel had brought his lithe body and his mobile feet and hands, dance had been a matter of mere stamp and chant. Now these youngsters danced as if it was their idea; or that what they were doing, their re-enactment of the capture, the choreographic expression of their glad feelings, was a tradition whose roots were buried in the depths of time. They were wrong of course. And Cuspangel was no longer here to tell them so. Only one short season ago he had still been dancing with them. One day they too would follow him and also be forgotten. Suddenly the dance changed and moved slowly towards them, the dancers flipping sweat from shining brows and offering smiling faces to the old men. Lug and Ratts looked at each other again. Was this homage? Perhaps the youth weren't as bad as all that. But the dance was turning melancholy; they were honouring the great Dance Master. Silently the Elders, Triple no more, took the danced praise for him and remembered. Old Ratts and Lug remembered Cuspangel's agile beauty as if it were yesterday and grieved his death as if today.

It was of course a great capture. Bandits were not easily snared. How do you catch a bird twice your size; one with razor sharp claws? On the other hand it was the Chief Bandit. No one had worked that out yet. Another sigh. So few had ever seen him. The captive shivered in the tangle of the net. Some of his feathers were gone for good. His beak clacked and he lifted his great head and looked at Lug. Do beaks smile?

He had wondered why they had only tied one of his legs to the post. And why by such a strangely particular length of line. His Bandits, he thought, would have trussed him up good and tight and rolled him into a deep pit while they considered his future. But here he was at last, prisoner of his old enemies, only half tied and with enough length to step a little back and forth. He smelt torture or at least games. He was right. And after a time he found out about the line. At first he had obeyed his eyes strutting to the end of the line's length and back again. To the end and back, to the end and back. Until something made him stretch his foot a little beyond the given length. There, instead of the tightening jerk he might have expected, he found a softening and a giving that let him outside its apparent reach. He had heard of such things though he'd never seen them. A miracle of invention that was at once what it was but could be other. Both short and long in the same thing. And then he knew what games were to be played.

It was useful stuff. Some little squirt had found it on Morn when he'd run off, away from a well-deserved whipping. Running back with the news and, the boy was smart, a small sample, he'd sprained his ankle in the excitement. He only got half a beating; the other half cancelled in acknowledgement of pain already endured and of the potential his foresight promised. The properties of the new material were soon appreciated and put to use. Those with the skills were soon knotting and netting and doing a great trade in head and prong covers. Though after a few jokes about worms in a net and bong-fruit bouncing in a storm the latter were soon discarded in favour of the old fashioned loin bindings.

Le Duk refused from the very start to do what they asked. He had to be very careful. Before him, there had been no one Master. He had changed that and now he wasn't sure what a

Master was free to do in such circumstances. They laughed when he explained, politely at first, that if they hadn't known it they had collected Le Duk, Bandit Master of this territory and it was not appropriate within the laws of warfare to humiliate him. When they had finished with the laughter they simply said, 'Now you fly for us'.

'No', again and withholding anger.

'You our captive. We say fly. You fly.'

With a sigh that croaked in his long neck he explained the difference in meaning between the words capture and collect. Capture, he said, as gently as he could, only referred to a denial of liberty resulting from a fair exchange of battle tactics. Netting, he couldn't help spitting his contempt, was the trickery of youngsters with no battle skills. There was a long, quiet pause after he'd spoken as they looked at him and then at each other. As one they puffed up their skinny chests and thrust out bottom lips and walked away with some show of dignity. He watched them, heads together conferring. Some shouts splicing the air. It was a short victory, their discomfiture, and he knew that whatever happened next would happen to him. After the third refusal they stoned him anyway, some half-heartedly and some, disappointed, more viciously than if he'd flown into the air on the end of their soft line. And then they cut his wings off.

They did it when no Elder was in sight. The general opinion, later, was that it was only a Bandit and youth must cut its teeth on something. Lug kept his mouth shut and sat in the hut of the Elders with Ratts listening to the scream of Le Duk. He cried out only once. Lug remembered how he hated the old men telling him what to do when he was young. But this was different; it was Le Duk, he was sure. How could he forget? Ratts, next to him sighed. To be young again. Lug looked down at his scaly arm and at Ratts' twisted leg: when had they got old? Bandits were different. Le Duk looked the same as he had forty seasons ago. Until someone had reached for a knife. Very improper. Not the thing to do to a great leader. Now they had less than bargaining power. They might have to pay recompense. Something had gone wrong. Youngsters didn't listen as they had in their day. Well, they'd learn. As if he'd spoken aloud Ratts said, 'Come rescue arrive what say we then?' And he shrugged, his shoulders answering his own question.

And come they did. Though too late; their Master damaged and made low with pain and shame. Plenty of warning from young Crow, they arrived; black specks in a thundering sky scarcely seen at first against purple and indigo clouds. Then they were there; great black wings blotting out the remains of the light, screeching and wailing at what they saw. As thunder crashed, great gobs of moisture rained down on the scattering youngsters, then feathers, tears and long strings of gluey shit. The sky filled suddenly where it had been empty. The air now thick with the movement of flight. One youngster, presumptuous or stupid, flung a remaining stone at the angry mob above him. Seized, he was lifted and shaken with such frenzy that splinters of white tooth flew from his mouth like drops of water from a wet dog shaking.

Le Duk would only speak to Lug, the made-good slave he'd lost so long ago. He took some water from him and told him his decision. He saw the workings of fate and knew at last why the slave had escaped him then. Such clarity was rare, he realised, and was grateful. Pain will pass. And the knife bearer was inexpert. Only the feathers had been cut, the main cartilage and flight tendons were still there and would regrow. Probably. Until that day shame was wings enough. He turned from the tardy rescuers ignoring their clamour and entreaties. They would have to manage on their own for a while. Barziley would see to them all. A Hoof would show them what they'd lost.

After they'd pulled down most of the huts and pissed in the water barrels the rescuers left. Slowly and reluctantly lifting into the darkening sky, circling the compound time after time calling and clicking to him, some bud playing a dirge on a nose pipe. But he had dug himself into the dirt and had his back to them. The stumps of his wings were splintered and flies buzzed above his head. Finally when the sky was quite empty and quiet he put his head in his hands and wept.

It was Ratts' idea. Elder Ratisbon. The Old Crow who knows things. Throughout his life he'd had several good ones. Like matching men to jobs that suited. A simple concept but one with far reaching consequences. Now food was frequently palatable, messages arrived on time and roofs stayed tight in a tempest. What's more there was a lot more meat to be had when the hunting party was composed of Boys who had good sight. Of course others, like his suggestion to abandon the compound and go to live by Paradise, were not so favourably received and were allowed to slip away with only a few jokes in his direction. But this latest seemed to solve several problems in one hit.

The first problem was how decently to dispose of the mutilated Bandit. The delicate balance of plain raid and revenge had been nearly destroyed this day. Whose fault it was that Le Duk, most reasonable of Bandit leaders since who knows when, was not recognised, would be determined in the very near future. But re-building came before punishment.

A rattle of tutting went round the hut as a shower of debris fell from the broken roof and a young worker's face smiled down at them. The men rose frowning and smile was wiped. The Council of Elders considering cost was no light matter. Outside, their view fell onto the wounded Bandit who was huddled some way distant, pitiful, and a reminder of the cruelty of fate. The sight of him focused the collective mind swiftly to the problem. The Bandits' response to a simple mutilation had been destruction and pollution. They had to move very carefully.

The second thing was honey; they were nearly out of it. And the third, was Lug's unending grief for Cuspangel. Ratisbon turned to his old Triple-mate and said, 'Hey, Runner, when you go Triple-sister see?'

Lug looked at Ratts and then at Le Duk and smiled a brief smile. As the idea filtered from one to the other, slowly from man to man, they stood grouped together culpable, gently nodding at the possibilities of this excellent idea. Lug said to no one in particular, 'There healer in Paradise.'

Someone added, 'And honey.'

Le Duk was not so heavy as Lug had imagined. But honey! If there were boys ready to leave Paradise then they'd have all they wanted. Otherwise it'd be what he could lift and no more; his legs were not what they once were. Alright for Ratts to have ideas when others, as usual, had to carry them out. He laughed at the word joke and thought of the books in Paradise. His reading was nearly gone now. Cuspangel had passed him a book the last time he'd been to Paradise with him. He'd hardly understood a word. Cuspangel had shrugged and pointed to his heart. He loved him with or without printed words. To visit Lady Ren would be hard for them both. She had had many lives already. He himself remembered two. Her loss had been more gradual than his for she'd already given some of Cuss up to the Triple. Sighing he shifted the Bandit's weight. Not so heavy, for an old man. His body with its fragile bones was light without the great wings. Lug's mouth turned down reflecting the heaviness of his heart. Did he ever do such a thing when he was young? Probably.

Still unspeaking, Le Duk had understood when he was told about the journey and had obligingly sheathed his claws and was using his long fingers to clutch Lug's shoulders. The rest of him was shamefully in a bag strapped round the slave's body. He was entirely dependent on him for all basic functions. The very thought made him dizzy. He couldn't remember if he'd had this old man beaten when he was a slave. He thought it likely. He worked to adjust himself to the slow rocking gait of the slave beneath him. The noise of the flies around both their heads and the invasion of his body by their offspring called for all the discipline of his training. He concentrated on what was beyond torment. Through the slave's back he could feel every step, every stone, every stumble. He allowed himself no more tears, dry or wet, but felt with his remembered wings the ripple of wind through fluttering remiges. Bitterly he noticed that without flight the warm disc in the sky was burning him like a cinder. Never before for so prolonged a period had he so close an experience of the desert floor. Often he'd listened, sceptical, to Barziley and other Hoofs tell stories of life on the ground. They had all been true, every word, he knew that now. Now he too felt the tyranny of white and longed for shadow. He felt his eyeballs shrivel in their sockets and his shallowest breath was full of dust. He heard the dry earth complain as they crept over it and saw rocks crack from just the pressure of his regard. He tried to be light, to lift himself when the slave stepped heavily and jarringly, but it was too tiring. The slave groaned quietly and Le Duk, Lord of the Skies, remembered other slaves groaning; he remembered other Carriers he'd known too, from the place by the forest. They were better built than this kind. Stayed strong even in age.

After several days of shared discomfort Lug and Le Duk reached a kind of companionable routine of walking, resting, eating. When they stopped Lug was careful with his handling of the Bandit and established no eye contact until he had attended to necessary functions and was rested. That Lug could only carry him and their supplies, and not the usual gifts to Lady Ren, did not occur to Le Duk. He was used to the sacrifice of others, and pain. Neither troubled him. And Lug? He wondered what Lady Ren would think of this particular gift.

*****

No one minded as long as Lady Ren was prepared to look after the creature somewhere out of sight. Another benighted male. Another tragic result of male interaction. Of course the heart was moved. One of the angels brought to earth. A sign from the Faithful Healer? If so, what the slek did it mean? Was it a warning to remember the basic rules of our life, remember how and why our foremothers had come here in the first place? That all males are by nature dangerous, and if they do it to their own what might they do to us if we let them near? Or was it lesson in compassion? To forget in this case our most deeply held beliefs, to put aside theory and find love in out hearts even for the enemy?

Well for the life of me I didn't know. But then that's the

Faithful Healer for you; as I said, I'm only a simple gardener not a cleric. They were all pale with thinking by the time he'd been taken to Lady Ren. Two outcasts together. It wasn't said but I knew they were thinking it. Of course she might like the company since she was due a visit from her dead brother, though she never struck me as a lonely sort of person.

She didn't turn a hair when they brought him to her, and it wasn't easy. He was a foul looking creature. I managed to look at him and not laugh at my own joke; I don't suppose anyone else'd get it anyway. No sense of humour, most of them. Anyway the first thing she did was to slap on some herb honey, for not only had the monsters torn off his wings, which everyone knows are a sign of great beauty and purity amongst the flying Bandits, but his remaining feathers were stained and twisted by the journey. In a bag on the shoulders of Lady Ren's brother's second Triple. The Bandit was constantly twitching as if he had a bad tic; fleas and shock I should imagine. But worse than that was the expression on his face, if a winged Bandit can be said to possess a face capable of expression. It was a terrible cross between arrogance, agony and humiliation. He was a most unlovely creature. The bearer was no picture either. Then he was a man and couldn't help it. There were stories about all three of that particular Triple. Rumour had it that Lady Ren's brother had once been a woman. Now how do you begin to think about a thing like that? Lady Ren herself was the centre of some similar scandal and no one knew the truth of it though when she was by we were all lip clamped, no smirking and eyes down. If not I'd have had something to say for I knew her well and was quite a good friend of hers, being a gardener and having often needed her honey salve on injuries. Anyway, the bearer took the Bandit to her almost straight away after apologising for the lack of gifts. As a man, as is proper, he would have the habit to bring gifts to make his welcome strong. Hut crafts. Woven things and wooden toys and dolls, things off Morn. Sometimes beautiful polished sand stones. This year, he said, his burden was other. That was a good one, and he caught my eye. The Bandit, this other bird, was done indeed. This time I did laugh, though I got elbowed. They didn't see it. Burden; bird done. Too clever. I tell you, none of them are half as sharp as a gardener. It's the isolation I suppose. Gives the brain space to think.

*****

After he'd arrived in Paradise Le Duk had been in almost too much pain to notice his surroundings; huts grander, he soon realised, than any he'd seen as he hovered over the compounds of his enemy. And even in his first aching fever he marked in some quiet quarter of his brain the abundance of their doors. They were mouths under the sloping brows of the huts and he was at once terrified and moved to tears by them. Then, before he could count them he was somewhere else more open and set apart where the air was filled with insects. There was a woman he remembered from long ago and he saw she remembered him too. Several saw to his needs, all following the same procedures of healing and nurture. Some were gentle, some saddened by his condition, some impatient and repelled by him. He knew them soon, as if by name, according to their touch and he grew a little better though his wings were still gone.

There were fewer hut doors here, though still more than he was used to. And some in the broad open spaces; doors that were no doors. They were simple frames of different materials; some sturdy, some flimsy, shaking in the breeze. It seemed that they grew from the earth, for they sprouted, some of them, with fruit and flower. He was amazed. But it was the doors in the woman's house that affected him most. At first he hid from them shivering, but soon he felt a longing greater than any he'd felt since his downfall. To move beneath that wooden arch, to perform the act of going out and going in and to wonder which it was he was doing. On the wing he knew bliss; but this was wonder. Pausing under a lintel he felt the enormity of the empty space bearing the weight of all that hung above it. And he wondered how it could be and for the first time in his life he knew the impossibility of moving through the air as he used to do. Air, he saw now, was both empty and full. How was flying possible? How had he ever lifted off the earth so easily? Why hadn't he fallen?

And then he saw that he had. Fallen away from the old ideas. He had told them, long ago, that they needed a Master. That he would care for them. Now it was plain he had not; he could not even look after himself. How long had fate waited to show him this lesson? He doubted he could wait so long to teach a bud who needed to be taught. So dazzled was he by these ideas that he felt dizzy and would have fallen if not for the solidity of the door posts that held him. He longed for Barziley's wisdom, for the comforting sound of Wing clatter but there was only the woman human.

She was changed, as did all her kind with time. Her colours, her bearing, her strength and vigour. Though what good, he thought to himself, was his slow ageing to him now? He had been so young and sure of himself then. She had been little more than a chick. She was family with the one who brought him. That slave never came though the terrible, wonderful arches, but met with her at some distance where they sat and talked. Le Duk watched them part. They were fond just like they were at home, hanging on each other's neck just as Hoof and Wing. They parted and turned heads and ran back for another embrace; a familiar ritual. Then came the final stiffness of two turned backs and he knew it was over; but not quite. For when the woman came towards him he saw in her eyes some wet. When would they meet again, he wondered, and why did they part? Their kind could fail at any moment. How sad it was to be apart from your family and kind. Then he saw the house of the insects and forgot the troubles of the woman. Here again was the same thing copied small. These furred and striped creatures, with wings like once he had, were busy passing each other going in and going out of the tiniest arch in the straw house. Inside he heard the roar of their life, and it reminded him of the roar of wings when he'd flown in formation, wheeling and spiralling close but never quite touching another flyer. And he wished more than anything that he could transform himself into one of those creatures and vanish into that horde.

'You weep.' Le Duk spoke the barely remembered language for the first time in nearly a whole season. In her mind's eye Rena saw Le Duk as he'd been the last time they'd met. Before things had changed again. When Ash had brought her here and when Cuss had become a Triple.

'They said you'd lost your voice as well as your flight.'

Le Duk lowered his great head and studied the ground. The silence was not a hard one. Two sets of eyes glazed for a moment as old friends and enemies paraded their stories and whispered familiar memories. They were both together and both absent for a while, and when they returned blinking and sighing and swallowing back what they knew about themselves and each other, not long had past in the day, though thirty or forty seasons had raced by in memory. Rena smiled at the broken creature and he returned the look as well as he could for smiles are a learned habit with Wings, even those whose bodies are not mutilated. They were like old friends for though they'd met just once before, their lives had been woven like a plait.

'If you remember Ash,' said Rena, 'You could come with me. I'm going to visit her grave.' The bandit nodded; Ash, the clever one. He remembered her especially well. She had beaten him in a word battle for the very slave who'd brought him here.

'In our tradition,' said Le Duk, getting the feel of words once more, 'in our tradition we give our dead to the air, on a high place somewhere, for fox or flesh-wing to send them home.'

'I think Ash would have liked that. But she made no provision and so had no choice.'

'Is it true,' politely now, about the strange customs of other nations, 'that you lay your dead deep in a box under ground?'

Rena laughed. 'No. Once they did that. Now we wrap our lost in cloth and cover them with a little earth so the worms can give them a quick push through the door to their next journey.'

Le Duk said no more. The pleasure of speech had dried up on him and he took it upon himself to think about her words. Suddenly death seemed too close. Was it the thought of the dead Seer or was it the clamour of the doors?

Some time soon after their conversation about death the woman began to talk of her family; of one young girl in particular. She described her in detail both her appearance and her character. And where and how she lived and how easy the journey was to reach her. That's all she said. Le Duk knew he was a guest with the woman of the insects for as long as he wanted. He also knew that he was free to go.

*****

Often the hogs would rattle their bells in the night as they heaved against each other in slumber. Sometimes a brief dreaming scuffle would shatter the deep quiet of the dark mountain field. But it was a sudden squall, swiftly over. So when Roseen woke for the third time she knew something was different. This night she sensed that the air itself was restless, as if its black eyes reflected more than hogs. She sat up and peered out of the window. Black as it sometimes was: no stars, no moon to light her disquiet. The door suddenly swung open and banged shut and a scuttling dark shape skittered towards her. With a rattle it leapt onto the bed and at her.

'Button', she exclaimed with relief, 'I was scared.' As she sank back onto the pillow the little hog burrowed its snout under her knees and soon his soft puttering breath soothed her light mind. Her hand caressed his firm little body and she felt his chest rise and fall and shudder with contented breathing. She liked to feel his body, loving its solid warmth along hers. Sometimes she was filled with an inexpressible feeling of melancholy which his little shape helped dissipate. Now she moved her knee and felt the hog's fluttering breath on her calf. As she fell step by heavy step into the torpor that would obliterate all sense, she remembered a previous resolution to stop the little pig's visits. He wouldn't be so sweet to sleep with once his tusks and bristles grew.

It was in the morning she saw him. In the distance a crouched, still figure through the scramble of the morning feed.

'You were right,' she said to the hogs, who weren't listening now, 'there was someone.'

She took a branding iron and walked carefully towards the figure. If she hadn't already heard the story she would have remembered him anyway. He too must have had a bad night but she could see it was still her angel. But what was the Lord Bandit doing in her hog field snoring the day away? She coughed and immediately he was awake, his startled morning eyes blinking in the light.

'Good morning, Lord Bandit. Are you waiting for breakfast?' And as if to answer for him, his stomach rumbled loudly. 'I'm glad you called, Lord. Two is always better than one.' Roseen smiled and chattering brightly she slowly led the way up the green slope past the hogs to her hut. His eyes flicked warily at the short four-footed creatures. Hoofs and yet not Hoofs. He sighed. 'They won't bother you, Lord, I keep them well fed and their noses are most often stuck in the ground.' She was being polite of course. They had both sensed the shiver of anticipation that had run through the herd as they passed it, notwithstanding all heads to trough. Still, even with his great wings gone, he was big enough for the biggest of them and while they had tusk and tooth, he had claw and beak. Anyway he knew herds; who better.

The morning was a hard one for Roseen. She knew who had done this terrible deed; stories of the Boys and the Bandits made good tales in the old cafe in town. But while she had laughed aloud with the others at those stories of their primitive behaviour it was different to see the results here before her. She had seen him, Lord of the Bandits; seen his glittering wings and his swooping dancing flight. She had been Sol dazzled that day staring at his progress in the sky above the mountain. She remembered his blissful shut-eyes and how, catching his pleasure, she had felt, for a moment, the ecstasy of flight. The few shining feathers that had fallen to earth were safely in a box beneath her bed and she blushed now, making his meal, to think of the pain it would give them both if he knew. After that first meal he sometimes ate with her, sometimes not. Days he spent wandering the mountainside; nights, restless and painful, in the same spot she'd first found him. Slowly the raw look of the torn wings softened as some fluff formed. She saw him flex the stumps and twist his neck to preen the small new growth. After that he was easier and would talk to her. She learned a little about his life. About his friend Barziley, who was his second. About the responsibilities of a leader and the terrible events that had robbed him of his wings. She grew used to this new companion and she saw he looked for her whenever he was near the hut.

One night when his moaning was too much to bear, Roseen brought him into the hut and sang him to sleep. The next night also. Soon after, she took Le Duk into her bed, and reversing Bandit tradition, made one where before there had been two.

*****

Barziley Dvek was not known as a Seer. Not officially. Not as such. But his instincts were always more than sound and he knew better than to ignore them. Many a disaster had been averted on his say so. The slave uprising in the season of Le

Duk's coronation. The dreadful flash flood that would have drowned them all if he hadn't heard the clouds gathering in the dark. Countless other things; lost kid and kin, trapped hooves, broken wings. Sometimes he tired of it, the noise of it in his head; the smell of it under his nose. Then he shut it off with an effort and cantered away into the sand, trumpeting his exhaustion, picking up speed and galloping, galloping until he was miles away from duty. That's where he was the day his dearest friend was captured by the enemy; miles away from duty. Since then, in the two and a half seasons they had been parted, since grief and shame, which had been of his making, had been the bed mates of his friend, duty had been his, every moment, every day. He had gathered the Bandits together, he alone had seen to their repair, to the rebuilding of their rituals and routines. No easy task with a tribe grown crazy with disbelief and despair. Tron and Fremzle had been punished though it was hard to say if they were aware of it. He too demanded a forfeit for his absence and omission and bore the scar still on his back. And all the time he waited.

Barziley knew that Le Duk would recover his dignity once his wings re-grew. No easy growth for one as old as Le Duk. Slow. About now, he thought, Le Duk will be ready. So he too was ready for anything. Slept light, kept his ears pinned and his nose keen. Waited. When it came he was unprepared. He had expected the sound of growing triumph or pleasure. Irritation; anger even. But what he sensed was none of these. What he felt made him rock heavy. His limbs grew weary and his spirit dry as dust. He lay down in the dirt and wept and didn't know why. Above him, as though a swarm of locust covered the bright disc in the sky, it turned dark, blue was gone and life, and all he had ever done was of no value. Anxious kindred gathered round and no amount of cajoling or reasoning could lift his spirit. Only when his youngest cousin, Egg, sat down next to him and burst into tears did he realise all was not well. Then he rolled over and dragged himself upright. Listening deep he knew he had wasted time on himself. Careless again, he thought, and giving the little Hoof a caress with his long tongue he set off, hearing only the terrible sense of doom that he knew was his friend Le Duk.

If circumstances had been different he would have paid the Boys' Huts a visit. It was night as he trotted past their enclave. He heard the warning whistle and knew he'd been noted. If he'd had more time, he thought, what I'd do to you, savages.

On and on, the wretchedness gnawing at him like insects. Why, friend, why? Surely you have your wings now. Fly home to us. It was plainly time to be firm. No more sorrow. No more shame. The past is over. We need to make profit again, to hear applause. The tribe needs you to turn us from flock back to warriors. I shall be severe with him. Make him return with me. I shall carry him if he will not fly.

After a few days of hard travelling he came to a forest where huts nestled like birds in a nest. This was a place he'd heard of. Scouts had told of it. Here were human creatures. Not too dangerous, so it was said. He remembered seeing some long ago when he and Le Duk were young. Some fuss about a slave. The human had been tepid. Clever in tongue but no threat. Still, Barziley was cautious. There was no time to make mistakes now. The trail was heavy on him. He kept his panic carefully squashed. Skirting the place he cantered on and the path lead him up. This slowed him for it was stony and full of holes. If I break a leg we're all done for, he thought, seeing himself dying alone on an unfriendly mountain slope. Enough, he told himself, this is just the spell of Le Duk. Follow it, don't feel it. And step by step, sometimes pulling himself along by branches and tree stumps, sometimes stopping, sniffing the air his keen ears pinned back and twitching, he slowly worked his way up, cool rain now on his back always following the direction of his friend's sadness.

*****

They sat once more together on the little wall, a soft drizzle beginning.

'So, tell me what's on your mind.'

'Let's go inside, Grandma. There's nothing.'

Rena didn't reply to this, merely looked away and waited in silence.

Roseen sighed. Of course, her Grandmother would know. She knew everything. Everything of worth. And there was the vow of truth. 'I don't know how it happened.' Another lie.

This time Lady Ren laughed. Roseen was about to get indignant at the laughter when her Grandmother said, 'You know they'll send you away, like they did me? They won't let you stay together, not even here. As for the child...' Her voice trailed away leaving the sentence unfinished.

'But I can come here, with you and the bees, can't I?' This was a plaintive question.

'I won't always be here, you know. In fact some day quite soon ...' Another unfinished sentence.

'Where are you going?'

'I'm an old woman, Roseen.'

'Don't you feel well?'

'Tired, sweet girl.'

'Don't leave me, Grandma. Not now.'

'It's not for me to arrange.'

Roseen put her two hands on her belly and began to rub it, round and round, massaging the little bulge. Rena saw that there was more of a hurry for Roseen to learn the bees than she had thought. But first things first.

'You must tell him to go, Roseen. Back to where his real duty lies. He has a people. He was a good leader; let him go.'

Roseen wasn't crying; the tears trickling down her face were nothing to do with her. She refused to acknowledge them in any way. Rena leaned across and wiped the girl's face, but there was no stopping them. The river would flow for a good bit yet.

'He went,' she said. She stood and turned to face the mountain behind them, staring up at its heights. Rena followed her glance. How high and still the mountain was. The eye was drawn to the slightest movement. They stood together for a while in silence looking upward. Watching. When her face was dry Roseen said, 'His wings grew, then he went. He said what he'd done was wrong. But it was my idea, not his, yet he still blamed himself. I think he means to damage himself. He was so sad. I don't know how to save him.'

The drizzle now was rain soaking them to the skin. The bees made no comment. If a little smoke convinces them that their home is on fire then rain or maybe tears renew them. But while the two women sat silently grieving for loss to come, the one petitioning the Holy Maker and the other calling on the Faithful Watcher, the rain dried up and Sol came out and the wet around them sparkled like stars.

And below, in the field where the path skirting the forest ended, they saw a strange being burst out of the trees and step carefully but urgently over the rutted soil.

*****

In a bright wet place that begged him to rest he came upon two of the creatures of the area. One, he thought, was younger than the other, though it was hard to tell. Barziley Dvek stopped to catch his breath and wondered how these creatures were so content with neither enough legs nor any wings to propel them. He would have liked to ask them many questions but he had neither the time nor, unlike his friend, much of the tongue. Have they seen Le Duk, he wondered, did they even know who he was, and how could he put this to them in a way they could understand? Even if they could speak like a Hoof, he was fixed to the spot by the sight of the swarming insects around the heads of the two creatures. They didn't seem to care, but Barziley knew them and swished his tail just in case. Then he saw something that made his heart jump. In the hand of the smaller one was one of Le Duk's feathers. He was sure. That particular brilliance and iridescence could only be his. He trotted forward a few paces but the insects, picking up his scent, rose excitedly with a great noise and he retreated in fear. But they saw his attention, both of them, and jabbered at him, the words going too fast for any understanding, and gesticulating with the feather. He wanted to snatch it from them. How did they get it? Was it found, or stolen or given even?

Where is he, where is he? I can't hear him any longer. He felt his eyelids drooping and his head reaching for the ground. And he realised his powers of concentration were waning with his tiredness. There was a flurry of quick movements from the two creatures and the sound of water splashing. Then the older one, a she, he thought, though tall for her kind and like a bunch of twigs, moved on her two legs with surprising agility towards him. Barziley backed anxiously away. Before her in her fingers was a bowl full of liquid which rocked as she stepped. Suddenly he remembered his body. The liquid shone in the evening light and his mouth watered. But was it safe to drink from the hands of strangers? The smaller one spoke with agitation until the older one nodded and looking him straight in the eye she lifted the bowl to her own mouth and sipped the liquid. Then she swallowed. She did a creature thing with her lips stretching them up towards her ears, showing her teeth then she offered him the bowl.

Barziley found that he couldn't care if it was poison, he needed to drink and eat and sleep. And drinking, was the best he had time for. He bowed his long neck and sniffed the liquid. It was golden and he remembered some story about these creatures and the insects. Carefully he put his hands over those that held the bowl and he lapped a little and swallowed. The creature's lips stayed up and he saw that her eyes were the same colour as the drink. It was sweet and a little sour. And as he lapped and lapped he felt strength returning. When the bowl was empty he made a bow of gratitude and swept up his head flinging his mane into the air feeling alive again. Then the two of them came together making their strange noise, their heads close. They beckoned to him, the two of them, wanting him to follow. Now it comes, he thought, the trap; the drink was a lure or the poison is slow, soon I shall be in their power. But he followed them anyway until they stopped where a gap in the trees made a perfect circle. Through the gap was a clearing with a lake, and beyond the lake the green slopes of a mountain that grew craggy and stony as it neared its peak. He stared at it. It was a good sight. Then he turned and meant to continue up the way he had been going but they were shouting again at him and pointing. Pointing at the mountain. Yes, yes. How can I tell you, I have no time, creatures, to admire your homeland. Again he turned to go when the small one thrust the feather at his face violently and pointed with it. Her face had become wet and her little shoulders were heaving as if she could no longer breathe. The feather nearly went in his eye and he reared back, his eyes sliding along its length. Then he saw. Movement. An insect high up on the mountainside. Then he knew; and the feeling, the dead sense he had been following flooded into him again and, as if it was the ecstasy of mating and not the pain of affliction, he trumpeted loud as though Le Duk at that distance could actually hear him.

When night fell Barziley was forced to stop, and at last he slept, at first restlessly, unwilling to cease the chase. What was the purpose of Le Duk's long expedition? If his wings were repaired why did he not fly home? There was no sense that Barziley could see and that in itself was ominous. But no one could climb without seeing and the moon was somewhere else tonight. If Barziley rested, he thought Le Duk was probably forced to do the same. Then before daybreak he dreamt a dream.

He was falling to earth leaving his home behind, his heaven. He felt his breast, his brow, belly all to be tenuous, almost untenanted, and disparate, unjoined. His transparent hooves touched the alien ground and through the exquisite veil of his being he felt the imposition of an unknown other;

corporeal, soft, warm. There were sounds, cries of some kind; delight, distress. He could not decipher them. But as he reached his journey's end and his body congregated together he was intact despite intrusion. And soon, after rest, he began to learn the language for important things; beauty, translucence, proximity, death.

As he uttered the new word, Death, he was Le Duk lying on piercing stones and halfway to dead. They had left him to rot; left him to lie where he had fallen because it was his choice, plainly made. Beasts of the field were approaching to make an end of him and a gravedigger was flinging clods of earth on him. Suddenly the girl of the feather came running, running hot foot, her belly big with child. She points the feather at the earth and the clods vanish then she flings herself on Le Duk and puts her feather in his mouth.

'Eat, eat,' she cried. 'You have to eat.'

Then he woke and knew his friend was in terrible danger.

*****

From the peak Le Duk saw deep into the ravine below. He hoped that as he fell he would feel some peace before he died. But how could he fall and not fly? How could he go through that door? This was what he needed to ponder. But quickly before the Hoof could find him. The pest was full on him devouring him with its teeth. He was a tree whose branches were full of them. How swift they could cover the land, even a desert where at first sight there was nothing growing. After their passing you knew what nothing meant. One crime after another. Done for. Ruination on all he touched. Had it been like that before? Perhaps always he'd been in the grip of this ague, perhaps always he'd brought a curse to the tribe.

Perhaps they'd always known and his going was a blessing. He gripped the crag with both fingers and claws, holding steady to the rock. The wind blew through his feathers and his new winglets flexed on his back. Now, before they grew too big, too much of their own will. Now.

But a picture of Roseen came to his mind and he paused a moment remembering her. How hard it had been to make his tongue say the unknown syllables of her name. How hard to leave her. Her soft hands, her laughter. She had laughed when he'd told her about the doors, and danced in and out of them pulling him with her. How he had enjoyed being her chick, something he had forgotten over the long years of leadership. Then he remembered the terrible nights and how she had lightened them with her pale body. What harm he had done her; she was an innocent who would be punished for his crime; for his indulgence and lust. He pushed from him any thought of the offspring. He was no better than the breeders of Tron and Fremzle. How seductive was the forbidden. How seductive that soft painful feeling in his breast. Again she had laughed when he had complained about it. 'We call that love,' she had said, 'I feel it too.' And then another image obliterated the ravine and he cried aloud to see the Wing who'd hatched him. Where had she come from? Dead since many a long while; but there she was clicking her beak at him and scratching his wing root. That also was love. And unbearable; he retracted his claws and waited for his fingers to tire. It was time to do what he had come for. And then he was at last in the air.

It was much more painful than he had expected. And why did it hurt so soon? Where was the long peaceful drift to earth? Where was the sweet whistle of wind in his ears? And what was that terrible noise? Suddenly he jumped alert.

This was no peaceful fall. Something had his tail fast in a painful grip. And surely he'd heard that noise before. Straining behind him he caught sight of that devil, Barziley, and the noise was the trumpeting of an angry Hoof. And he was in the air no longer. Tossed like a chick away from the edge, with one flick of that strong neck, his body banged painfully on the stony slope. He bounced and before he could right himself he began to roll back down. Over and over he went, dizzyingly, the edge once more in sight coming up fast to take him to his destination. He smirked to himself thinking that he would get his way despite this interfering Hoof. He would get his way. He would make his quittance and discharge his sins, this was the only correction he could see. He shut his eyes as the edge spun nearer and nearer. He took a deep breath, saying silent goodbyes. But instead of the great space of the ravine he banged against a set of strong legs and came to a stop.

His friend's voice was cracked as if his throat was full of dust. 'Now you must ride on my back. The way home is not so easy'

*****

Another hot day. What the slek's happening to our weather? Not enough drip hose to go round, so who gets to do the watering! Not that it means any extra credits; all part of the job according to them. Never mind that there's so much I end up doing it in the dark and can't see where I'm putting it. And then I'm at fault for water waste. Of course, that's what I love to do. I get up every morning and I think, now how can I waste some water today? Why don't I wait till dark and let the precious stuff leak all over the path. If I was allowed to get on with it I might finish it in the light and then I'd see what I was doing and it wouldn't get spilt. But oh no, she hasn't got enough already. Don't want her to feel she's got nothing to do. Let's see, what else can we give her? I know, the gravedigger's a bit short staffed, send her there. Don't forget your spade, will you, dear. I mean, own a spade and any hole that's needed and you're on it. Or in it. A grave joke, that. In this heat, too.

At least I was on the spot to say goodbye to the Lady Ren. Pay my respects. A sad loss there. For all the so-called difference, she was one of us. They didn't reckon her value till too late. It's always the way. Won't obey the rules so you're not fit company, off you go. And now it's how wonderful she was, what a shame she lived the hermit's life. Enough to make you sick. She and I were alike. Outsiders. I'm definitely one. Get it? Gardening; outside? Oh dear. No joke, her granddaughters condition. Don't tell me children are born innocent. That one was doomed before she started, poor thing. In my opinion, not that anyone's asking me, it's a community crime. We're all at fault; should have kept her close to town, with her background. Kept an eye on her. She stood there with no shame. You got to hand it to her. Didn't care who saw her. Wept like a river. Got a lot to weep on, no doubt. Now there's someone yet to arrive who's really going to be different. Make Lady Ren look an old stick in the mud. Anyway at the end she bent over, if you can call it bending, belly big as a gourd, and put something in the grave. A feather. Must have been one of his. Off his wings. She'll be safer with bees' wings. If she gets too close they'll let her know it in no uncertain terms. If she don't know already about being stung, if you catch my drift. Got a nasty swelling from somewhere. Some bee that was, eh? Left her with more than a feather to remember him by. Hope it was a flight worthwhile. Bit of a gorgeous creature; those wings, how they shone in the air above us. I remember staring up at him that day. We were all entranced. 'Look at me, look at me.' Kids are still playing that game. Damn bird gave me a neck ache. Bad day for her, though, the day that angel came to Paradise.

Chapter 9

Explosions in Syberia

~ ~ ~ ~ ~

No one knew what they were, the flakes, when they came drifting down from the pale sky. Like a lunar landscape the world was suddenly grey. Hills and valleys, trees and turrets all glittered dully; blue seas rocked, leaden with this new burden, a silver negative of their former brightness. No one knew what it was; ash, dust, pollen, dirt, spores. Minute particles of nearly white; like town snow. Unlike snow it neither stayed in cold white drifts, nor did it melt on the skin with that icy patch of wet. It vanished, true, but with a point, a pinpoint of pain. At first when it dusted the globe, people dashed it away with a hand or a broom. But then hand blistered and bristle melted, and swathe after swathe fell, and soon too did the creatures it touched.

Sometime later a bitter wind blew, cold and sharp as teeth. Those who were left lifted their heads. Life began again.

It took time to get it going; the systems, the machines, the governments, the armies. At first business was slow, but the human animal is resourceful, determined and full of impatience. They cleared up, buried the dead. They rebuilt lives and buildings. Scars healed and those that remained, were ignored. Good looks were no longer the point. Leaders began to investigate causes with a view to prevention, and perhaps punishment. Little was discovered apart from evidence of explosions in a distant quarter of the globe. People, men and women, thought it better to invest in the living and forget the past. And then, with the sun rising and setting and the moon waxing and waning, all back to normal, a discovery was made. Not by the scientists, not by experts, but by the ordinary man and woman in the fresh swept streets. The children. Where were the children? In dreams children grew healthily, tumbling about, crowing with laughter; indefatigable and numerous. In truth, those who were born were small and weak. Mothers held them tightly in their soft knitted shawls even as many drifted away, as if death were less trouble than life. Worse, it was discovered that the generative powers of one half of the human race were no longer reliable. The flakes were not forgotten, but apart from the usual denials governments were silent. With the future of the species in danger reproductive programmes were introduced, with financial incentives. To no avail.

But cruel Nature, once called Mother, found a way to bless her children. Where before the two halves of the creative puzzle had fitted more or less satisfactorily, to bring forth and increase, as many of the holy books of the time instructed, now those halves were no longer neat, nor satisfactory. Yet while the species faded, barely replacing its number, some of them found the means to continue. They found within them, an untapped force; a switch that had been waiting for millennia to be touched. To reach the switch, several methods were employed. Some, made longing the force. Some called upon the sun. But most delved deep within themselves to find the element that once another had provided. A dangerous activity; soon cursed and forbidden by those it excluded.

And so it came to pass, that little bands of women moved away by night, looking for safety and sanctuary. For each other. And perhaps for Paradise.

Arkady was a very long way away. Five days on a horse, ten by dogcart and a month on foot. Of course the dogcart idea was just that, an idea. I mean who would put a dog through such a mountainous journey. My name is Babs, by the by. I nearly became a Storyteller once, here in Paradise. I was the youngest in the whole competition that year. Got to the last three. I was so upset when I didn't win. When I was practising everyone said I was the best and the funniest. And I know I looked good, which isn't supposed to count, but you know how things are. Mother thought I'd win too. She wasn't so pleased about it, but she'd hired a new apprentice so I wasn't needed. When I lost they gave me a shell necklace as third prize. It was a pretty thing and the big centre shell was curved and creamy and had a mark on it like a mountain. I could see it was an omen and I thought that's what I'll do, I'll leave them all. This miserable so-called Paradise.

Me and Yatty, who was in my twig class, used to wonder a lot about Arkady; how we'd get there, and why it was so far away.

'You'd think they'd need to be near each other,' said Yatty. 'They must have had a fight. That's the only reason I can think of.'

Years later, we fought ourselves, over nothing, but we didn't speak any more so I couldn't tell her she was right. Just think, if I'd been born in Arkady instead of Paradise, how different things would be.

'If there are no boys in Arkady,' Yatty said, looking at our Teacher as if she really wanted to know, 'How are babies made?'

The answer was no secret, though we didn't truly understand, but we were daring each other not to giggle. The Teacher said we should ask The Mistress of Questions. I knew then we'd never get an answer.

When I got back from Arkady not much had changed. The second well was finally built; there were new chairs at Eye; babies had grown.

'Who are you?' said one cheeky pigtail, almost the moment I arrived. I knew her from my sleep-sit days; she had too much spark in her, even then. They all seemed to be waiting for something. Not me though. No one seemed very surprised to see me and I'd thought to startle them.

'We were expecting someone,' said Big Manjit, ' but we didn't think it would be you.'

It was April-Mae they'd been waiting for. Not back from one of her trips. We're still waiting.

'You're home then,' was all I got from my Mother. She said I could have my old room and soon it was like it always had been. I settled down to the old ways. To the old work. Took my hands a little while of course before they didn't blister. The new apprentice, who wasn't so new now, gave me a look or two, but I soon brought her round with a few compliments and I'm-so–silly-I've-forgotten-how . . . which she was only too pleased to hear. As for Hazel, Mother sniffed a bit, and looked at her very hard, but another pair of hands in exchange for a bed in the barn, well she'd not say no to that, would she?

Then one evening, while Hazel was doing the meal, and I was working some grease into my hands, Mother plumped down beside me.

'Well?' she said. 'When are we going to hear about this

famous trip of yours?'

'It was hardly a trip, I was gone long enough.'

'Came back soon enough though, didn't you.'

Personally, I don't think anyone would call a year and a half soon. But she was right, I did come back.

'You went off in a good sulk, when you lost that competition; I nearly felt sorry for you.'

She's must be getting soft, and it wasn't true about the sulk. Anyway, that night, when the soup pan had been washed and we'd licked our lips, I began.

'Well,' I said, when they were both paying attention. 'When I get to Arkady, it's freezing and there's no one there. My bag's very heavy all of a sudden, after the long climb, but I stumble around in the snow calling, "Hallo, anyone here?" like a fool. It's true there's a deep layer of snow over everything but everywhere's perfect; clean, no mess or droppings, neat curtains, no chips in the paint. Do real people live here? But everything's battened down and shut up. Perhaps they're expecting an invasion. Perhaps they've all left. Then there's a movement, and I see on the very top of a crag, a figure with a long, thin whistle lifted to it's mouth. It's the thinnest whistle I've ever seen, like a thread of straw. And the whistle-holder's slender as a boy; but it has to be a woman for this is Arkady. Anyway, I soon find out why nobody's there. From out of nowhere, from the skies, from somewhere, slowly and gathering force, comes the thinnest, sweetest, hardest, highest note I'd ever heard. It's hardly in my ears; except they feel pierced and bloody, and the note is so deep in my chest and my head, so deep except it's so high and I'm trying to sort out what's happening, when I go fuzzy and everything goes black.

The next thing I know, I'm surrounded by these mad Arkady women, dressed in bright colours, and all clapping and cheering Lady Skinny-Whistle . Some of them kneel down and pat me and talk over me as if I am a child.

"Did you see that! A true shock"

"She's bound to fall."

"She didn't even know it was coming. Did you?" Then they're talking to me. Not asking if I'm alright, or even who I am, but suddenly very strict.

"Of course you shouldn't be here."

"She's not even wearing boots."

"It's very dangerous."

"Where are your gloves?"

"If Lynel had reached the note, you could be dead."

Here, I feel my ears. Do I still have them and are they really bleeding? Yes and no, thank goodness. I ready myself for more of this mystery when Lady Skinny-Whistle is here, down from her crag looking as miserable as a sheep-lost-lamb. She's shaking her head and they're all saying: "it was wonderful" and "never mind" and "you'll get it next time". They're speaking all at once, but soft to her, making the words big on their mouths, so I think she can't have any hearing. Though whether that was because of the note, or whether she made the note because of her silence, I don't like to ask. I'm rubbing my poor old ears and my knees where I fell when one of them, in red and lavender, turns to me again but I go in to fight before she can.

"Why is Lady Whistler crying?"

As if I'm a fool, she says, "She's trying to make light."

I look puzzled, I'm sure, and with a rather rude sigh, she says, "If she plays the right note, high enough, it'll become a beam of light." And gives me the sort of smile you give to children who ought to know better. Then turning to Lady Whistle, she says,

"Look, Lynel, this stranger; you felled her. It was a true shock, unplanned."

At this Lynel starts to cheer up; almost smiles at me. I'm very pleased to be the cause of such delight, except I don't know what I've done to deserve it. Until, turning again to me the woman says, "You probably don't feel it yet, stranger, but we think you are now most likely carrying." She smiles triumphantly, and there's some clapping, like stones falling.

"Carrying?" I go. And Red and Lavender looks at me again as if I'm stupid and pushes the word right into my face.

"Yes, carrying. Carrying."

I still don't understand until a voice in the crowd says, "With child."

And before I can turn to see who my teacher is I promptly faint again. And that was how I came to Arkady.'

*****

Hazel in the corner, by the sink, is peeling something for the morrow. Making herself useful so she'll fit in. She's smiling tightly at the story; she was there.

'That was Auntie Elin. I lived in her house for seven years.'

My Mother frowned, and said quietly, 'I used to know a girl called that; pretty name, strange though. Stop working now, Hazel. You don't have to work every hour the Maker sends. Take a rest; get some air before you sleep.' And taking off her apron, Hazel said goodnight and thank you, and left for her barn. Mother turned to me and said, 'Why does she act like that? They don't have slaves in Arkady.'

Well, how would she know that? It's me that's just been there not her.

'More story tomorrow,' I said. And she pinned her lips together very thin.

The next night it nearly didn't happen because it was Story Night at Eye The Girls. Hazel and Mother and I went together but Story Night was cancelled for some reason. Afaf must be ill. Mother and Hazel were being such good friends that after a beer I went home. I was just unbuttoning my jerkin when the door downstairs burst open and I heard the noise of a crowd of people.

'Babs, Babs . . . Are you sulking again?'

It was my dear Mother, frizzled with the beer. 'We want the rest of the story.'

When I put my head out of the room, Rena nearly bumped into me. 'Babs, dear,' she said, 'please come and entertain us. Afaf's throat is hurting her and Noor won't stop worrying about April-Mae.'

I felt heartsick for Rena and Noor; they had enough troubles without April-Mae being one. So I followed Rena down and they smiled as if they were really glad to see me. I'm about to fill the newcomers in but Mother says she's told them and to get on with it. So I do.

*****

'When I come round from the faint I'm sitting in someone's house, getting warmer, drinking something strange, and clutching the strings of some old boots someone's given me, when a Queen Bee type of woman enters. She looks me up and down, but not before I do the same to her. The orange and yellow is hurting my eyes when she says,

"What do you do?"

So I stick out my hand being polite, and she takes it as if she doesn't know what to do with it. It turns out it wasn't "how do you do?" she meant, but "what do you do to earn your keep?" I keep quiet for a moment while I think. I passed their sheep on the snow ledges; I think they have filed teeth. And their fields are terraces of ice and snow. How do you mow ice? The silence is going on too long and I'm as surprised as anyone when "Storyteller" slips out and can't be called back. But I don't expect the commotion that lie brings forth. "Storyteller!" they yell. "Storyteller. You're from Paradise!"

How do they know that? A few draw away from me with looks of horror. "That dreadful place." Well I don't like to hear others say what before I'd thought myself, and I get upset and tearful thinking of my home. Queen Bee seems sorry for me and there's an arm round me and apparently I'm a refugee Storyteller from Paradise. It's a bit more than I expected.'

****

'Don't call her Queen Bee,' Hazel says, smiling to make it better.

'Sorry, Hazel.' And I really am.

Then turning to Mother, Hazel says, 'Her name was Suniva, and she and Elin and Ylva, cared for me, and Flot.'

It was actually more complicated than she made it sound. Ylva and the scarlet haired Flot also lived somewhere else some of the time with another woman whose name I never got to know. It didn't seem so shocking there.

'Ylva was the best mother. I shouldn't say that, should I?

She was quiet and you never noticed how she got things done or how she got you to do what she wanted. I miss her the most.'

There were yawns. My audience was getting cold. Mother made the fire up and Noor told me to go on. I'd learned much about storytelling at Arkady, one thing being, to end on an itching note to bring them back the next time for me to scratch. But I was nearly at the end of the beginning of this story, and I knew I wouldn't sleep if I didn't get it out.

'Finish then,' said my mind reading Mother. 'Some of us have got to work tomorrow.'

Noor looked at her sharply. So I began, before we all got upset.

*****

'I'm to stay with Suniva and as she takes me to my new home I hear the sound of the whistle again. It's not so thin or high this time. Suniva shakes her head and some of the women following cluck and tut. Suniva says, "It'll be a great day when she succeeds."

I'm looking puzzled again, I know. I spend much of my time in Arkady looking puzzled. Suniva tells me that Lady Whistle is the Chief Clock. She and her team blow time. It's a lonely job, and dangerous. Several clocks have lost fingers to frost. Why don't they have a mechanical timepiece like we do? I don't ask. Suniva shivers in her padding and continues. "Not just fingers, Storyteller. Some Clocks have been lost to sky creatures."

And this big bright, queenly woman looks fearfully skyward and points a gloved finger. I follow the direction of the point and there far and high are dancing dots you'd never see unless you were looking.

"They're not birds," she says. I know. We've heard of them in Paradise, though I've never seen one close.

"We hope to play the same game as they do with us. A beam of light would reveal them and confuse them."

I'm suddenly frightened and think of the clacking beaks I've heard of. Then as if one, we both shake off the nightmares and stride ahead. Suniva smiles at me.

"You mustn't worry, you'll work up till your time, and then you'll be cared for."

"Time," I say, "what time?"

Confused again. Is it something to do with the Clocks. Not as impatient as Elin, she replies, "Till the child arrives." I've forgotten that. I want to make a joke. But I mind my manners and stay silent.'

*****

And I show my audience what silence is. 'More next time.' I say, trying not to yawn.

There was no storytelling the next night. Noor had taken Roseen from the nursery so she could be grandma and wouldn't have time to think. Rena was exhausted with trying to be cheerful as she watched an empty horizon. Afaf's throat was worse, Mother and Hazel had decided to bake and Lis was being courted by someone the other side of town. I went to bed early; I wasn't sulking, I really was tired. Later, I woke in the dark. When my eyes lost their sleep I saw there was a glimmer of flickering light beneath the door. Someone had forgotten to bank down the fire. Cursing, since someone else would have to do it, I struggled into my slippers.

My door swung open silently as I pushed it and I trod softly to avoid the creaking beam. I had no idea anyone was still up. I wasn't trying to hear what wasn't meant for me; I was quiet out of care for them sleeping. The sound of soft voices below soon revealed that mistake. Since there was now no danger of unattended sparks using our wooden floor for kindling, I turned back for my bed. Then the word Arkady stung the air and I was fixed to the drugget. For a moment, I back and forthed in my head with the right and wrong of it; but I sat down anyway in the dark corner outside my room, and strained to hear the discussion, my head on the quiet banister, like a child spying with its ears when it should have been sleeping. What secrets I overheard.

Hazel was yawning, but I heard her ask, 'Why didn't she stay? You must have both been welcome.'

My mother's voice comes floating up to me, unfamiliar, soft with recollection. 'I think we were by some. I never knew why mama wanted it that way. Perhaps the old way didn't work for her anymore. Perhaps she disliked it too much. Perhaps she just wanted to be part of something miraculous. I tried for her. But, I hated it there. I was teased in the nursery; you know how children are to outsiders. Those Arkady sprouts knew about Paradise and told me I had been made by a foul act. I knew, of course, how we got babies in Paradise but I'd never thought wrong of it. Till my new companions made it clear that it was and wouldn't let me touch them. I knew then without any history lessons why Paradise and Arkady were two and not one.'

For a moment there was a sad silence between them which I joined, though they didn't know. Through the banister I saw that the fire was fading; fighting with itself to stay alight, sending sparks up the chimney with the thin

233

smoke. Mother was turned away from me; it was only Hazel's face I could see, lit strangely in black and red. Their heads were close, Hazel leaning towards Mother to catch her words. If I hadn't known, if I hadn't proof, just then I might have been jealous. I wondered what Mother would say when she knew we'd both suffered the same in Arkady. And the other. The thought of Flot haunted me, though understanding didn't make what she'd done any better. Then mother went on, not seeing Hazel's sleepy eyelids.

'And then Aunties began to make a point of telling mama how to bring me up and what was wrong with me. Neither of us looked quite right either. One day mama couldn't find me until she heard my cries and came rushing in. One of the Aunties was standing over me with some shears about to cut my plaits off. It was the fashion in Paradise, in those days, to let children grow their hair. Even the boys. Then you'd get a big ceremony and a celebration when you cut it. I'd been growing my plaits for several years. Mama got there just in time. I think that was the moment she decided to go.'

I was thinking of creeping back to bed before my stifled yawns turned to loud snores when the discussion changed direction.

'So she never made the baby she came for?'

'No.'

'Did she believe?'

'I think she did. She talked to me on the journey about why we were going. I think she said "miracle". And I still remember the story of Sun making a child. It was beautiful; Barbara loved that story when she was little.'

I did too. The sun taking off her trousers and lifting her arms to the sky. None of my friends knew it; I quite wore it out, telling it, over and over. That's when it started. Seeing my friends still and listening, with their mouths all open.

'No one tries that, not up a mountain,' Hazel even sounded cold. 'Imagine baring your belly to that icy Arkady sun. We do it the other way.'

But before she gets to the real point Mother interrupts. 'I never really understood. If you want a child, doing it with men is so much easier and it doesn't have to last long.'

She laughs quietly. Not to wake me I suppose. And even before she starts I know what she's going to say next. Something she told me long ago when she was explaining babies to me and I have to stifle my own laughter.

I remember how I thought it would be when mama first told me. That you'd stand against a wall with one of the men facing you and very close, and a teacher with a pointy stick says, 'Put that, there.'

And then suddenly I remember about Grandma Jo and feel sorry for Mother and laughter dies in me. But Mother is laughing louder now and Hazel shushes her and asks her if that's what it's like. Mother says, ' Well, almost.' Hazel shakes her head and begins to talk about their way.

'Shocking your body into maleness, that's what we all do. Did. The Games were the best way, because of the danger. You had to really want to do it. I wasn't quite sure yet, but my sister was sure enough for me. I was in Gree-Grip. We got the best Carrying results and the fewest deaths.'

At this I shot upright. Gree-Grip was the ledging team Hazel was in. Sweat broke out all over me.

'It's strange to hear you talk about the place.'

I couldn't tell who said this and I thought I'd behaved badly long enough. So I four-footed it back into my bedroom before anyone else got to agree with me. I lay awake, thinking about Granma Jo, and how I missed her, anything to stop thinking of Gree-Grip. I'm still sweating with remembered fear, when the sun cracks the dark through my curtains.

The first time I met Hazel she was dressed like a barrel in cold-clothes, full of smiles with sparkling hair curling out of her helmet, and we liked each other straight away. She poured me into some of her padded spares and raced me up the path to an edge I thought I'd fall off, if I looked right down to the bottom. So that's how the young people kept themselves warm and busy after work. Ledging, which I refused to try, ever, the whole time I was there, was a madness danger sport where you stood on a small length of polished wood and slid to the edge of the ledge launching yourself into the air hopefully to arrive on the ledge below. This certainly was a shock to the body, and I could see that several of Hazel's team were indeed carrying. And also in other teams. Hazel's sister Flot, the one with the bright hair, was Captain of Fizzy. When someone threw up over my feet they all laughed at my face, Flot loudest, because the sick was frozen in a moment. She kicked it off my boot and it sailed over the side of the mountain.

'Food for the lammers,' Flot said.

I wasn't going to let that go. I could feel my face flushed; who likes to be laughed at? 'I thought lammers liked bones.'

She went a bit pale when I said that and too late I minded Hazel telling about deaths. I knew I shouldn't speak about bones. Flot didn't like being corrected, so we didn't say much to each other after that. They said I should be in the third team, Snow-Kindle. But once I realised it was so dangerous, I decided I didn't want to be parted from Hazel. A few scornful looks came shooting my way, but I needed to be looked after, that much was clear if I was ever to return home in one piece.

Ylva, their mother was noticeable because she only wore brown. She was reputed to be descended from a wolf-child. It was her eyes; while you wouldn't exactly call them animal, to me, they said forest quite plainly. But wolf or not, or perhaps because of it, she was what Hazel had said and Hazel favoured her. Not Flot. For sisters who looked so alike, their natures were strangely different. You know how it is when someone hates you, but you don't know why? So it was with Lady Red and I. I called her that, once as a joke. I didn't do it again. I'd turn and catch her putting her mouth in order like she'd been laughing at me behind my back. And once later on, coming out of the Archive, I saw Ylva angry with her. I then I heard Flot say, 'but mother, they're disgusting.' And I understood.

In the summer it was even worse: Fall-tumbling. I couldn't watch to see Hazel do it. When she told me about it and showed me her beautiful Egret and the other canoes stacked in the boat shed, I thought of the games we played with ours, in Paradise. Rolling over and over and using the paddle to right ourselves. Wonderful wet fun when you're hot. Of course it's never really hot in Arkady and I discovered Fall was short for waterfall and there was nothing short about any of those that fell down the mountain and disappeared into the clouds. Fizzy usually won this, Hazel said. A simple game of getting in the canoe and heading downhill. Tumbling wasn't an obligation but it happened anyway. In Paradise we canoe horizontal; in Arkady they did it vertical. But then we didn't do babies their way either.

The unspoken fight between me and Flot came to a terrifying head at the end of that summer. It was warm enough for once to have bare arms; pads were left behind. We were at the edge of the bank on the flat pool before it fell roaring into nothingness. Flot was being unusually nice and I thought Hazel had spoken to her. I had been seduced into a canoe to show Paradise style, when Flot leaned over and pulled the buckle on the boat skirt tight. The sound of the falls was tremendous, but I heard her say, 'Safety,' with a smile. Suddenly the sun went in and over Flot's shoulder I could see Hazel running and waving, running and waving. I was about to laugh and wave back when I looked into Flot's eyes. There was the animal. 'She's my sister, not yours,' with a growl at the back of her throat. 'Let's see Paradise style now. Seen my double rotation?' I had. And her front-flip. I'd seen her fly into the empty air, no handed, paddles held aloft, and vanish though the spume, to death surely. But quickly, the sound of cheers rewarding her fearlessness came faintly up over the thunder of the waterfall. Now it was my turn, and surely my end. I was shaking as she was smiling. She had hold of the front of the kayak and gave a little push. It swung forward trembling in the current. But with that one glance of her eyes I'd wedged my paddle deep into the sludge by the bank and held on for my life. Slowly my grip slipped and slowly the back of the canoe swung round. I kicked at the skirt that held me in so snug and waterproof, but that buckle was firm, and the canoe joined the fast water that would take me to my death. Ahead was nothing but the spume of the fall, and the roar grew more deafening as it approached. I side paddled and back paddled with all my strength, but there was no denying my fate.

My legs were at breaking point; my arms screamed at me to be nice. The canoe spun with my efforts and briefly I saw two figures fighting on the bank. Their two red heads gleamed through the spray. Almost suddenly Egret was gaining on me and thrusting me with it's huge nose. Careful, don't hole it, I would have screamed if I'd had breath. But Egret had a skilful beak and together, with much effort, we gained the bank. As the current still pulled fast and determined, two of Gree-Grip and the Fizzy prentice swung ropes and secured us. It was then a matter of disentangling myself from the skirt and crawling precariously over Egret to safety. I lay on the bank trembling with more than muscle fatigue. Hazel stumbled off with a look on her face I'd not want to see again. I lay there and tried to translate it; anger, disappointment, fear? When I saw her again I could do no more than thank her for my life, not speak about the other.

Afaf was back in fine form after her little holiday so I never got to finish the story of my adventure. Just as well. I knew I wasn't a real Storyteller anyway. They soon knew it in Arkady too; though they didn't know much about it themselves; at least the rules of listening. But Paradise was no better than Arkady there, always throwing in remarks and laughing at our own jokes. I quickly learned the itch trick though they grumbled and groaned. I told all the stories I ever heard; all those that I remembered from the days of Storyteller Meriam; Oumou and Loumou and the dogs. They gasped at the dogs.

The months flew by and I started inventing some of my own, but they weren't very good. Finally I ran out of stories and they ran out of patience with my belly. It might work for young Arkadians but my body was not interested, which was a relief because I wasn't either. Perhaps I just didn't long enough. But forget I couldn't because they would pat my belly every time they met me. I rather wished they knew how to shake hands.

'She's not ...' Pat, pat.

'No bump.' Pat, pat, pat.

'No child?' I backed off a hand's length.

'How disappointing.'

Their sadness was something to be seen, but after a while they left me alone and I felt they didn't like me anymore. They took me off storytelling and put me in the Archive. Something to do with my skill at the pen. I didn't mention my skill with the spade. I was just better at copying and letter writing than the other job. Better at memorising some of the things I read there too. Well, no one tells stories in Arkady now so they're back where they were before I came.

And then one day Ash came to get me. 'Last time I do this, I'm too old for trekking up hillsides.'

Seemed I was needed at home. Ash wouldn't say much and she's a bit grumpy which I put down to old bones and wonder why she didn't send her apprentice.

'Is Mother alright,' I say.

'I'm Carrier, not Messenger,' more grumpy. 'So you're not bumped then?' This time with a smile. 'Good.'

Later, when April-Mae is long lost, I'm sorry for my selfish thoughts. And, too, when I speak about Mother to Ash, hoping for sympathy. There's a long pause and I think she's ignoring me which is what I deserve, but she says, 'You were a very precocious and pretty child, and Johana showed you too much favour, right from the moment you were born. Your mother never got over it.'

But it was something to do with the tree fairy wasn't it? Aunty Susa told me once. Now I didn't know what to think. I thought Granma Jo was perfect. Nothing changes. She and Mother, then Mother and me. That's something to ponder on. And now there's something stranger than a baby in my belly; couldn't be sympathy, could it? I hadn't come to Arkady for that.

But something happened to wipe all that from our thoughts. As we're talking about the journey ahead, and I start to put things in a bag, Suniva and Elin appear. How those Arkady women know things; they pretend it's a magic sense, but I think they listen round corners.

'We've come to say goodbye.'

They don't look very sorry, but they give Ash a parting gift which I hope is food enough for going downhill.

'It's from Ylva,' they explain.

It seems she's binding Flot's leg, and regrets she can't come herself. A near escape for Flot, they tut. I don't say a thing. And while I've grown to like their madness, and the brightness and the whiteness of Arkady, I suddenly felt a terrible yearning for my green home and the shadowy forest. But then I'm torn, for Hazel rushes in wanting me to stay. Ash takes one look at her, before I've even said their names to them both, and says, 'You coming too?'

Suddenly it's just what she's always wanted. Then for a moment a magic sense hits me, just like an Arkady woman, and I know that Hazel's looking for a near escape too.

The two bright birds say many big Nos and wobble their heads and shake their feathers. But Hazel is sure and full of smiles at them; and us.

'Just for a visit,' she says. 'To see what it's like.'

That's nice I think. I like Hazel, she'll be better company than a grumpy Carrier. And we'd march back into Paradise, three, where once there was two. After a while there seems to be an agreement, that Hazel shall come for a visit. She's full of smiles as usual and it seems easy. Why then is there something crawling up the back of my neck? And why isn't Ash smiling? It seems discourteous, when they beg for one more day with Hazel, to refuse. It seems even more so to refuse their invitation to a goodbye supper. So Hazel has one last day with her mothers and sister and saying farewell to her team and we lounge around waiting for the meal, me wondering where the parting gift went.

I stop wondering when we're called to supper. What a spread. I never saw even birthday celebrations that fine in Arkady. Food is not luxurious up a mountain. But Hazel's not there; she's spending a last while with Flot, Elin says. So we feast, the four of us, on fruit soup, river fish and, rare for Arkady, fresh green vegetables, almost as good as we harvest in Paradise. Then there are cream puddings and a sweet pie and even some wine. At the sight of the feast I'd forgotten the creature on my neck, so when Ash whispers, ' Be careful.' I don't know what she means unless it's the health of my belly. But I'm a farmer's daughter; strong as a horse in all my parts.

I awake in darkness later, sick in my belly part and apparently with that very same horse on my head. Someone else is groaning too.

'I'm too old for this sort of thing. It'll kill me. Barbara, help me up.'

Eventually I find her and help her to sit. Her warning, now I see her meaning, had not been enough for either of us.

'It must have been in the wine. I didn't eat the sweet things.'

And from inside her robes she brings out her light maker. Not strong enough to light up sky bandits, but good enough for here. We've time enough to look around and find ourselves back in Suniva's guest room where I had stayed, along with the bags we'd packed the day before. Ash laughs softly.

'They not much used to doing this, then,' she mutters, and flicks it off with the sound of a key in the lock. I'm dazzled by daylight as Elin enters and sits firmly on the bed. I look at the open door frame but there's a shadow I know is Suniva.

'What this, then?' says Ash. 'Hospitality Arkady style? Things are different in Paradise.'

'We know that.' Elin looks tired. 'But we're owed. You may go, Carrier Ash. But this girl owes us.'

What the slek does she mean? I don't remember any promises. Yet once more I'm confused. Suniva is leaning at the door. She answers me when I didn't speak; like Mother does.

'It was our daughter Hazel's turn to carry. But she wasn't ready.'

Elin sighs, 'She'll never be ready.'

Ignoring her, Suniva continues, 'She was excused when we had hopes of you.'

Ash and I look at each other. I need to think about this thing clearly. 'If I'd fallen for a child,' I use the Paradise words for spite, 'I would have taken it home.'

'Her.' She corrects me. 'Always her.' And again. 'No, the child would stay here, wherever you went.'

I see. Ash and I look again at each other. 'Where's Hazel, now?'

'With her sister.'

Oh dear. Oh dear. Will I ever see my dear friend again? Then Ash says, 'If she isn't bumped by now, how long are you going to keep her trying? I don't think she's the bumping kind. It runs in the family. I'm the same and I'm her aunt.'

Now it's their turn to exchange worried looks and they

leave hastily without speaking to us. The door bangs shut and there's that key sound.

After two more days of this confined living, bowls of food that are not from the feast and daily lectures about duty and motherhood and longing, I know I'm in trouble. I've called them mad before, but I meant it as a joke. I must be careful what I tell the world to do in future.

'You'd better go home, Ash.' I'm being as good as I know. She's an old lady. Doesn't deserve this.

'Shush your nonsense,' is all I get back.

'You can; I'll understand.'

'Just wait. Find your patience. Something's coming.'

Yes, I think, a damn baby. And then Ash smiles, puts her finger to her lips and seems to sink into herself.

That night a miracle happens. At first, I'm truly pleased for Lynel, and surprised that I have good feeling for any of them here, except Hazel. The Clocks have blown time on time as if everything is normal. I hardly notice the pitch any more. This night it's as ever, high and sweet. And then suddenly it changes. There's pause like a heartbeat and the note creeps a fraction higher, and then higher and then it swoops up and up. And it happens. The sky outside our curtains is suddenly lit by a flickering beam like a ray of the sun. The noise is mighty. The noise of jubilation. Screams and crying and women beating drums and logs of wood. So that's the end of those sky snatchers. I turn to wake Ash from her sleep, but she's up and reaching for the few things we've unpacked.

'Quick,' she hisses, 'it's now.'

I try the door, but it's still locked of course, but as I move away, the key, barely whispering, unlocks and the door opens. In the crack Ylva's face looks at me. She opens the door wide and I see the flickering beam outside and hear the joyfulness. Ylva touches my hand and I look into those forest eyes. She's sad.

'Take care of my daughter. She's waiting beyond the bend. Quick,' she echoes Ash, 'now while they're with Lynel.'

Ash pushes me through the door, and with scarcely a brief smile at the wolf woman, I'm dragged out of the house on to the path. No time even to say our thanks. For an old woman Ash runs fast. I have a job to keep up with her and not drop the bags, which I somehow I'm carrying.

'How did you know?' I gasp. She's panting like a cat having kittens.

'Save your breath.' She sounds like a bagpipe. ' Just run.'

And there, round the curve in the path that protects Arkady from the world, is Hazel and a mule. What a story this will make, I think. Perhaps I'll be a Storyteller after all.

Mass Dreams

By
Berta Freistadt